ALSO BY KIT FRICK

THE
SPLIT

A NOVEL

KIT FRICK

EMILY BESTLER BOOKS
—
ATRIA
NEW YORK LONDON TORONTO SYDNEY NEW DELHI

EMILY
BESTLER
BOOKS

ATRIA

An Imprint of Simon & Schuster, LLC
1230 Avenue of the Americas
New York, NY 10020

First Emily Bestler Books/Atria Books hardcover edition February 2024

EMILY BESTLER BOOKS/ATRIA BOOKS and colophon are trademarks of Simon & Schuster, LLC

Simon & Schuster: Celebrating 100 Years of Publishing in 2024

For information about special discounts for bulk purchases, please contact Simon & Schuster Special Sales at 1-866-506-1949 or business@simonandschuster.com.

The Simon & Schuster Speakers Bureau can bring authors to your live event. For more information or to book an event, contact the Simon & Schuster Speakers Bureau at 1-866-248-3049 or visit our website at www.simonspeakers.com.

Interior design by Erika R. Genova

Manufactured in the United States of America

1 3 5 7 9 10 8 6 4 2

Library of Congress Cataloging-in-Publication Data is available.

ISBN 978-1-6680-2247-4
ISBN 978-1-6680-2252-8 (ebook)

*To the Stewart sisters, Pat and Sally—avid readers who
introduced me to the joys of a great mystery*

ONE

This is the place where memories go to die.

Officially, Monte Viso's sixth floor is the memory-support wing, but strip away the top-notch doctors, the warm and earnest aides, the cheerful signs in their block letters and bright primary colors, and the naked truth is: you're in a vault of forgotten pasts.

There was a time when Mom remembered, and then a time when she did not. Her move here was a stark inflection point for both of us, the acknowledgment that a different future, one in which she spent her golden years rattling around her too-big house with its stately bones, was no longer possible.

I suppose all lives have such pivotal moments, paths diverging, cracking in two—though the finality of the split registers only when we take stock of the universe we now inhabit, surrender to the swift death of the other.

"Where are you taking me?" Mom's voice is sharp, shaking me from my reverie. Her eyes dart around the off-white hallway, its fresh coat of paint and pale rose carpet failing to counteract the harsh, institutional glare and faint smell of spray cleaner that permeates the sixth floor.

"We're going out to the courtyard," I tell her again. "It's finally cooled off. I brought pomegranate iced tea."

Slowly, she nods, allowing me to take her elbow and guide her gently toward the elevator.

Seven o'clock is a sleepy time in memory support. Dinner has finished. The more social residents gather in the common room, watching TV or working at jigsaw puzzles. Many are already in bed. Over the past two months, the staff has grown accustomed to my daily routine, my insistence on taking Mom outside unless it's pouring rain.

I call the elevator, and Mom straightens beside me. Tonight, like every night, she looks impeccable. A healthy shine brushed into her long, brown hair, the gray dyed away. Clothes selected to accentuate, not hide, her tall, upright frame. And just enough makeup to draw out her delicate features.

I take after her—tall, brunette, small features that look refined when made up and mousy in any other light—whereas my little sister, Esme, shares a lucky list of attributes with Dad: blond, effortlessly slim, undeniably attractive, disinclined to ever truly grow up.

The consistency in Mom's outward appearance is a comfort when the changes to her brain have been so staggering. Familial Alzheimer's. Early onset. The first signs began at forty-eight; maybe even earlier. In review, I amass a collection of moments of confusion, missed appointments, muddled memories that revealed their importance only in aggregate.

The elevator doors part, and we step inside. I type the access code into the keypad, eyes lingering on the small gray-and-white monitor strapped to Mom's ankle. At sixty-three, she's one of the youngest residents at Monte Viso. Unlike many of her peers, she is fully ambulatory, a flight risk. Hence the ankle monitor and access code, insurance she won't wander away from the sixth floor unaccompanied, or worse, out of the building altogether.

"Hold that!"

The doors jerk back open, revealing Dr. James Paulson's surprised face. It's been a month since our breakup, a month during which I've carefully arranged my visits around his work schedule, intent on giving him space, on avoiding just such an awkward run-in.

"Oh," I say, words failing me. My gaze darts from his name tag to his crisp white jacket to the small patch of freckles dusting his nose, unsure where to land.

Jamie recovers first, eyes resuming their familiar, amiable glow as he joins us in the car. He turns to my mother.

"Marjorie Connor. Always a pleasure."

"You remember Dr. Paulson, Mom?" I ask, knowing full well she does not. On good days, Mom knows me. Close family, old friends. But new faces rarely stick, even the neurologist she saw for a year before his relationship with me made it necessary for her to switch doctors.

The elevator begins its descent, and Mom turns to me as if we are alone in the car. "He's very handsome. And a doctor."

I resist the temptation to roll my eyes. Mom's family didn't come from money, but marrying Dad—marrying Carl Connor's wealth—changed everything. If it wasn't for the favorable terms of the divorce settlement, she would have spent the past two decades living somewhere far more modest than the grand, rambling house on Boneset Lane.

Mom never made a secret of the fact that she wanted Esme and me to marry up. Unsurprisingly, she loves Esme's husband, Mark Lloyd, of the New York Lloyds, who has been in my sister's life long enough to stick in Mom's brain.

Her comment about Jamie lingers in my ears. She has no idea how many months I spent wondering if he might be the one, if marriage was in our future. But not because he's a doctor, or makes a doctor's salary. I do just fine on my own at Empire, the private lender in Lower Manhattan to which I commute an hour and a half each way, every day. My job is the only way we can afford Monte Viso. All the time I spent on Jamie had nothing to do with career or money; I simply loved him. And it hasn't been so easy to leave those feelings in the past.

When the doors open on the ground floor, I motion for Jamie to step out first.

"I didn't know you'd be on the floor tonight," I apologize, taking in his achingly familiar crop of brown hair, warm brown eyes, the dusky scruff along his jaw.

He shrugs. "My flight doesn't leave until almost midnight. Haruto will be covering for me all next week."

"Of course," I say, guiding Mom out of the elevator and toward the courtyard doors. "Your trip," I add, hoping it sounds like I've just remembered. Tonight, Jamie is leaving for San Francisco to visit his parents. For months, the trip sat on our shared calendar. For months, I hoped an invitation to join him might materialize. When he unlinked our accounts a week or so after the breakup, all of Jamie's plans vanished into the ether, leaving my calendar the same uninspired clutter of work meetings and doctors' appointments and visits with Mom.

Back when I first began bringing her to Jamie's neurology practice on the Upper East Side, the best in the tristate area, I was still living in Brooklyn and working twelve-hour days, only starting to wrap my head around the reality of Mom's diagnosis. How she'd require constant supervision, how I would need to return to my Connecticut hometown.

We began dating shortly before I moved back in with Mom. In

the little over a year we were together, Jamie was sweet, thoughtful, kind—always there for me, even in the tough times, *especially* in the tough times. He thrived on being my support as Mom's health worsened and I struggled to keep her safe at home; I imagine all doctors have a bit of a savior complex.

But eventually, when Mom was settled into Monte Viso, I was no longer someone in crisis mode, nor was I free to move back to the city. Seeing Mom every day was part of the deal I made with myself when I finally opted for long-term care. My life was in Branby now, my time in the city constrained to work.

When the dust settled, what Jamie and I had wasn't enough: me here and Jamie based primarily in New York City, save for his two days a week at Monte Viso. I would have fought to make it work, but Jamie didn't see a future for us. I thought our lives made sense entwined, but when he made it clear he didn't see it the same way, all the fight went out of me.

Jamie reaches over to key the access code into the pad on the wall for Mom and me, and the courtyard door glides slowly open. Mom is already striding out into the warm evening air, but I stand at the threshold, not quite ready to let him go. *I miss him.* And the fact that my mother doesn't remember Jamie at all is a cruel twist of the knife; our relationship is squarely in the past, it will never matter. He's going to San Francisco alone tonight, will go on with his life, and there is absolutely nothing I can do about it.

"Well, it was nice to see you," I say weakly. "Have a good trip." *A good everything. Without me.*

"Right. Enjoy the time with your mom." His eyes travel beyond me, then skyward. His lashes are unfairly long. "Nice weather tonight."

He takes two steps back into the hall before turning toward the lobby. Then he's gone, and my heart is floating freely in my chest, untethered and aching. Apparently, we are now people who comment politely on the weather.

"Esme," Mom says from the patio chair where she's settled herself across the courtyard, chin tilted up toward the sun still lodged in the late-summer sky.

"What about Esme?" I ask, unsure if Mom has mistaken me for my little sister. The fact that Esme and I look nothing alike is no guarantee against the ravages of Mom's Alzheimer's.

"She said she was going to visit, a week ago, maybe two," Mom says, "but she hasn't come. She canceled."

"I'm sorry." Mom's words have alleviated my fear that she has mixed the two of us up tonight, but all the same, I have to wonder if this conversation with Esme even took place. Just as easily, Mom could be remembering one of my many calls, her memory recasting my confirmation of an upcoming visit in her younger daughter's voice. She is no longer a reliable narrator of her own life.

I take a seat in the patio chair next to her and pull a thermos of the pomegranate iced tea Mom loves from my tote. Maybe Esme did call, dangle the promise of a visit, then flake. I'm very familiar with the sting of my sister's last-minute cancelations. The last time she came to Branby was the day we moved Mom into Monte Viso, two months ago. I've become intimately familiar with Mom's sharply deteriorating neurological health during the year I've been living at home, caring for her, while Esme has managed to avoid the harsher realities of Mom's decline. It would be nice if she'd help me shoulder the responsibility from time to time, but that's not Esme.

I unscrew the thermos top and pour the tea into two plastic cups. Mom sips hers, and a smile creeps across her face. For the first time since I got here tonight—perhaps for the first time all day—my shoulders relax. It's been ungodly hot since midweek, and if the hurricane currently making its way up the coast arrives tomorrow, the rain will drive Mom and me back into the frigid air-conditioning. But this evening is perfect, and I won't let my sister's absence or my run-in with Jamie ruin it. I let myself sink into the cushion and enjoy the warm sun on my skin.

There is a particular kind of darkness ushered in by a late-summer storm. It's not the dark of nightfall—dusky, gradual, accompanied by the low hum of cicadas and a meandering breeze—but sudden and all-consuming, the sky clear one moment and then inky, grim, swollen with threat.

The evening after I bump into Jamie at Monte Viso, I arrive home to 16 Boneset Lane right as the clouds rupture, rain beginning in earnest. Thankful to be in for the night after an early dinner with Mom, I pull around the parking circle and past the lush bed of succulents and hanging vines that was once a perpetually leaky fountain, fat drops splattering against the windshield of my Subaru sedan.

The house sits on several acres of manicured property secluded at the end of a tree-lined cul-de-sac. It's an updated 1920s affair, over four thousand square feet of stone and wood with four bedrooms and five baths. My sister and I christened it "Old Boney" many years ago after boneset, the tiny white flowers for which our street takes its name, or maybe for the way the walls shift and creak late at night, like an old woman settling into her bones.

Esme and I grew up here together, but my little sister has never felt the same love for the grand old house, or our small Connecticut hometown. The mortgage is paid off, thanks to Dad, but the upkeep and taxes are a significant monthly expense on top of Mom's care. I should really sell it, but I can't bear the thought.

The garage door slides shut behind me, and I switch off the ignition just as my phone begins to bleat.

Esme's name flashes across the screen, and I hurry to answer. Sometimes, I miss our old closeness with a ferocity that knocks the breath from my lungs. But it's been years since we talked every day, since we went to each other with our problems, since she called me out of the blue.

It's not surprising, given what I did . . .

"Hello?"

"Jane, thank god you picked up."

Phone cradled to my ear, I step out of the car and clamber up the stairs to the kitchen.

"What's going on?" I ask.

"I left Mark."

The almost flawlessly Michelangean face of my sister's husband flashes across my mind—the chiseled jawline, not a hint of stubble to be found; straight nose; icy blue eyes; closely clipped brown hair. It's nearly impossible to picture Mark Lloyd cast aside, his confidence shaken.

"Are you okay?" I ask. "What happened?"

"Nothing happened."

Mind churning, I cross through the kitchen and into the foyer, flicking on the overhead lights and dropping my bag in its regular spot on the ornate console table.

All her life, Esme has been lucky in love. Lucky, in fact, in everything. The things I've worked so hard toward—financial stability, a lifelong romantic partnership—have been handed to Esme, seemingly on a silver platter. I feel terrible that her marriage is on the rocks, of course I do. But for the first time in a long time, I feel something else. The possibility of a connection to this woman who used to be my everything, who has made herself barely more than a stranger in recent years. Suddenly, I feel a little less alone in my uncharmed life.

"I've been bored for a while, and I finally woke up," she continues. "Marrying Mark was a mistake. Now you can gloat about how right you were."

I start down the hall toward the living room, kitten heels clicking on the Italian marble floor. "I never—"

"Of course you thought it was a mistake. I was twenty-four. Everyone thought it was a mistake."

It's true I worried about her decision to get married so young; I've always wanted to spare her from any sort of pain, heartbreak or otherwise. I was happy for her, and maybe a little jealous, but mostly I didn't understand the rush to marry Mark Lloyd, six years her senior and firmly established in his career as an investment banker. Esme was barely out of college when they met, and the power dynamic in their relationship was worrying. But I knew she'd take my criticism badly, and I kept my mouth shut.

Clearly, my discretion didn't matter. Esme has always been able to read me like a book.

I sink into the living room couch, dark leather cushions shushing beneath me, and let my eyes fall shut. At twenty-eight, my sister still looks like a child playing a very stylish game of dress-up. Wavy blond hair and sparkling green eyes. Pale, blemish-free face. Soft makeup. Tiny frame, unique in a family of formidable height, with the delicate features and high cheekbones to match.

Only the jagged pink scar that runs all the way from her shoulder to her elbow mars the doll-like effect. The cut healed years ago, but the scar's indelible presence is a reminder of how badly I hurt her, how I will forever live in her debt.

"I thought you were young," I say, choosing my words carefully. All her life, people have wanted to take care of Esme. Perhaps me, most of all.

"See? Gloat away."

"I'm not gloating, truly." The last thing I want is for this rare phone call to turn into a fight. My gaze travels across the living room, past the entrance to the three-season porch, to the wide picture window overlooking the patio, the grounds, the small stone cottage. Thunder rumbles overhead, and a thin blade of lightning splits the sky.

"Anyway. I need some time to clear my head," she says, "and nothing exciting ever happens in Branby."

My chest swells with the knowledge that she wants to come here, to me, to weather the storm. Is it too much to hope that her return home will open a new chapter for us, one in which we start to mend? I want it so badly, my throat aches.

"You can stay as long as you want," I say.

Esme doesn't respond right away, and it hits me that she didn't actually say she wanted to stay at Old Boney, with me. Laughter erupts in the background, and the clinking of glasses. It sounds like she's at a party, or out at a restaurant, and the noise reminds me I haven't gone out on a Saturday night since Jamie ended things between us.

My sister and I have always been so different. While Esme is a social butterfly, I am reserved; while she thrives on drama and secrecy, I am practical and measured. Even our names are uncanny reflections of the women we've become—plain Jane after my paternal grandmother; then Esme, Mom's fanciful choice for her second daughter after ceding to Dad's strong will when naming their first.

Just as her silence is becoming unbearable, Esme clears her throat. Then her voice cuts through the background noise, carrying an obvious note of tension. "Thanks, Janie. I might take you up on that. But I need you to come get me."

"You still haven't told me what happened with Mark," I urge, pressing the phone to my ear, hoping she'll open up to me, like she always used to.

"I did though."

"You realized it was a mistake," I say. But something tangible must have happened to prompt her to leave him. "Did you have a fight?"

"No fight."

"If Mark was hurting you, you'd tell me, right? If he did some-thing—"

"It's nothing like that," she cuts in, voice clipped. "I left Mark on Thursday, and I've been figuring things out. I said I'd meet him for dinner tonight. He wanted to talk."

"Okay," I say slowly. "It went badly?"

"It didn't go at all. Mark wants the impossible; I'm done. Din-ner would have been a senseless agony. And now I really need a ride."

My eyes travel again to the back of the house, rain pummel-ing the picture window. Water streams down the glass in sheets. "Where are you?"

"Thanks so much," she says, although I haven't agreed to any-thing. "I'll text you the address."

The call ends, and a moment later, my phone chimes with a new text.

420 Madison @ E 48.
Txt me when you're here.

I blink at the screen, pulse ticking in my throat. It feels good to be needed, like old times.

But this is a bad night for a drive. I squeeze my eyes shut, and I can almost feel the steering wheel bucking in my grasp, the tires beginning to hydroplane. Then I'm back there, fifteen years ago. Scared out of my mind, totally out of control, screaming at the top of my lungs while Mom's car spins and spins, hurtling toward the grim promise of impact . . .

I pry my eyes open and shake the memory away, but I'm left with the reality that Esme's not exactly nearby; it's an hour's drive to Midtown Manhattan in the best of weather. My fingers hover over the screen.

It's storming! I can't drive into the city
right now. Don't you have a friend you
can stay with for the night?

Jane, come on! I have
nowhere to go.

That cannot possibly be true. After all, she's been staying *somewhere* for the last two nights. But something is going on with her, more than she's letting on. My stomach clenches with nerves—for what she's not telling me, for what I need to do. Because I am incapable of ignoring her cry for help, a truth as elemental to our relationship as the molecules of our DNA.

I picture her then in the days after Mom and Dad's divorce, a fragile ten-year-old in black leggings and a shimmery gold tank top that makes her look older than her age. She sits outside, on the patio wall, looking away from the house and chewing her fingers raw. I join her, and for a moment, we sit there in silence, staring at the lawn, the stone cottage in the back, the unblemished blue sky. Then she rests her head on my shoulder, a signal I can wrap my arm around her, draw her close to me, that she will let me absorb some of the hurt into my skin.

The memory fades and I head back into the foyer for my keys, torn between two competing urges: to tell my sister firmly but gently no for the first time in my life, or to get in the car and rescue her.

TWO

GONE

Five minutes later, I'm back in the garage, door up, sitting in the driver's seat of my Subaru. The key is in the ignition, but I can't bring myself to turn it. In the rearview, water streams down the driveway, gutters in the succulent fountain. Relentless.

Thunder booms overhead, and my palms go clammy against the wheel. A whimper escapes my lips.

I nearly killed my sister that night fifteen years ago, driving recklessly in a thunderstorm on the highway. I could have chosen inertia, but instead I chose to act, grabbing the keys, then Esme's hand, my mind made up. From there, the consequences seemed to flow as through a broken dam into a new universe of my creation, wave after unbridled wave, no return.

My heart was in the right place, a fact I have clung to all these years. But beside it is the unassailable truth that I almost destroyed everything.

The old questions rattle around my brain, restless ghosts. Did I do more harm than good that night—to Esme, to who we are to each other? If I could go back, what path would I choose?

But I don't have time to dwell in the past. Right now, Esme needs me.

I suck in a deep breath and try to reason with myself. I know these roads; I drive around Branby in bad weather all the time. It's getting on the highway that terrifies me, but maybe the storm will pass. Maybe I'll drive out of it. All I have to do is turn the key.

Hand trembling, I start the car, shift into reverse, back out of the garage. As I ease around the parking circle, lightning flashes, filling the sky with sharp white light.

A series of angry beeps blares from my phone, and I slam on the brakes.

> Flash flood warning for Fairfield,
> New Haven, Middlesex, and Hartford
> Counties.

Perfect.

I can't do this.

I shift back into park and call Esme.

"Are you on your way?" Her voice is eager, impatient.

"I'm sorry," I tell her. "I just can't."

For a moment, she says nothing. Her disappointment radiates through the phone. "So what am I supposed to do?" she finally asks.

My eyes lift to the car ceiling. I want to be strong for her, to come to my sister's rescue like I always used to. But the old fear is paralyzing. "I'm sorry. Can you take the train?"

"Janie, that's *why* I called. Metro-North is down."

Of course. "Then you'll have to take a cab."

"There are no cabs! And both Lyft and Uber are giving me a two-hour wait."

Tears prick the corners of my eyes. I feel like such a failure, but surely I'm not her only option?

"Look," she wheedles when I've been silent too long, "I know you hate storms, and you're probably all shaken up, but—"

"*Esme*," I cut her off. "Please understand." My sister, better than anyone, should not require an explanation.

"What am I supposed to do?" she asks again, voice small.

"You have so many friends in the city. Can you go to one of their places for the night? If the trains are still messed up tomorrow, I'll pick you up. We'll go—"

"Not an option."

I shake my head, at a loss for what to make of her claim. Of course she has friends she could call, of course she could crash somewhere in the city. Something very strange is going on with my sister.

I open my mouth to suggest she book a hotel room for the night, but what comes out instead is: "Why are you lying to me?"

On the other end, there's a muffled gasp, as if Esme can't believe I've flung such an accusation at her. I can hardly believe it myself.

"Go look in the mirror," she snaps. "We're all fucking liars."

Then my phone screen goes dark. My sister has hung up on me.

The next morning, I pad downstairs, poorly rested. My jaw aches from a night spent clenching my teeth, still wired from the fight with Esme. I half expect to see her sprawled on the living room couch, a throw pulled over her delicate frame, the evening's raiments discarded in a sopping heap in the hallway. But there's nothing—no Esme, no evidence she found another way up to Branby. Guilt knifes through me.

I drop a bag of orange pekoe into my favorite blue-glazed mug and assure myself that Esme is fine. Despite her claims to the contrary, by the time I switched off the light, she was most likely fast asleep on the futon—or more likely spare bed—of one of her equally well heeled friends. My sister has lived in Manhattan since college; she has a wide net in the city.

Even so, I need to check in. The rain has long cleared, and if she still needs a ride, I can go get her now. While the tea steeps, I run upstairs to grab my phone, then right back down when I find the charger empty. I lift my purse from the table in the foyer and dig around. I'm about to dump the contents onto the couch when I realize that, in all of last night's agitation, I must have left my phone in the car.

I pound down the stairs to the garage and slip back into the driver's seat. There are no texts from Esme, but I have two Monte Cares alerts from last night—a power outage at Monte Viso, then another letting me know the power has been restored—and two missed calls and a new voice mail, from Mark. That's a surprise; I can count on one hand the times my brother-in-law has called me.

Jaw ticking, I take the stairs back up to the kitchen and check the time on the calls: 8:45 and 9:25 a.m. I take my tea out to the three-season porch and settle in on the love seat. After I've taken a sip and set the mug down on the wicker table, I play the voice mail.

Jane, hi, listen. Esme was supposed to meet me at Oma last night, but she never showed up. I've called several times, and she's not answering. She mentioned going to stay with you, so can you let me know that she got there? It's been a difficult few weeks, and I'd feel better knowing she arrived in one piece. Okay, well. Call me right away when you get this.

I should be sympathetic to his concern, but it's hard to get past the smug banker's tone, the way he addresses me like a subordinate. *Call me right away.* Mark Lloyd is a person accustomed to getting precisely what he wants, when he wants it. I'm sure he *would* feel better knowing Esme got safely to Connecticut, but the fact is, she's not here.

I try Esme instead. The phone rings several times, then switches to voice mail: *This is Esme. I probably won't listen to this, so text me.* Beep.

My sister has had the same outgoing message for years; she hasn't had to change it because she has never had to worry about sounding professional. Almost as soon as they got engaged, Mark encouraged her to quit her entry-level position at a literary agency "to pursue her writing full-time," a lifestyle that has included hosting exclusive literary salons and mentoring student writers, but which has never seemed to involve much in the way of actual writing. I start composing a text, then decide to try calling her again.

This time, someone answers on the second ring with a terse "Hello?"

"Esme? That you?"

"No." The voice is female, but throatier than my sister's. Older too. "If Esme is the owner of this phone, she left it on the bar last night. Tell her to come pick it up."

"Wait," I say quickly, sensing she's about to hang up. "Did you see the woman who left it? Do you know what time–?"

"Didn't work last night," she cuts in. "The Monarch will hold the phone in lost and found for a week. After that, no guarantees."

Then she's gone.

I stare blankly at my screen. Esme didn't come here, and she didn't go home.

She drinks, sometimes a lot, but she didn't sound drunk when we talked last night. That said, it was still early, and she was at a bar. I picture Esme staying for another drink or three after we spoke, then stumbling into a cab. Most likely, the driver delivered her to a friend's apartment, as I suggested, where she's currently sleeping it off. Leaving her phone behind probably doesn't signal anything's wrong. She'll wake up, realize it's missing, and swing by the Monarch to retrieve it on her way to Branby.

I left her hanging, but she's *fine*. Almost certainly. Unless my instinct last night was right, and something else really is going on . . .

I shake the feeling off, convince myself to get in the shower and go about my day. If she hasn't turned up by this evening, *then* I'll worry.

At noon, I meet Mom for omelets and orange juice at Monte Viso, then head to the grocery store, then Target. When I get home, there's still no sign of Esme. She has keys to the house; if she made it up here, she'd have let herself in. I call her phone again; this time, it goes straight to voice mail. It's ten after three. Surely she's awake by now, but if she got brunch in the city, if she's with her friends, it's entirely possible she hasn't gone to the Monarch yet. The address she sent me last night is in Midtown, and I highly doubt any of her friends live around there. I resolve to put away the groceries, then I settle in at the dining room table to tackle a few work emails. If I haven't heard from her by five, I'll call Mark, see if he has any updates.

At five on the dot, I snap my laptop shut and pick up my phone. My finger hovers over Mark's number, but I find myself scrolling through my contacts instead, unsure exactly what I'm hoping to find. I barely know the names of Esme's friends, let alone their numbers. There's Whitney, her best friend from NYU, but Whitney moved to Vermont or New Hampshire a few years ago. And once, soon after Mark and Esme were married, I joined them for dinner with a few of Mark's investment banking colleagues, but I can't imagine Esme went to stay with one of Mark's friends. Esme is always going out, always flitting from party to party, but the composition of her social circle is a mystery to me.

Then I remember Kiku, her cohost from the literary salon she runs. I met her only the one time at a dimly lit speakeasy in SoHo, probably three years ago, but I know she works at an agency, so

I google "Kiku" and "literary agent," hoping to find her contact information. My search locates Kiku Shima easily enough, but if she's on social she keeps her profiles private, and her agency page instructs writers seeking representation to contact her through a query manager. I click the link, half-heartedly thinking I'll fill out the form and hope she sees it, but a note pops up on my screen telling me, *Sorry! Kiku Shima is currently closed to queries.*

I'm out of ideas. Unless—Instagram. I open the app, then click on Esme's account in hopes she's posted since last night. To my surprise, her page is nearly empty. In place of the hundreds of carefully curated and beautifully edited shots of her life in the city that my sister has cataloged for years, a single post sits at the top of her profile. A pair of slim legs shown from the knee down, feet in a pair of pretty gold Balenciaga slingbacks. They're lovely, delicate, the kind of thing I'd never in a million years buy for myself. A massive cream-and-blue carpet bag rests on the cobblestones beside her, washed in sunshine. The messaging is clear: the shoes, the travel bag, the picturesque street. A new path, Esme style. I tap open the full caption.

Time for a fresh start. I'm archiving all my prior posts (!) and embarking on a new chapter. This is a little bit scary, but I've been overdue for a change. I've got so much in store, so thank you for trusting me and sticking around. More to come!

There are no hashtags, no further clues to demystify what kind of "fresh start" she's talking about, but the post is dated Thursday—the day she left Mark.

Since then, it's accumulated over three thousand likes. My sister is far from famous, but becoming a Lloyd has made her a bit of a society darling among a certain New York set. Her account is followed by a truly mind-boggling number of aspiring writers and would-be socialites, all of whom seem to hang on her every move. I scroll down to the comments. Hundreds of Esme's followers wishing her well, bemoaning the loss of the posts she's archived, asking where she's off to, what's next for her, if she has a discount code for the Balenciagas. As far as I can tell, my sister hasn't responded to any of them. I look for familiar names among the handles, but there are none I recognize. Instagram is a dead end.

Feeling a sudden prickling anxiety, I resign myself to calling Mark. He picks up before I even hear it ring.

"Jane, finally. Is she with you?"

My jaw clenches, and I try to relax. "No, I'm sorry. I just got your message."

He groans. "Shit. I've been calling around, but I've come up empty. I hoped she was in Connecticut with you."

"Unfortunately not. She called me from a bar near Grand Central a little after eight last night, begging for a ride. But it was the middle of a thunderstorm. I told her to go to a friend's."

He clears his throat. "Right. Well, she was supposed to meet me for dinner at eight. She didn't cancel, she just didn't show up. And she *definitely* didn't come home."

Does Mark sound a touch defensive, or is that a hint of anger in his voice?

A lump lodges in my throat. For the first time, I'm starting to really worry. "I'm sorry, Mark. If she shows up here, I'll call you right away."

He promises to do the same, and then I'm left blinking at the dining room wall. I should know what to do in this situation, but my mind is blank.

For once in my life, I need someone to take care of me.

I pull up my favorites and stare at the list. Mom and Esme are followed by Alisha and Claire, my two best friends. At least, they used to be. Alisha and I were still pretty tight until last December, when she left Empire Lenders to move on to a new job. I look at my text history with Claire with a guilty twinge; my last message to her is an apology for canceling on a plan nearly two months ago. Ever since Mom's diagnosis, my world has narrowed: work, commuting, caregiving, and for a blissful year, Jamie. He fit into my life in a way that made sense even when nothing else did, but in the meantime, I let everything else fall by the wayside.

Now the thought of catching up with either Alisha or Claire so I can lay my Esme crisis at their feet feels equal parts shitty and exhausting.

Below their names is Jamie's.

Before I can think too hard about it, I press Call.

When the phone has rung four times, I almost hang up. He won't pick up. He's in San Francisco. Christ, I shouldn't—

"Jane?" He sounds distracted. In the background, I can hear someone talking.

"I'm sorry," I say. "It's a bad time. You're with your family?"

"Hang on." There's a brief, muffled pause, then he's back. "It's fine. What's going on?"

It doesn't sound fine. He sounds annoyed, which—of course he's annoyed. We're broken up, and I'm calling on his vacation.

"Why are you calling?" he continues when I fail to say anything. "Is everything all right?"

"No, not really . . . Um, how's San Francisco?"

"Jane. What's going on?"

"I'm so sorry for bothering you, but I didn't know who else to call," I blurt.

"It's okay," he says, voice reassuring now. "I'm listening." Of course he is. Jamie may no longer see a future for us, but he will always be there for me in a crisis. He thrives on it.

In the early days of our relationship, Jamie shared that his grandmother's swift descent into dementia, something he was powerless to stop, inspired him to become a brain doctor. Since childhood, he's been wired to help others, to problem-solve, to step up in an emergency. My guilt over interrupting his vacation fades a little.

I tell him the whole story, starting with Esme's call last night, and he listens patiently. On two occasions while we were together, Jamie and I were supposed to get dinner with Esme and Mark. Both times, Esme canceled at the last minute. Jamie doesn't know my sister, but he knows she can be flighty and hard to pin down, that I have longed to be closer to her in our adult lives and struggled to find a way.

When I finish, he clears his throat. My heart is pounding, but just knowing I'm not alone in this anymore is comforting. Jamie is a highly capable, levelheaded adult. Jamie will help.

When he speaks, he's switched on his Dr. Paulson voice. Calm, reassuring, in control. "Esme's probably fine, but I think you should start calling hospitals."

"Hospitals, right." Of course Jamie knows what to do. The relief is instant.

"As a precaution. You said she was in Manhattan when she called?"

"East Forty-Eighth and Madison."

"Okay. We'll split it up. I'm going to text you a list of numbers."

"Right. You're right." I would have figured this out on my own. Of course I would have. But letting someone else take charge right now feels impossibly good.

"And call the bar again. Not her phone, but the line for the Monarch. See if she's come back for her phone."

"Yes. That makes sense."

"It's going to be fine. But Jane?"

"Mm-hmm?"

"Has Mark notified the police?"

My breath catches in my throat. "I don't . . . He didn't say. I don't think so, not yet."

"Hmm."

"You think that's strange?"

"I don't know, maybe not. But it's been close to twenty-four hours since anybody's heard from her. If I were her husband, if it was my wife, I would've reported her missing."

I get off the phone and google *how long do you have to wait to report a missing person in NYC?* The results take me to a police site. Clearly I'm not the only person who's had this question. *Please call 911 or notify the NYPD Missing Persons Squad as soon as possible to report that a person is missing because late notification can cause loss of valuable time in conducting a search. There are no requirements to wait a specified amount of time before contacting the NYPD.*

A text from Jamie comes in. *I'll take A-M. It'll be okay*, followed by the promised list of Manhattan emergency departments and their phone numbers.

I look at Jamie's list, then I close the text and dial the number for the Missing Persons Squad. While it rings, my heart begins to thud. Last night, I *knew* something strange was going on with my sister. She asked for my help, and my last words to her were an accusation: *Why are you lying to me?*

The operator picks up and asks how he can help.

I swallow, hard. "I need to report a missing person."

2

HOME

I'm still in the garage when thunder rumbles, loud and angry. Reflected in the rearview, water streams down the driveway, gutters in the succulent fountain. Relentless. Every muscle in my body tenses; I feel like I'm going to snap.

Hand trembling, I start the Subaru, shift into reverse, back out of the garage. As I ease around the parking circle, lightning floods the car with an intense surge of white.

A series of angry beeps blares from my phone. Eyes locked on the windshield, I scrabble around on the passenger seat with one hand. My fingertips graze the case, succeeding only in knocking it to the floor, where it promptly slides beneath the seat. Perfect.

I can't do this.

I shift back into park and press my eyes shut. I should call Esme, tell her to take a cab or find a friend's couch to crash on for the night. Surely I'm not her only option.

But she asked *me*. She wants me to swoop in and save her like I always used to, when we were kids. It's a role I know how to play, and it's been such a long time since she's needed me like this. Fear pricks at the back of my neck, but beneath it, there's the hope I've felt since her name flashed across my phone screen—that this could be a fresh start for us.

Fifteen years ago, I nearly killed my sister, and every day since I have lived in her debt.

I pry my eyes open, focus on the windshield wipers battling the rain. I remind myself that I am not seventeen, am not operating on cold dread mixed with bad judgment—others' and my own. But the old questions rattle around my brain, restless ghosts. Did I do more harm than good that night—to Esme, to who we are to each other? If I could go back, what path would I choose?

I don't have time to dwell in the past. Right now, Esme needs me.

And I am perfectly capable of making the drive into the city—a drive I've done a thousand times before. If I leave Esme to fend for herself tonight, she'll feel abandoned. Who knows what rash decisions she might make, what trouble she might get into. How she might come to resent me, crushing any possibility that her time in Branby might spark up the old closeness again. It occurs to me, not for the first time in my life, how much can ride on a single moment, the way one choice can pave the path forward.

My phone chimes, and I dig it out from where it's slid beneath the passenger seat. Dismissing the flood alerts that have collected on my screen, I open Esme's text.

Are you on your way?

I press my lips between my teeth.

Yes. I'm coming.

I breathe in, reset, and shift back into drive. Soon, I'm making my way through Branby and onto I-95, where traffic is stop and go, but moving. I'm still on edge, but I'm fine. The rain lets up a bit on the highway, and by the time I pull up to the corner of Madison and East Forty-Eighth, the storm has abated to a steady drizzle. I double-park in front of a tall building with a charcoal-gray awning jutting over the sidewalk. The Monarch Hotel, a landmark if some-what touristy Midtown institution.

This must be it, although what brought her to a hotel bar of all places, I can't imagine. It's nowhere near the Village, and the Mon-arch is a far cry from the trendy nightlife spots Esme's always show-casing on Instagram.

My gaze lands on the hotel's name illuminated in marquee lights above the revolving door. Perhaps she's been staying here, in which case keeping her room for the night would have been a great idea. Why the sudden rush to come home to Branby, a place she typically avoids?

But I'm here now. My sister is an enigma, and I've long ago given up on trying to figure her out.

I put on my flashers and text her.

Thirty seconds later, she's bursting through a door to the left of the lobby entrance in a sleek rose cocktail dress and a pair of pretty gold Balenciaga slingbacks, no umbrella. Behind her, a bellhop lugs a massive cream-and-blue carpet bag and twin roller cases, gleaming black Louis Vuittons. So she has been staying here. I pop the trunk.

Esme darts into the passenger's seat and drops a boxy gold-and-white handbag, probably vintage, onto her lap. "Christ, what a fuck-ing night."

When the trunk slams shut, I put on my signal and pull back into the street, prompting a series of honks from a cab in the other lane.

For the next couple of blocks, Esme stares out the window, silent. Finally, I clear my throat.

"So you stood Mark up for a twenty-four-dollar martini, huh?" I can't keep the amusement out of my voice.

Esme doesn't answer. The rain has stopped completely now, and traffic is moving at a clip as we head toward the parkway. Ever since we were little, my sister has always held her secrets close. In school, she'd drive her little friends crazy, spilling her guts one day, then refusing to share even the most inconsequential details of her life the next. *It builds an air of mystery*, she told me once, tucking a single blond wave behind her ear.

But she'd come home and tell me. She always used to tell me.

"So you couldn't have stayed the night?" I try again. "I would have gotten you in the morning."

"I checked out hours ago, and then they were fully booked. Saturday night." She shrugs. "I was planning to see Mark, then collect my bags and order a Lyft up to Branby, but Mark was being a dick, and then the storm . . ."

She pulls out her phone and starts scrolling, shutting the conversation down.

When my phone shrills from the nightstand, the room is still cloaked in darkness, the work of thick curtains blacking out the bank of large windows overlooking the stone patio. I scrabble for it, adrenaline coursing through my veins. At night, I leave the ringer cranked up in case there's an emergency with Mom. Last night there were two Monte Cares alerts—a power outage, then another letting me know the power had been restored—but now, the name on the screen isn't one of the several Monte Viso numbers I have programmed into my phone.

"Mark. What's going on?"

It's before nine on a Sunday morning. My brother-in-law is not in the habit of calling me at normal times, let alone early on a weekend. The hairs on the back of my neck bristle.

"I woke you."

He doesn't apologize. I press my thumb and forefinger into the corners of my eyes. "It's fine. I'm up now."

"Jane, listen. Esme was supposed to meet me at Oma last night, and she never showed up. I've been calling, and . . . Anyway, she mentioned she was planning to stay with you."

I wonder once more what's been going on in their relationship, why she left, exactly how messy things got between them.

"Esme's fine," I assure him. "I picked her up from some bar near Grand Central. I'm afraid she got cold feet about your dinner."

Through the phone, I hear a loud crack. Mark's dropped something, or hit something. "Fuck," he says sharply, then draws in a noisy breath. When he speaks again, his voice is measured. "Good, fine. I'm glad she's safe. Your sister likes to make me worry."

My fingers dig into the blanket. I don't like his casual dig, but at the same time, I can relate; I worry about Esme all the time. And I don't want to relate to Mark.

"Right, fine," he says when I haven't responded. "If . . . Well, Esme knows how to reach me."

And then he's gone. I stare numbly at the thin line of daylight bordering the blackout curtains. After the drama of last night, I'd been looking forward to sleeping extravagantly late. But I'm fully awake now. And despite the fact that I know Esme's fine—I tucked her into bed myself—Mark's call has set me on edge.

I throw back the covers and slide my feet into my sandals, then I pad down the hall toward Esme's room.

We got home at a few minutes after one, following a stop at her favorite all-night diner outside Greenwich. When we were kids, Mom and Dad used to take us there on the way home from our family cabin in the Catskills. Back when Mom and Dad were still Mom and Dad, when we were still the Connors, party of four. Last night, the place felt haunted by the ghosts of our never-perfect family, the wholesome faces our parents wore with Esme and me, until they cracked.

After the divorce, I could have easily soured on marriage. But if anything, reflecting back on Dad's temper, Mom's coldness, and their mutual infidelity—Carl through affair after affair with a string of wide-eyed graduate students, and Marjorie through a spate of retaliatory cheating of her own—only turned me into that much more of a romantic. Since childhood, a *good* marriage to a *good* partner has been the thing I want most in life. Perhaps wanting it too much is precisely what's kept the dream at bay.

In a move I think shocked Marjorie to her core, Carl eventually walked out, proclaiming his latest affair was something different, impossible to let go. That relationship imploded three months later, but Dad didn't come home. Instead, he retreated further and further into his work, displaying almost no interest in spending time with his daughters even during our weekends at his new house in New Haven. The person he became after the divorce only further served to highlight how little stock he'd ever put in our family.

But last night, Esme was in a great mood by the time we got out of the city, laughing at everything I said, ordering pancakes and chocolate ice cream at the diner. She didn't seem to notice the old lies chilling the air.

Now I twist the knob of her bedroom door and push it slowly open. Esme's room faces the front lawn, which gets the brunt of the morning sun. Nevertheless, she's left the curtains flung wide, and she lies sprawled on top of her covers in tiny floral shorts and a cream cami, a sleep mask covering her eyes. She's breathing deeply.

Silently, I pull the door shut and head for the shower.

I spend the next few hours at Monte Viso, then the grocery store, then Target. When I return home to fix myself a late lunch, Esme hasn't so much as emerged from her room.

The afternoon is swallowed up by work, getting a jump start on tomorrow's emails. Every week, I tell myself I'll stay away over the weekend, and then every Sunday I take a peek at my inbox and resign myself to the fact that Monday's going to be a lot less miserable if I spend a couple of hours taking care of things now.

By the time I come up for air, it's nearly five. I shut down my VPN and close my laptop, then I grab my phone and before I can stop myself, I'm opening Instagram and pulling up Jamie's account. He's been in San Francisco since sometime late Friday night (the flight details, while expunged from my calendar with the rest of his appointments, remain burned on my brain)—ample time for him to have begun documenting his trip. Jamie's Instagram is set to private, but so far, he hasn't booted me off. I try not to look too often, and I never like his posts or comment for fear he'll remember I still have access to this glimpse into his life. Maybe it would be for the best if he severed that tie, but I can't bring myself to unfollow him.

I'm rewarded by a post captioned *Vacation so far! Good to be back, San Francisco.* I scroll through a few landscapes of the bay at sunrise, a selfie of a slightly bleary-eyed Jamie in front of a coffee shop, a posed family photo of Jamie and his equally good-looking parents smiling for the camera on what looks like the deck of an upscale seafood restaurant, and a slightly off-center shot of a fancy-looking brunch plate and a glass of champagne. The post has fourteen likes. Unlike Esme, who treats Instagram with the seriousness of an artist at work in her darkroom, filtering each post through her own soft, dreamy presets, Jamie pays no attention to the frequency of his posts or their artistry. He's just a regular guy with zero social media savvy and 210 followers made up of his real-life family and friends. It's one of the many things I found—and truthfully, continue to find—so charming about him.

A memory. Jamie and I had been together for two months, maybe three. One Friday evening, when everything still brimmed with novelty and promise, I'd met him for dinner at Carmela, a rustic little

Italian place near his apartment on the Upper East. Over arancini and caponata, we'd talked about Marvel movies; there was a new one releasing, and a long line of moviegoers stretched down the sidewalk across the street. I'd watched a couple with Alisha, who'd grown up reading the comics, but I'd never really seen the appeal. Jamie—this dedicated, earnest, warmhearted doctor—surprised me by saying he'd seen them all.

"It's partly about wish fulfillment, of course," he'd said. "Who doesn't love fantasizing about the power to fly or bend time or heal in an instant? But there's more to it than that. There are so many injustices in the world with no easy solutions. Imagine if one man, or a small team of heroes, could right those wrongs in the span of two hours."

Jamie had the real power to save lives, of course, or at least improve them. But his work with dementia patients was slow, often frustrating, the opposite of magic. That he could consider a world of superheroes, and not dismiss it as childish or silly, said so much about who he was. A man who had dedicated his life to the hard work of patient care, who could still find joy in the impossible, the fantastical, the electrifying.

Now my finger hovers over the comment icon. My hope for a single, shared future has faded into the dull reality of two detached lives. But on Friday evening, lingering outside the elevator at Monte Viso, we'd talked about his trip. I could write something breezy and upbeat. *Hope you're having a great time! Looks fun! Have a blast!*

Inwardly, I groan. Each possibility is worse than the next.

"Whatcha doing?"

My phone clatters to the table. Esme stands beneath the arch beside the pass-through, one shoulder pressed against the wall. She's freshly showered, dressed in a little pink top and impeccably fitted joggers.

I reach for my phone, but not before I catch Esme eyeing the screen, where Jamie's face is prominently displayed.

"Sorry. Didn't mean to startle you."

I flip it face down on the table. "I didn't hear you come down-stairs."

She shrugs and pushes off the wall. "You know me. Like a cat."

For the past couple of hours, while I've been absorbed in work, I'd honestly forgotten she was home. Now I'm filled with the itchy desire to get up, entertain her in some way. "Have you eaten?"

She shakes her head. "Can we order Mario's? I haven't had a clam pie for ages."

"You're staying in?" I shove up from the table. Driving in the storm last night lit every nerve in my body on fire, but I'm glad I didn't back out. Because now my sister is here. Choosing me.

I give her a smile. "I'm going to change out of these jeans. Then I'll order."

When the pizza comes, Esme takes our food into the living room.

"*Hart of Dixie?*" she asks gamely, scanning the list of shows I'm currently watching.

"Have you seen it? I'm in the middle of season two." When it comes to entertainment, I can't resist a rom-com. The meet cute, the misunderstandings, the happily ever after. So different from the way my life has turned out.

She shrugs and selects the next episode in the queue. "I'll catch up."

I eye her suspiciously. "What's going on with you?"

Esme has long been the light of my life, but my sister is not with-out her faults. She can be perfectly polite when it suits her, but when it comes to the big stuff, she never apologizes, never says thank you, and always puts herself first. I admire her self-assuredness, a quality she's had since a very young age, but the imbalance in our interac-tions wears on me from time to time. The accident tipped the scales forever in her favor, but on more than one occasion, I've longed for her to admit when she's wrong, to put my needs before her own.

But that's not her way. Selecting a TV show I like may seem a small showing of kindness, but it's big to me.

She takes a giant bite, and oil drips down her chin. In this moment, she isn't Esme the host of Scribe Society's cliquish salon or Esme Connor-Lloyd of the New York Lloyds, or Esme the beautiful young socialite, living her best life on Instagram. She's just my sister—the girl I used to know.

She gives me a small smile and swipes at her chin with a stack of thin paper napkins. "Real talk?"

I nod, hope swelling in my chest. Finally, Esme's going to open up, allow me access to the events of her life.

"I saw your phone earlier. The photo of your ex?"

"Oh." I pause the episode, which has just begun to play.

"We're both going through breakups. I'm here for you." She puts her plate down on the coffee table and springs from the couch. "You know what we need?"

I give my head a slight shake.

She crosses into the kitchen, clocking the empty wine rack above the stove, then peering into the fridge. "Do you have any white?"

A memory. Esme was nearly ten and I was thirteen, both of us sprawled across my bed while our parents entertained thirty or so of Dad's most esteemed Yale colleagues and their partners downstairs. Ladder faculty—the tenured, the ascending. Esme called it a gathering of snobs, and we passed the fancy wine we'd sneaked from the bar back and forth between us, taking swigs straight from the bottle, then screwing up our faces at the bitter taste, every time. On nights like that, my sister and I shared one mind, would have given up our many advantages for two happy parents, no questions asked. We had grown to despise Dad's distinguished professorship, his family money, Mom's dogged, middle-class determination to fit in with the society set. All that striving, that ascending, drained Mom's spirit and made Dad mean.

We'll never be snobs, I told her, reaching under my bed for a box of oatmeal creme pies and tossing her a cookie.

We both knew how the evening would unfold. Dad would stay civil while his colleagues were present, but when they left, he'd snarl about someone who'd gotten too big for their britches. Mom would try to soothe his ego, and he'd take it out on her, shouting while I made a fortress from the covers for Esme and me and played DJ on my iPod until the house was still again.

"You know I don't drink," I tell her now.

She sighs. "Guess I'll fix us some tea." She plucks the kettle from the countertop. "Orange pekoe, lemon ginger, or cinnamon?"

I can't remember the last time my little sister has pampered me in any manner, large or small. The last person to take care of me was Jamie, and my heart can't afford to spend any more time dwelling on what I've lost. As she digs in the cabinet for mugs, it hits me that this is the closest I've felt to Esme since before the accident. After that, everything changed between us. My eyes travel automatically to the jagged scar gleaming on her arm.

On the cushion next to me, my phone hums softly. I tear my eyes away to glance down at the text.

> **You'll ruin everything. Don't fucking
> do this.**

It's not a number I have saved. What the hell? I lift my phone to unlock it, and that's when I realize—it's not mine. It's Esme's.

"Janie? Hello?"

"Sorry." I drop Esme's phone, and the carnelian red case tumbles to the cushion. When I raise my eyes, Esme is lost to the kitchen cabinet, rooting around for honey.

"There should be some mint on the second shelf," I say. "I'll take that."

Through the wide arch, I watch her stir honey into her tea, then pluck a bag of mint from its box and drop it into my favorite blue-glazed mug.

"That's better." She walks back toward the couch, then sets our mugs down on two coasters. "Shall we?"

Before I can respond, the remote is in her hand, and the episode has resumed. I try to focus on the show, but every few minutes, the text needles at me.

Someone is threatening my sister.

THREE

GONE

By Monday morning, no one has heard from Esme for thirty-six hours. I didn't go into the city to pick her up, and now there is no question left in my mind: she is missing.

I take a long, hot shower and apply two layers of concealer that don't begin to compensate for the sleep I've lost. When I contacted the NYPD yesterday, I still felt half-sure she'd saunter through the front door by nightfall. That after I lectured her for making me worry and she inevitably stalked off to her room, I'd have a good laugh at how badly I'd overreacted to a misplaced phone and a few lost hours.

But I was right to trust my gut. Esme hasn't been admitted to any of the city's emergency departments. She hasn't contacted me. She hasn't contacted Mark. Could she be off on some adventure, the "new chapter" she alluded to on Instagram? I try to picture it. She's impulsive, sure, but even Esme would have to register that I'd be worried by now. It's hard to believe she'd leave me mired in anxiety for the sport of it, but it's been years since she's let me in. How well do I really know her?

I can't focus on work. I can't focus on anything except Esme. She vanished *on my watch*. Because I couldn't swallow down the old fear, make a drive into the city that probably would have been fine.

This is my fault.

I message my boss, Nabeel, letting him know what's going on. What begins as a notification that I'll be using a personal day quickly turns into a phone call, Nabeel insisting I take the week. More, if needed: "You never use your vacation. I will handle your loans. Jane, unless your sister is found safe, I don't want to hear from you until next week." *Click.*

I head down to the garage and climb into my Impreza. At noon, I will be meeting with Special Investigator Jay Marrone of the Missing Persons Squad, a specialized unit of the NYPD Detective Bureau. I have a healthy distrust of cops, but something about all the official-sounding titles calms me. New York is no small town with an underprepared and overwhelmed sheriff at the helm. There's a whole squad dedicated to these kinds of cases. And, much as I feel ill acknowledging it, Esme is a wealthy, beautiful white woman. Her case will be a priority.

In the car, I plug the Monarch Hotel into Google Maps and get on the road. It's the same address Esme texted me Saturday night, 420 Madison, which tells me only that her phone made it no farther than her last known location. I'm sure the detectives will have already picked it up, but I want to get a look at the place for myself.

As expected, Caitlyn at the reception desk informs me that an officer was here earlier, which is reassuring.

"He collected her phone, but I assume you'll be taking her bags?"

My eyebrows arch.

"I'm not sure the officer knew they were here," she says, registering the puzzled look on my face. "Her phone was behind the bar, and I don't believe he stopped by reception."

I nod, my confidence in the investigation thus far dropping by a few degrees. "And, sorry, but why are her bags down here in the first place?"

"Ms. Connor-Lloyd checked out on Saturday morning," she explains, "but she left her things at reception. I have a note here saying she'd collect them that evening, but she left the bar without stopping by the desk. I'm not sure what happened, but we can't hold them forever."

"Of course," I say, processing this new information. If Esme was a guest at the Monarch, presumably since Thursday, when she left Mark, why did she check out on Saturday instead of staying an additional night, given the storm and her lack of a ride?

"Did she say anything else?" I ask. "Inquire about extending her stay?"

"I'm not sure," Caitlyn says, "but we were fully booked on Saturday, so staying an additional night wouldn't have been an option, I'm afraid."

"I see." I press my lips between my teeth, thinking. My eyes stray toward the bar.

"The bar's not open yet," she tells me, following my gaze, "but Jody's in there setting up. You could ask her if she remembers anything from Saturday."

Gratefully, I step through the adjacent door and take a moment to look around. Along the wall to my right is a sleek black bar, a small leather-bound menu at every seat. Black-and-white photographs of theater darlings from decades past line the walls. The floor is carpeted in an abstract cream, gray, and green pattern. Everything is a little too bright. The place isn't entirely tasteless, if you favor the kind of guidebook New York experience that involves a trip to the Met, a quick gawk at Times Square, and a Broadway show. But this is not Esme's scene.

The woman stacking glasses behind the bar looks to be in her midforties. I make my way across the carpet and introduce myself.

"This is Esme." I pull up three photos from Thanksgiving, the most recent ones I have on my phone.

"Sure." She taps the screen with one long silver nail. "She was here on Saturday. All made up, pale pink dress."

"Was she with anyone?"

Jody shakes her head. "Not that I remember. She was nursing a cocktail at the bar for a while, but I don't remember her speaking to anyone."

"Do you know what time she left?"

She shakes her head again. "Nine or ten, maybe? It was before eleven, because we had a large party come in around then, and someone handed over her phone."

As if on cue, the phone behind the bar rings, and Jody wishes me luck before raising the receiver to her ear.

I walk back through into the lobby, where a massive cream-and-blue carpet bag and two gleaming black Louis Vuitton roller cases await me. I lug them out to the car.

An hour and a half later, I'm seated in a small, well-lit conference room at One Police Plaza with Special Investigator Jay Marrone, a stocky man with tan skin and thinning black hair who looks to be around my age. The room is newly updated; we're sitting in comfortable roller chairs, not the rickety metal kind I'd imagined, and the floors are a soft blond wood. Esme's phone sits on the jet-black table between us. I take the investigator through the events of Saturday night and Sunday morning while he listens carefully and takes notes.

SI Marrone asks for a description of what Esme was wearing that night, and I feel a surge of importance disclosing she was in a pale pink dress, per Jody at the Monarch. He gives me a smile that's hard to read, either grateful or bemused by my detective work.

"I need to be transparent with you, Ms. Connor. Our division handles active Amber and Silver Alerts—that's abducted children and missing dementia patients—and cases where a person goes missing under suspicious circumstances. At the present time, there is no evidence of suspicious circumstances surrounding Ms. Connor-Lloyd's disappearance."

My jaw hinges open. Before I can say anything in protest, he holds up a hand.

"Please keep in mind, we are in the early stages, and new information may very well come to light. I'm just letting you know where things stand."

"Okay," I say hesitantly.

"This morning, I met with your brother-in-law, Mr. Lloyd. He let me know that his wife disappeared once before, for three full days with no word."

I sigh. Three years ago, Esme and her friend Whitney took an impromptu girls' trip to a remote ski lodge, and the power went out. She'd left a note for Mark on the kitchen table, but apparently the housekeeper had sorted the note into a stack of mail, and Mark hadn't seen it. He called me, mildly concerned, but the absence of Esme's carry-on suitcase, winter coat, and ski gear was a strong suggestion she wasn't in danger. When the power came back on at the lodge Sunday night, Esme charged her phone and called Mark, and the mystery was solved.

"That was a misunderstanding," I say. "This is entirely different."

Marrone jots something down on his notepad. "Understood. Mr. Lloyd also showed me this." On his own phone, he opens Instagram and pulls up Esme's "time for a fresh start" post.

I roll my shoulders back and force my voice to stay steady. "I saw her Instagram. But that post is dated last Thursday, the day Esme left Mark. Did he tell you that?"

"He did," SI Marrone confirms. "He said Ms. Connor-Lloyd had been staying at the hotel, and she was planning to go home to Branby, Connecticut, for a while."

"That's right. So the new chapter she's referring to, that's about leaving Mark. It's unrelated to her disappearance." Even as the claim spills from my lips, I'm not entirely sure I buy the lack of connection, but I need this investigator to take the situation seriously.

"That may be," he says, "but unless we find evidence of foul play, we have no reason to believe your sister is not acting of her own accord. Adults walk away from their lives more often than you'd think. It's cruel to the family, and we're very sympathetic to the hardship these circumstances can cause, but it's not criminal."

"But she called me an hour or two before she disappeared," I counter, chest tightening. The ski weekend does *not* establish some kind of pattern, nor does the Instagram post. Heat rushes to my cheeks, and I jam my hands beneath my legs to keep them from visibly shaking. "She wanted a ride up to Branby, but it was storming. Are you telling me she left her husband, spent two nights at the Monarch, and made plans to come to Connecticut, just to abandon everything at the hotel, including her phone? Has anyone checked to see if she's used her credit cards?"

He nods. "Mr. Lloyd provided us with access to your sister's financial records, and we have not detected any new activity on her accounts. But she was in the process of leaving her husband, which both you and Mr. Lloyd have confirmed. Women who leave failed marriages seeking to start over often open new accounts. It's likely your sister is using a new card, possibly even new credentials. She may have left her phone behind on purpose, out of a desire not to be followed."

I sit with this information for a moment. Could Esme really have gone dark like that? Left behind her life—left *me*—with no explanation?

Marrone nudges Esme's phone toward me. "I don't suppose you have your sister's password."

I shake my head back and forth. "You can unlock it though, right?" My eyes linger on the carnelian red case, the black screen gaping blankly up at us.

He gives me a noncommittal shrug. "In certain cases, the NYPD contracts with digital forensics firms to access locked data. If it becomes important to the case, we will pursue it."

"Her laptop," I add. "It's not in her luggage."

His gaze is steady on me, but his eyes lack the flicker of interest I'm hoping for.

"It must be with her," I press. "If she's using it, you can track it from her phone, right?"

"If it becomes important to the case," he repeats, "we'll look into it."

"You have—" I start to protest, but he cuts me off, clearly done with this line of inquiry.

"Do you have reason to believe your sister's relationship with Mr. Lloyd was abusive, Ms. Connor? Physically or psychologically?"

My eyebrows shoot up. "Physically, no. She insisted nothing like that was going on, and I believe her. But psychologically?"

How well do I really know Mark Lloyd? I know facts *about* him: his family wealth, his investment banking job. But in the five and a half years he and Esme have been together—a year of dating, a brief engagement, and four years of marriage—Mark has largely kept his distance. He is a man used to getting what he wants, personally and professionally. Beyond that, I don't know much.

"Ms. Connor?" Marrone asks.

"Maybe psychologically. I'm not sure she'd tell me." The shame of admitting to this near stranger how distant Esme and I have become, how much she'd be likely to withhold, knifes through me.

He nods and jots something down. "There is of course another possibility." His tone is gentler now. "Mr. Lloyd let us know that his wife has been abusing alcohol and prescription drugs lately and isolating herself from her friends. Were you aware of this?"

The implication hangs heavy in the air. Substance abuse, self-isolation. Mark was suggesting she may have ended her life.

My gut says to dismiss the suggestion of suicide, but I force myself to consider it. Esme was "troubled" growing up; after she recovered from the accident, she transformed seemingly overnight from the sweet, sensitive girl she'd once been into a bit of a wild child, intent on doing whatever she wanted. New friends, constant partying, a cool irreverence to any rule Mom tried to instate. So the drinking Mark's mentioned is nothing new, and I'm not shocked to hear about her popping pills. But prescriptions indicate to me she was seeking treatment for conditions she's kept close to the vest. I can't objectively refute the possibility that she wanted to harm herself, but it doesn't sit right with me either. On Saturday, my sister wanted a ride. She was upset when we spoke, but not despondent or out of control. Not suicidal. She wanted to come home, not end her life.

There, I've considered it.

"I'm sorry, but I don't think that's what happened."

This conversation is not going as I'd expected, and there's a reason for that—Mark has steered the NYPD's thinking. First he brings up the ski weekend, which he knows as well as I do was a communication snafu, not an attempt to run away. Then the Instagram post, which was so clearly about her decision to leave him. Now this? Why lead the detectives to these conclusions, unless he has something to hide?

I fight to keep my voice under control, but it's a losing battle. "You don't think it's *a little bit suspicious* that all this information about self-medicating and isolating herself from friends is coming from the husband she was in the process of leaving?"

Marrone softens. "I know this is very upsetting." He picks up Esme's phone and places it on top of his notepad. "We are looking into Mr. Lloyd. I can assure you we are taking your sister's case seriously, and we will be seeking further information in her disappearance. It's our job to ascertain everything we can about the situation without ruling out any possibilities. As I said, it's still very early."

I nod, processing, but his words don't fill me with confidence.

Then Marrone is standing and sticking out his hand. Unsure of what else to do, I push my chair back and accept it.

"The lack of suspicious circumstances is good news," he assures me, walking to the door. "In all likelihood, your sister is fine. She may reach out to you of her own accord over the coming days. If she does, if you hear anything at all, please be in touch immediately."

"Right. Okay," I mumble, unmoored by the sharp pang of true worry. Until this moment, I'd been able to partially stave it off, believing, perhaps naively, that the Missing Persons Squad would be the solution, that as soon as this meeting took place, their work would kick into high gear and I could rest assured knowing Esme's case was in the hands of the experts.

"I know this isn't easy, Ms. Connor." The creases around his eyes relax, and he gestures for me to step through, into the hall. "We're going to do everything we can to find your sister. You have my word."

3

HOME

Monday morning, I wake before my alarm to the sound of the floors creak-creak-creaking. Old Boney, shifting her weight. Half an hour remains before I have to start my day, but my ear is tuned to the sounds of the house now. I'm up.

I take my time showering and getting ready; with Jamie on the other side of the country, I no longer need to squeeze in visits with Mom before work to avoid his shifts. At seven, I descend the stairs and head toward the kitchen. Esme has been home for less than forty-eight hours, but evidence of her presence marks every facet of the house. Discarded clothing droops from the sofa, the wide banister rail, the backs of the stiff dining room chairs. The contents of an entire Sephora store are strewn across the coffee table, and a deep berry smear mars its white marble top. She must have stayed up for hours after I went to bed, and I wonder if she went out.

I'm in the kitchen checking Slack and waiting for the kettle to boil when Esme's voice floats in from the three-season porch, sending my phone tumbling to the counter.

"Morning!"

She appears in the living room then, wearing a pair of dress shorts and a lacy top with a deep V, hair swept up in a twist, face fully made up. Given that I've barely seen Esme in daylight since she arrived, the sight of her up early and ready to greet the day is more than a bit jarring. She's holding a coffee mug and a leather-bound notebook with the year embossed in gold in the top right corner—an analog day planner, the kind of writerly accoutrement my sister loves.

Seeing her this way, it's hard not to feel a little jealous. There was a time when I, too, wanted to be a writer. We were both raised by Professor Carl R. Connor after all, who, for all his flaws, is a renowned scholar and tenured professor of contemporary American literature at Yale. But my literary attempts stayed between the pages of my journals, scenes from my life I'd narrate in blunt, economical prose (Raymond Carver phase) or through carefully observed and recorded dialogue and an attempt at dark humor (Flannery O'Connor phase). Even those I eventually stashed in a box on the top shelf of my closet when I got far enough along on my business degree to admit I'd chosen my path.

Journaling was a way of coping with my parents' split, with the accident, with the accumulated stress and deep uncertainty of my late childhood and teen years, but writing was a shot-in-the-dark kind of profession—and if a Connor girl was going to take that kind of risk, it wasn't going to be me. *Esme* was the daughter Dad encouraged, in his way. Perhaps he saw something in her, a raw talent I never possessed. Or maybe he knew I'd be miserable with the highs and lows, the criticism, the financial uncertainty, and as soon as I showed an interest in more stable, lucrative ventures, he steered me away from a road he thought it best I didn't start down.

"You okay?" Esme asks, drawing me from my reverie.

"Fine." I recompose my face into a smile and scoop up my phone. The creaking that woke me was probably my sister moving around down here. "Just startled. I had no idea you were up."

She crosses into the kitchen and deposits the mug in the sink. "I have an appointment."

"Oh." The kettle hisses, and I pour the steaming water into a fresh mug. "In the city?"

"Wouldn't you like to know." She hugs the day planner to her chest in a display of childish secrecy. Her green eyes flash.

"Oh my god, I'm not trying to pry." Although I am, a little bit. Esme and I haven't spent any real time together in ages, and I'd love to know her plans. And then that text message I accidentally intercepted last night . . . *You'll ruin everything. Don't fucking do this.*

But this morning, she seems far from upset or anxious. What is going on in her life that could possibly make a message like that feel routine?

She gives me a skeptical look.

"I'm leaving in twenty. If you're taking the train in, we can go together," I offer. "That's all."

"Thanks, but I'm not going to the city. I'm good." She spins on her heel and crosses back into the living room, heading toward the stairs.

"Wait!"

With an exaggerated sigh, she halts and turns back to face me. Last night, she was attentive, motherly even, but this morning, she is as shuttered as ever. My vision of the two of us growing close again stretches between our bodies like a precious, fragile web. One more step, and the strands will snap.

My mind flashes to Thanksgiving, nine months ago, the last time my sister stayed here at the house. We both remember how that ended: Esme in a snit over something she wouldn't share, storming out before the turkey to take an overpriced Lyft to join Mark's family in Old Westbury. She opted to return to the Lloyds' Long Island home for Christmas, despite repeated complaints about her husband's heated spats with his father and her mother-in-law's disapproving jabs targeting everything from Esme's partying to the cut of her top. When she came up to help with Mom's move in June, she booked a hotel.

The fact that she's back here now *must* mean something.

"I just . . ." I start, then trail off. If she won't even tell me where she's going, she's definitely not going to open up about what I saw on her phone. She has a right to her privacy, but that text was *threatening*. It's hard to believe Esme walked out on Mark out of a simple change of heart or sheer boredom. There's something else going on, but my sister has never been one to talk it out, has never responded well to confrontation.

A memory. We were in high school, ninth grade for Esme and senior year for me. It was a Dad weekend, which meant entertaining ourselves at his big, modern house in New Haven while Dad shut himself in his library to work, then banged around the kitchen for two hours, playing Stravinsky, drinking red wine, and cooking an elaborate meal we wouldn't sit down until after nine to eat. We were always bored, kept away from our friends for three nights. We hated how he grilled us about school, then lambasted the education we were getting, how he inevitably found ways to make us feel unwanted in his house, unworthy and small.

On that particular weekend, first-semester grades had just come in. We were both doing well in school, but it wasn't good enough for Dad. We should have been excelling, teaching the teachers, not coasting by on our intelligence and the shortcomings of the local public school system. It was well-worn territory. I was practiced at holding my tongue until Dad had found a new target for his ire, usually an uppity dean or a scholar at another university he suspected of sabotaging the peer-review process for his latest work of literary criticism. But Esme was thin skinned, not capable of such patience.

On that night, Dad held our latest English papers in his hands. He performed an unkind reading, then tore into our teachers for going too easy on us. He was disappointed in his daughters, in our predictable, uninspired drivel. He expected more from his girls. He was, as always, exceptionally hard on Esme. She could do better than this, couldn't she? I sat there and telegraphed my mind elsewhere, but Esme was stung by his hardness. She burst into tears at the table, then stormed out of the house, into the biting December night, and I ran after her. *He's got issues*, I told her when I had her wrapped in my arms, and she was gulping big, shivery tears into my shirt. *He acts this way because he hates his life, and he hates himself. He's an overeducated asshole. You're brilliant, okay? A star. Let's not let him ruin the night.*

When we went back inside, Dad was locked in his library again. Esme and I both changed into warm pajamas, then I went downstairs to load up the dishwasher and pack the leftovers into the fridge.

For a long time, the night slipped into the recesses of my memory, and I thought Esme had forgotten it too. Soon after, Dad started receiving postcards at work. Snide comments about his published work, barbs about his teaching. Nasty, searing stuff meant to get under his skin, hit him where it hurt the most. For two years, the mysterious correspondent taunted him, driving Dad into fits of fury. It wasn't until Esme was in her third year of college that she told me, with a smug grin, that she had sent them all.

Esme doesn't forgive and forget, and she doesn't do direct confrontation.

She lashes out.

Now I let my gaze float from my sister up to the high white ceiling. Pressing her about the text, or about Mark, would be futile. If I don't want her to shut me out completely, I'll have to tread carefully.

"You have a lot going on," I say gently. "And I just want to see if you're okay."

She tilts back her head and lets out a loud, throaty laugh.

I cringe. "Did I say something funny?"

"Jane, I'm about to be a twenty-eight-year-old divorcée. I'm sleeping in my childhood bedroom. Of course I'm not okay."

"Fine." I draw in a deep breath, forcing myself to quit while I'm ahead. I am, of course, also sleeping again in my childhood bedroom, but there's no use in pointing that out. You have to wait for Esme to come to you. "We can talk later, if you want. I'll be home from Monte Viso by nine. We could have a late dinner."

She shrugs. "If I'm home. See you." Then she vanishes into the hallway, and I'm alone in the kitchen once again.

Despite waking up early, I'm late leaving the house, and by the time I pull into the park and ride, the last spaces available are in the farthest row from the platform, against the thin grassy strip separating the parking lot from Caldwell Boulevard. The temperature has already climbed past eighty; it's shaping up to be a brutally hot day. I'm closing the car door and mourning the loss of the AC, hair suctioned to the back of my neck, when a white work van slows to a stop on Caldwell, directly across the grass.

A grinning face leans across the cab to wave at me through the passenger's side window. "If it isn't Jane Connor."

"Dylan!" The twinge of old heartbreak is fleeting. I'd heard that Dylan Greer was back in Branby, but I haven't seen him in ages. I break into a wide smile.

Growing up, I couldn't imagine a future without Dylan prominently featured. His father, Hank, was the full-time caretaker at our house, and until five or six years ago, Hank still lived in the old stone cottage on our grounds. As children we were inseparable; Dylan, just one year older than me, was like a part of the family, and then he became more. My first friend, first love, first heartbreak. When we got together, it was intense, all-consuming, and then over far too soon. He faded from my life when he left for ESF, the environmental sciences school at Syracuse. We've overlapped in Branby at various times over the years—holidays, odd weekends here and there—but we haven't really *talked* in more than a decade.

I rush across the grass and lean through the open window to give him a very awkward hug. He's tall and slim, tan as ever, blond curls sticking out beneath a beanie, despite the August heat.

"I can't talk," I say, overcome by a wave of disappointment. "My train's about to pull in."

"Bummer. You headed into the city?"

I nod. "Work."

"Well hop in, I'll give you a ride to Grand Central." He stretches across the seat to open the passenger's side door. It swings out toward me.

"Really?" I cast a look back across the lot, toward the platform. It's teeming with commuters sweating through their business attire.

"It's barely a detour. Started a new contract with the city to transform an old industrial lot in the east twenties into green space."

While Dylan and I haven't kept in touch, I've followed his impressive career in landscape architecture from a distance. A brand-new riverwalk in West Hartford, a campus revitalization initiative at a small central New York liberal arts college, the addition of an urban garden to an outdoor art center in the Bronx. It would be good to catch up, wouldn't it?

I look once more between his van and the platform.

"Get in," he says, patting the passenger's seat. "I'll tell you about it on the way."

I get in. Twenty minutes later, Dylan has told me all about his new project, his years moving around after college, then settling in the city before returning to Branby. He tells me his father has been battling prostate cancer, which comes as a surprise. Hank and I have run into each other around town a handful of times in the year I've been back, but the elder Mr. Greer has always been very private, perhaps a holdover from his desire to keep his personal life separate when he was living on our property. Dylan tells me he'd been going back and forth from the city to help his father out, but Hank began a more intensive course of radiation recently, and Dylan decided to rent a cheap place in town for the course of the treatment. It's a story all too similar to mine, and I feel my throat constrict as he talks.

When it's my turn to play catch-up, I fill him in on my own move back to Branby from the city last year, Mom's transition into memory support earlier this summer, and Esme's surprise return home last week.

"Big changes," he says. He glances down at my hands, folded in my lap. "Thought you might be married by now, to be honest. Anyone special?"

My stomach gives a little toss. I, too, thought I'd be married by now; teenage Jane would be crushed to know I'm still single.

My mind travels back to that girl, to who she was with Dylan. In spite of the years, I remember every detail of the June afternoon when everything changed for us. I was seventeen, Dylan eighteen. He kissed me behind the stone cottage, the two of us lying in the grass. I can still feel the tickle of the blades where my shirt had scrunched up my back, then his hand warm and soft against my skin. For two magical weeks that I thought would last forever, we were everything I'd spent months longing for us to be, unsure if I was alone in my desire. After that first kiss, it was like a light switch flicking on, the world suddenly bold and bright. We made plans for the coming school year, when he'd be off at college while I was stuck in Branby, reassured each other that we would talk every day, that we wanted this, had always wanted this, in ways we hadn't known how to define, and we were always, always, touching. His hand brushing my hand, my knee, the small of my back. My shoulder pressed to his shoulder, my head in the crook of his neck.

Then he ended it at the lowest moment in my life, days after the car crash that nearly killed Esme. I needed him more than ever then; I was so guilty and confused, and Dylan was the one person I felt like I could talk to. But he shut me out. I knew why, of course: How could he stand to look at me after what I'd done?

But it still hurt as badly as any pain I'd ever known, as badly as the pain of what I'd done to my sister, a realization that brought on fresh waves of guilt. I held out hope he'd change his mind, that we'd reconcile before he left for school. But June turned to July, and Dylan was like a ghost around Branby, never home, never in any of our usual spots, and then suddenly he was leaving for a summer program in Syracuse he hadn't bothered to tell me about. He started his new college life without looking back, leaving me alone in my misery.

"Very single," I confirm, dragging myself from the old heartbreak to the new. "I was seeing someone, but we broke up about a month ago."

"That's too bad." He sounds sincere. I wonder if he's seeing anyone, if I even want to know. What happened between us was so long ago; we were so young then. But I decide it's best not to pick at old wounds.

"But since you have all this newfound time on your hands," he continues, "with Marjorie getting round-the-clock care and you being newly single and all, maybe you could fit me in for dinner some night?"

I bite back a laugh at the suggestion of extra time on my hands—I have always had a talent for allowing work to plug any holes in my schedule—and consider Dylan's question. Is this a date? Would I want it to be?

"Only if you'd want to," he adds when I've said nothing to fill the silence. He reaches down to crank up the air another notch.

I find myself staring unabashedly at Dylan's open, eager face. He's even more handsome now than when we were in school, same bright blue eyes and boyish dimples, but age has replaced the puffiness of youth with a sharpened jawline and neatly clipped blond scruff.

He hurt me once, badly, but that was fifteen years ago. And much as the memory still stings, I understand why he did what he did. I understood even then. Before that, we had an entire childhood filled with good memories, years when we meant the world to each other. I'm not the same person I was that summer, and I'm sure he's not either.

"Dinner," I repeat, stalling.

"Say yes. Please. I'd like to catch up, more than surface stuff. More than this."

More than this. Heat flushes down my neck, despite the air blasting in the van.

I smile. "Dinner sounds perfect. How's tomorrow night?"

FOUR

GONE

I can count on one hand the number of nights Esme has stayed at Old Boney since college, but now that she's missing, there is something eerie about stepping into her childhood bedroom. Part of me expects her to poke her head out of the attached bathroom, blond hair and green eyes gleaming, and snap at me for entering without an invitation. It's silly, but for a moment I hover at the threshold, fingertips resting on the doorframe.

Esme's never been one to lay all her cards on the table, to spell it out. But I should have trusted my intuition on Saturday. Something wasn't right, and *I left her there*. I wince, gaze landing on the two black roller cases I dragged up here yesterday, and the guilt pooling in my stomach gives a little slosh. I can't stop picturing my little sister, wherever she might be: alone, confused, hurt, or worse . . . How could I have let something that happened fifteen years ago, under entirely different circumstances, keep me from going to her when she needed me?

I take a step into the room, then another. All morning, anxiety has washed over me in wave after chilling wave, until my guts turn to liquid and I feel like I'm losing my mind. With Nabeel discouraging me from so much as returning a work email, I have too much time on my hands. Mark has agreed to meet me this afternoon to talk, but until then, I have hours to fill. I need to find a way to redeem myself to my sister, need to find valuable information I can hand over to Missing Persons.

Officer Marrone seemed uninterested in Esme's luggage when I mentioned my cursory search through it yesterday, but surely there must be something there that could lead the police to her. That could bring her home safe. I heft the suitcases onto her bed and unzip them. Out wafts something light and floral, whose source I soon identify as the bottle of Jo Malone London leaking slightly into her toiletry bag. Along with the perfume is a little embroidered pouch of jewelry, her makeup, and a few Duane Reade basics like deodorant and hand lotion.

Methodically, I paw through both roller cases, pausing to hang her dresses in the closet and fill the shoe rack. Perhaps unsurprisingly, beautiful clothes compose the bulk of what she's packed. I check the outside pockets, then run my fingers along the lining. They graze a slim rectangular object nestled in an inside pocket—Esme's passport. If she was headed somewhere on Saturday, she wasn't headed far.

I place her passport on the dresser and return to the suitcase. Inside another small pouch are three orange prescription bottles. One I recognize as a Xanax generic. I look up the other two; they're all medications commonly prescribed for anxiety or depression. J. Farahat is the prescriber, and 0 REFILLS is circled in green Sharpie on each label, typical for SSRIs, benzos, and the like. Several of Mom's meds also require a call with the doctor before refilling. I make a note to check the number of remaining pills against the fill dates to see if Mark's claim about Esme abusing prescription drugs holds any water. In any case, the bottles aren't empty. She definitely didn't pop a bunch at once, no matter what he's led the cops to think.

At the bottom of one of the two roller cases is a who's who of ultracontemporary litfic ranging from mainstream to experimental, a tattered copy of Denis Johnson's collected poetry, and Kahlil Gibran's *The Prophet*. I lift the slim volume, now missing its dust jacket, from her luggage and peek inside.

To Esme. Yesterday is but today's memory and tomorrow is today's dream. Always, Dad, July 8, 2005.

Esme's tenth birthday. Two weeks later, he would walk out on us, and Mom would file for divorce. Honestly, I'm surprised Esme has held on to it for all these years.

I clear the contents of the floating bookshelf by Esme's bed to make room for her books. When I've finished sorting through both suitcases, I stand, frowning. I'm not sure what I'm looking for exactly, but whatever it is, it's not here.

Back downstairs, I make a beeline for Esme's carpet bag, which still rests against the living room wall where I deposited it yesterday. I extract several sweaters, a couple of scarves, and a gorgeous camel-and-white winter coat. When Esme packed, she was thinking of the seasons changing. She was thinking long term. Why pack all this, then leave it at the hotel? Was she trying to throw everyone off course? SI Marrone's suggestion that my sister might have intentionally gone dark grips me once again. But more likely, she had no intention of going anywhere on Saturday night but right here—before something or some*one* got in the way.

I unpack the rest of the carpet bag's contents. Tucked into an outside pocket is a black leather-bound notebook with the year embossed in shiny gold numerals in the top right corner. I let out a slow exhale. In the age of Google Calendar, leave it to my writerly sister to keep an analog day planner. *Thank you, Esme.*

I walk into the library and draw the heavy silk drapes to get some sunlight into the room, then settle in on the padded window seat and crack the planner open, flipping immediately to Saturday, August 26. There's nothing, not even the dinner with Mark she chose to skip, and I wonder if she ever had any intention of meeting him.

The afternoon prior, she's written *Hunter Library 3 p.m.* This could be something. I pull out my phone and plug it into Google. The day before she disappeared, my sister met someone at the Hunter College library. The main branch is on East Sixty-Eighth and Park Avenue. It's not directly next to the Monarch, or Grand Central, but it's the same part of the city, a ten-minute cab ride away.

Flipping ahead to this week, *Hunter Library 3 p.m.* appears again on Friday. I suck in a sharp breath. That's three days from now. I pull up my own calendar and enter it in. If she hasn't surfaced by then, I'll show up to her appointment, figure out who she met with the day before she disappeared, who she was planning to meet again.

Flipping back, there's a lunch on Monday, August 21, a few days before Esme left Mark. *Victoria Polo Bar 12:30.* Google tells me the Polo Bar is a Midtown restaurant with a hard-to-crack reservation list, which is definitely Esme's style. More Midtown, too; maybe I've been wrong about my sister's habits.

Before that, there's another call with Victoria, and someone named Laura, on the previous Monday at ten a.m. Farther back are several more calls with Laura in close succession—August 11, August 9, August 7, and July 26. There's an appointment with Dr. Farahat on August 3; probably her psychiatrist, but I've seen enough TV to know he or she isn't going to release any information unless there's a court case or a police subpoena.

On a Saturday in mid-June, a few days after Esme last came up to Branby to help move Mom into Monte Viso, *Café Lisse* is written in at 7:30 a.m. I plug the café into Google. It's on First

Avenue, north of Gramercy, a long way to go from Esme's West Village brownstone for a weekend coffee date. I explore the map to see what's nearby. A hospital—maybe she had a doctor's appointment. There's a Hunter College dorm one block over. That could be something; I make a note to come back to it later.

Finally, the details of a party are scribbled in for tonight. I look up the venue online; the events calendar for the swanky downtown space lists a cocktail party being hosted by one of the major publishers. I don't know exactly why Esme was planning to attend—maybe one of her friends from Scribe Society, the literary salon she hosts, has a new book coming out—but someone there might know something, and I will take a stroke of luck, no questions asked.

I spend another twenty minutes scouring the planner, but nothing else stands out. By the time I close it, I'm feeling a little discouraged, but I remind myself I didn't come up empty. Far from it. Tonight, I have the publishing party. And on Friday, I've got the Hunter Library appointment. Something will shake out.

But first, I need to talk to Mark.

At four thirty, I stand on the stoop of my sister's Barrow Street brownstone, waiting to be buzzed in. Apparently, late afternoon was the earliest Mark could get away from the firm, and even that was an inconvenience. I live and breathe work, but when Esme went missing, I didn't blink before taking a leave. And yet Mark went right back into the office following his interview with the NYPD. There's something off about that, something that pricks the base of my scalp as I wait on his doorstep.

When the buzzer blares, I press through the front door and into the vestibule. The building is quaint outside—window boxes, wrought iron railings—but inside it's very modern and very white.

White walls, white drapes, white fixtures, white furnishings with dove-gray accents where the interior decorator was feeling a little frisky. According to Esme, the entire brownstone was a gift from Rupert and Cynthia when Mark graduated from Yale and gained entrée to the world of investment banking. The Lloyds are a family of earners, have been for generations. Mark's older brother Sean is the CFO of some tech firm, and Luke, the youngest, is a patent attorney, following in his father's footsteps.

Esme has complained more than once that Rupert disapproves of her "career" as an aspiring writer and socialite, buoyed in large part by the name she married into. But while Esme is lacking in her father-in-law's approval, she's snared the interest of thousands on social. A certain sector of New York society has long been obsessed with the Lloyds. And while Rupert and Cynthia produced three virile sons, this generation lacked a daughter— not to mention a photogenic, fashionable party girl. Esme's in-laws may not approve, but "the people" do, and for the past five and a half years, my sister has been more than happy to give them what they want.

Until she wiped her Instagram account last week. Until *something* changed with Mark. The itchy feeling at the base of my scalp starts up again.

My brother-in-law meets me in the entry with a curt nod, then beckons for me to follow him into the living room, a light-filled space with high ceilings, a hardwood floor mostly covered by an enormous, plush white rug, and a large white sectional sofa. Floor-to-ceiling bookshelves, also white, line the far wall. They're mostly empty.

Mark takes a seat on the sofa and I follow suit, leaving ample space between us.

"Can I offer you something to drink?" he asks.

I shake my head. "I'd prefer if we got right to it."

Mark sighs and settles into the sofa, crossing one black-clad leg over the other. The hem lifts to reveal a glimpse of deep blue between his suit pants and shiny black dress shoes, the sole hint of color in his buttoned-up wardrobe. He's just over six feet, his arms muscular and shoulders broad. An atypical hint of five o'clock shadow lines his wide, square jaw, but the offending stubble is offset by his impeccably trimmed brown hair and gleaming white teeth. Mark is undeniably a type—one that many find irresistible, but his Ivy-bred manner and aggressive charm have never worked on me. I'm honestly a little surprised they worked on my sister.

I produce Esme's planner from my bag and hold it out. A part of me wants to lay into Mark, blame him for hindering the investigation, but if I lead with accusations and anger, he'll shut right down.

Reluctantly, I scoot closer to him on the sofa so we can look at the planner together.

"This was in her luggage. I need some help filling in the blanks about the people she was meeting." I point to the several instances of Victoria and Laura. "Who are they?"

He shakes his head slowly. "I don't know."

I narrow my eyes.

"Really," he says, voice unruffled. "She's been impossibly aloof lately, more so than usual. I don't know who she's been spending her time with."

"Marrone said she'd been 'isolating herself from her friends,' according to you. What was he talking about?"

"That started a few weeks ago. Some dustup among the literati." He gives a throaty chuckle that sets the hairs on the back of my neck on end.

"Go on?"

"I don't know what it was about. She wouldn't tell me. And it's not as if I had many opportunities to ask." He sighs and pinches his brows together. "She's never home, and when she is, she doesn't want to talk. We sit down for dinner together once a week, if I'm lucky."

He's angling for sympathy, but I refuse to take the bait. This is about Esme's behavior, not Mark's feelings. "That started a few weeks ago, too?"

He shakes his head. "Longer than that. Months. Honestly, she hasn't had a real conversation with me since Christmas."

At least in the beginning of their marriage, Esme and Mark showed up for one another. She was downtown parties with a young, boho crowd, and he was society functions and stiff business affairs, but they both put in the effort, according to my sister. Despite my dismay at her choice in husband, I respected that about him, about their relationship.

Clearly, that has changed.

Mark exhales loudly. "The holidays were miserable from the start. Sean and Cora couldn't make it out to Long Island, which upset Mother. Esme was in a foul mood the whole time. She snapped at Mother, then I snapped at Esme. We left early. And with each passing week, she's become more of a stranger."

I press my lips together, processing that, then flip to one of the appointments with Dr. Farahat.

"Esme's psychiatrist," he says without hesitating. "She began seeing her in November or December, I think. Before Christmas. And for a while, I really thought she was helping."

"But?"

"This summer, she's been drinking more than usual. Which is saying something. And I overheard her on the phone with the pharmacy recently, arguing about prescription refills."

"So you told the NYPD she was abusing her meds," I snap, unable to keep my irritation with Mark's behavior at bay any longer.

He shrugs. "It seemed relevant."

"I counted her pills," I say, trying to keep my voice level. "She was short a few Xannys, but nothing eyebrow raising. Marrone put suicide on the table because of what you told him."

"I'm sorry," he says, sounding sheepish for the first time. "He was asking a battery of questions, and I was trying to help. Truthfully, I do think she's fine."

My brows arch. "You think Esme's holing up somewhere. Pressing pause on her life or starting a new one."

"I think it's the most likely scenario. More likely than her being, I don't know . . ."

"Abducted? *Murdered?*"

"Jesus, Jane. Yes, more likely than that." He rubs his hand against the back of his neck.

I've clearly made him uncomfortable, as if by invoking the obvious possibilities I might have made them true. Or because I'm dancing too close to a reality Mark doesn't want to acknowledge. The temperature in the room seems to dip, and I inch subtly away from my brother-in-law on the couch.

If Esme knew she was in danger on Saturday night, if she thought Mark was any sort of safe harbor, she would have gone to meet him as planned. Yet again, I wonder what exactly happened between them—beyond distance, beyond boredom—something Mark seems as reluctant to open up about as Esme did last week.

"So what now?" I ask, frustration washing over me. "Go to work, pretend everything's normal?"

"What else am I supposed to do?" Mark's eyes narrow, and his typically cool voice pitches up a notch. "She was obviously unhappy with me. She'd left me, in case you forgot. I think it's pretty clear I'm the last person she wants tracking her down."

"Okay, okay," I concede. His tone has set the hairs on the back of my neck on end, but the reality is that Mark may have valuable information to share. "Let's say you're right, and she orches-trated all this, for some reason known only to Esme. So, where is she?"

He shrugs, not offering up any answers. Something flashes in his eyes, confusion or helplessness, maybe, something a Lloyd probably rarely feels.

"She left her phone at the bar and her passport in her lug-gage," I continue, thinking out loud. "But no sign of a wallet or purse."

"Hmm," Mark grunts.

"Still no action on her credit cards? No money missing from your accounts?"

He shakes his head.

"What about your parents' pied-à-terre in the city?" I don't fully believe it, but if Esme is truly hiding out somewhere on a shoestring, she couldn't have gone far.

"They sold it when Sean bought the Tribeca loft. There's an attached suite where they can stay."

I snap the planner shut, defeated, and slide it back into my bag. What have I learned? Esme began cooling to Mark this winter. Dr. Farahat is her psychiatrist, which I knew already. Truly the single piece of useful intel is that Esme had some fight with her writer friends, which Mark either can't or won't say anything about. I can only hope I'll learn more at the party tonight.

"May I use your bathroom?" I say, standing.

Mark nods and gestures down the hall. "Use the one down here. The plumbing in the master has been on the fritz."

I walk slowly, taking in the rest of the downstairs. It's not just Esme's books that are missing from the living room shelves. The glass cabinet in the hall has been cleaned out; all my sister's novelties from trips to Italy and France and China are gone, sold or packed away. I know they're not in her suitcases. Where a fresh, lavish bouquet used to grace their dining room table each week, the wood is bare.

In the bathroom, the fancy hand soap and lotion dispensers have been replaced by a single bar of Yardley London resting on a teak holder. My sister has been gone a week, and Mark has wasted no time removing every trace of her.

I flush and switch on the water, a frisson of unease running through me. Maybe it was foolish to come here alone, to pump Mark for information. After all, whenever a woman goes missing or turns up dead, it's always the husband, isn't it?

Feeling suddenly tense, I leave the bathroom and walk hurriedly back down the hall to the living room, where Mark still sits stiffly on the white couch. I lift my bag from the cushion and sling it over my shoulder. "Thanks for talking to me. I'll call you if I hear anything, and I trust you'll do the same."

Mark nods, satisfied, then stands.

"Of course," he says, ushering me toward the entry.

I take two steps back, but hesitate for a moment beneath the living room arch. I know I shouldn't needle Mark any further, but I need to find out what caused Esme to leave her husband just two days before she disappeared.

"What did Esme say to you on Thursday?" I ask. "Why did she leave?"

His eyes darken, but his voice stays steady. "Come on, Jane. Walking out on me was a cry for attention, and so is whatever she's up to now. For months, your sister has been building some mysterious new life *I know nothing about*. And now, she's off living it."

His manner is calm, and it's possible he truly believes Esme is playing at something. But as he steps toward me again, as I edge over the threshold and into the vestibule, I can't help wondering if Mark believes everything he's saying—or if *he's* the one playing games.

He reaches around me to unlock the door, and I step out onto the stoop. Despite the oppressive late-afternoon heat, goose-flesh erupts across my arms. I take two steps down the front stairs, and when Mark shuts the door behind me, the whole building seems to vibrate.

4

HOME

I wake at six with that Christmas-morning feeling. For a moment, I lie in bed, trying to remember what there is to be so excited about. It's a regular workday. Staff meeting at nine, an increasingly chaotic to-do list as the end of the month approaches. But I'm leaving the office early today because . . . Ah. Tonight is my dinner with Dylan. My date with Dylan? My lips part into a slow smile, and I roll over, bury my face in my pillow to smother a squeal like I'm seventeen again.

Downstairs, Esme sits at one of the stools on the far side of the kitchen island, sipping coffee and crunching down on a piece of toast. Like yesterday, she's already showered and dressed. When I walk into the room, she closes her laptop and places her elbows on either side of its rose-gold lid, then rests her chin in her hands. She wants something.

"You're up early again." I switch on the kettle and pull the orange pekoe from the cabinet.

"I have plans," she replies. "In the city this time. Can I get that ride to the train?"

"Sure." I open the fridge and scan the nearly empty top shelf. "Did you eat all my yogurt?"

She flashes me a guilty smile. "Maybe? Sorry, I'll replace it."

I grab a banana from the counter and dig in the pantry for a cereal bar. "We're leaving in twenty. Be ready."

When the 7:42 to Grand Central pulls into the Branby station, I half-expect Esme to ditch me for a different car, but she follows me onto the train and picks out a two-seater for us. This morning, she's dressed in high-waisted linen pants, a pale blue blouse, and brown leather sandals. Her clothes are luxurious, but professional.

"You going to tell me where you're off to? Or are today's plans a secret, too?"

She makes a face. "I'm meeting Kiku, if you must know."

My sister hangs around with a large group of stylish, creative twentysomethings. Most are a revolving door of names and Instagram handles she'll speak of passionately once or twice, then never mention again. But through the years, Kiku has stuck around.

They met as assistants at the same Manhattan literary agency. Esme was a recent college graduate, and Kiku had a year or so of experience under her belt. Esme lasted less than two years; when she married Mark, she took him up on the offer to quit her miserably paying assistant gig and focus on her writing full-time. But Kiku stuck it out, eventually advancing to become an agent in her own right.

In the four years Esme has been "writing full-time," she has published one short story in the *Kenyon Review* online and a second in the *Virginia Quarterly Review*, both highly reputable literary magazines, but they were pieces pulled from her college portfolio. She has talent in spades—how many writers are able to place anything they produce in undergrad workshops, and in good publications at that?—but she's never had much of a work ethic.

The train pulls away from the station, and I squeeze my eyes shut, picturing the dozen or so journals I kept from the time I was eleven or twelve through the start of college. I poured countless hours into tending them, treating each entry as if it was important, something to be read by the world someday. Of course I'd never show anyone the results of my adolescent bleeding onto the page—those journals have long sat collecting dust at the back of my closet—but in a different life, one that didn't require caring for Mom and caring for the house, I would have loved to be a writer. I *love* to work. If I had my sister's time, her talent, her connections . . . I force my eyes back open and turn to look at Esme. She's absorbed in something on her phone. If I had what Esme has, I wouldn't be living my life on Instagram.

"Business or pleasure?" I ask.

"What?"

"Your meeting with Kiku."

"Oh, we're just hanging out. You know." She makes a little flapping motion with her hand, then returns to her phone.

Hanging out on a Tuesday morning. Must be nice.

That evening, I return home feeling frazzled and out of sorts. Nabeel had to practically shove me out the door at four so I could squeeze in a visit with Mom before my dinner with Dylan. With Jamie still on vacation, I have memory support to myself, and evening visits are far preferable to dragging myself out of bed in the dark. But leaving Empire early was a mistake I'll pay for tomorrow, and when I got to Monte Viso, Mom was in A Mood. Every option on the dinner menu was "repulsive." She was reluctant to get in the elevator, then reluctant to go down to the courtyard. The air was too sticky. The trees smelled foul.

Now I have an hour to shower off the stress, change, and drive over to the little bistro on Main Street that Dylan has picked out. When the garage door shutters behind me, I unclasp my seat belt and pull the lever to tilt the seat back, breathing slowly in through my nose and out through my mouth. I've been looking forward to this all day, but now that it's almost time, I'm starting to wonder if this, too, is a mistake. For years, I fantasized that Dylan might change his mind, find his way back to me. That he would see past what I'd done, see the rest of me again. I thought I'd buried those feelings long ago, but they're right here, simmering beneath the surface.

I pull out my phone, pull up Jamie's Instagram. In the two days since I last checked, he's added a bunch of new photos from his trip, including two of a grinning Jamie standing beside a pretty redhead with striking blue eyes, his arm wrapped around her in a way that might be more than friendly. She's tagged as @rachaelmeade, but when I click on her profile, it's set to private. Probably for the best.

I scroll through the rest of his new photos, waiting to feel the usual flood of longing and sadness and regret. What comes is a slow, muted trickle, not the usual pummeling rush. Jamie will be back in Branby on Monday night, a date I'm embarrassed to admit is burned on my brain. But who cares, right? He's off in San Francisco, possibly with the redhead, definitely not thinking about me. And I am seeing Dylan tonight. Maybe I am ready for this. I want to stop feeling so goddamn sorry for myself, don't I?

In the hall, I slip off my shoes and drop my bag in its usual spot on the table. Halfway up the stairs, hand on the curved wood banister rail, I freeze. The door to Esme's room is open, and her voice filters down into the hall. She's on the phone. I shouldn't eavesdrop, should say something to let her know I'm home. But in the days she's been here, she's been so furtive, so closed off, refusing to divulge the barest pieces of information. I still know nothing about her separation from Mark, about where she's been going when she goes out. This morning's date with Kiku is the most I've gotten out of her since she arrived.

"Do we have to do the whole library thing again?" Esme is saying. "It's just so . . . *stuffy*. And there are so many people."

I hover on the stairs, breathing softly, while the person on the other end responds to my sister.

"And we will totally do that, but no one's going to suspect anything! I want to get to know you—*really* get to know you."

I feel suddenly uncomfortable. Of course there was more to the Mark story than she let on. Whoever she's talking to is probably the something more to that story.

"Yeah, okay. Friday at three. I've got a little surprise for you."

Noisily, I clomp up the remainder of the stairs and down the hall.

"I have to go," Esme says quickly. "Talk later, okay?"

"Hi," I call out. I walk past my own room and down to Esme's, until I'm standing at the threshold. The door is wide open, but she looks up at me from her cross-legged perch on the bed like my presence here is some kind of violation. The room smells light and floral, a new perfume. Esme's linen pants and blue top from this morning lie in a heap on the rug between her bed and the dresser along with the rest of her laundry. She's changed into a casual slip dress.

"What are you doing home?" On Esme's lips, it sounds like an accusation.

Admittedly, this is earlier than I've set foot in the house on a workday in weeks, but it *is* my house.

"I left work early," I say. "I'm going out."

I wait for her to ask me where, for my turn to tell her it's *none of her business*, but she just sighs and shoves up from the bed. "Me too," she says. "In a bit."

"Who were you talking to?" I blurt out, even though I know she's not going to tell me.

But Esme is full of surprises. "My new mentee. He's a senior at Sarah Lawrence, a really talented young writer." She raises a finger to her mouth and begins to chew the cuticle.

I fold my lips between my teeth. Esme has been a mentor before; she's involved in a program that pairs working writers with students in the tristate area. With her sparse credentials, it's a wonder she qualifies. But what I just overheard sounded personal. Intimate. My sister would know better than to get involved with a college student, wouldn't she? Or is that exactly the kind of disaster she'd be drawn to, a fire she couldn't resist starting?

My thoughts turn again to the threatening text. *You'll ruin everything. Don't fucking do this.*

She drops her hand to her lap and gives me a placid smile. More likely, the mentee line is precisely that—a line. Something to get me off her back.

And fine, point Esme. I return her smile, then spin on my heel and head back down the hall. Forty-five minutes remain before I'm meeting Dylan, and I don't have time for any more of my sister's drama.

FIVE

GONE

The chill of my meeting with Mark still clinging to my skin,
I stumble down the steps and set off down Barrow, turning on Greenwich, then Christopher. For a few minutes,
I walk aimlessly, trying to shake off my brother-in-law's patroniz-
ing tone, the implication that I am somehow overreacting to my
sister's disappearance.

It's been *three days*. Three long days of worrying, of fearing
the worst. It's not *my* reaction that's off base.

The cocktail party I'm attending in my sister's stead is at six. I
have some time on my hands, so I turn another corner, then another, allowing myself to get lost in the spiderweb of West Village
streets. When my phone chimes, I pause to dig it out of my bag.

Jamie. Despite everything, a smile tugs at my lips.

> Just checking in. Any news about
> Esme?

I let him know there isn't, that I'm taking some time off work to
look for her.

I'll be home Monday night. So sorry
you're going through this.

My chest gives a little squeeze. Monday is Labor Day, a date that was already burned on my brain. I reread his text. He didn't directly invite me to reach out when he's back, but the implication is there. I thank him and drop my phone into my bag, keep walking. Jamie doesn't want to get back together, that's not what this is. I don't think. But would it be wrong to accept his help if offered, to not have to go through this alone?

Eventually, I find myself back at the corner of Christopher and Bleecker, a few blocks from Mark's house. Nerves still jangling, I step into a little café and order a chamomile. It's nearly empty inside, that dead time before the evening rush. I nab a window seat and blow at the steam, thinking. Mark's parting words won't leave me alone: *For months, your sister has been building some mysterious new life* I know nothing about. *And now, she's off living it!*

True, Esme has long traded in secrets and clung to her privacy. But a "mysterious new life"? When I try to visualize it, I come up blank. She would love the drama of disappearing, but a fake passport, plane tickets under a new name, siphoning money from their accounts over weeks and months . . . That all takes more work than I can imagine her putting in, when she could have come to me any time. Desperate people leave their lives behind, and Esme wasn't desperate.

I believe my sister was being aloof, furtive, downright cold to her husband. She has always avoided direct confrontation and is, after all, her mother's daughter. I believe she was keeping things hidden. But everything about my conversation with Mark left a bad taste in my mouth. I don't trust Esme to be forthcoming, but just as strongly, I don't trust Mark.

Then, as if I've conjured him, my brother-in-law appears on the corner, one storefront down from the café. My breath catches. He's changed out of his luxe black suit into something no less formal—a new suit, charcoal gray, paired with a narrow burgundy tie. He stands at the crosswalk, shifting his weight back and forth, waiting impatiently for the signal.

The light changes and he crosses the street, pausing when he reaches the sidewalk, then drawing his phone from his pocket. A second later, he jams it angrily back in.

Before I've given it much thought, I'm pushing through the café door and out onto the sidewalk. As I tail Mark along Christopher, the city hums around me—students grabbing pizza, tourists idling on the sidewalk, two gray-haired men, hands intertwined, reading a poster in the window of a cabaret club. I stay a block behind, following Mark to the Jefferson Market Garden, then up Sixth Avenue. As he walks, he shoves his hands into his pockets, then out again. Several times, he rolls his shoulders back. At West Twelfth, waiting for the light to change, he checks his phone again. If only I could get close enough to see who he's texting.

I keep moving until we're on the same block, reassuring myself that Sixth Avenue is a busy thoroughfare, its wide sidewalk bustling with pedestrians, and Mark is sufficiently absorbed in his phone. I'm hidden in plain sight.

But then Mark's head jerks up, and I flatten myself against a storefront, sure he's sensed my presence. He looks across the street, then over his shoulder at the Halal vendor three feet to my left. One more turn of his head, and his eyes will be on me. I try not to breathe.

The light changes, and a woman walking her bike bumps Mark's elbow as she starts to cross. His gaze snaps toward her, then he steps into the crosswalk, and I exhale slowly.

Maintaining a healthy distance, I tail my brother-in-law all the way to the northern edge of Union Square, where he stops beneath the crisp black awning of a Japanese steak house. I find a spot across the street, half-concealed in the shadow of a news-stand, and wait. It's not just my imagination. The whole way up here, Mark was acting twitchy. Nervous. *Which is exactly how I'd be acting if I just made my wife disappear.* I wait for five minutes that become ten, pretending to scroll through my phone, then actually buying a copy of *People* when the guy running the news-stand gives me a pointed look. Across the street, Mark is on his phone, too, busily typing.

Finally, he looks up, to his right, and I follow his gaze. Coming down the sidewalk is a tall, gray-haired man I recognize from Esme's wedding: Rupert Lloyd, Esq.

Mark shoves his phone into his pocket one last time and reaches out to accept his father's hand for a stiff shake. Like his son, Rupert is fit, broad shouldered, and smartly dressed in a suit, probably Italian silk, a button-down, and a tie. He reaches for the door, and the two men disappear inside the dark steak house, leaving me feeling let down—and incredibly silly. What did I think, that Mark was going to lead me to the place where Esme is being held, or worse, to her body? That the person on the other end of the phone would turn out to be a mafioso or hired hit? I turn and slink toward the subway, filled with the realization I've just wasted half an hour of my life following my sister's estranged husband to a not-so-clandestine dinner with his father.

At six thirty, I arrive to the airy SoHo loft where the cocktail party is being held and make my way to a row of tables staffed by a few eager young assistants encouraging everyone to locate their name tags and take a goodie bag. I smile, nod like I'm supposed to be here, and pin ESME CONNOR-LLOYD to my chest. The gold paper bag is marked by a round Brenner & Reed sticker. I recognize the name; it's an imprint of one of the few major houses left in the rapidly consolidating NYC book publishing world. Inside is an advance copy of *The Insouciants*, a literary novel by someone named Ben Latzer, a gold-stamped Brenner & Reed coffee mug, and a black fountain pen. An embossed card welcomes me to the imprint's twenty-fifth anniversary celebration.

Around me, a hundred or so publishing professionals wearing Ann Taylor and Banana Republic sip wine and Stella Artois at little round tables, making conversation. The literary agents are distinguishable by their fresh manicures and slightly higher heels; the authors have that teenager-in-a-bar look, clinging to their glasses as if they might get cast out any second.

Everyone appears to be deep in conversation. I walk over to the bar and select a prepoured glass of seltzer, then turn again to scan the sea of faces, seeking out someone, anyone, who I can approach.

This is going to be harder than I thought. No one is looking at me, let alone reading my name tag. Over a hundred people are already inside, and a couple hundred more tags remain to be picked up. No one is going to miss my sister in the crowd tonight.

I lean against the bar and allow my eyes to stray toward the elevators, wondering if I should go. Right then, the doors open, and out steps someone I recognize. Esme's friend Kiku Shima, whose contact information I had tried and failed to locate when my sister first went missing.

Kiku is talking to a young, scruffy guy in a brown corduroy jacket and jeans, probably one of her authors. They walk over to the welcome tables, then start toward the bar.

I touch Kiku's shoulder, and she turns to face me. She's Japanese American, black hair cut in a long, stylish bob, and square-cut nails painted a shiny eggshell blue. She gives me an affable smile, but it lacks recognition. It hits me that while I recently saw her photo on her agency page, we've met in person only the one time, when I came to see my sister in action at the salon, three or so years ago.

"I'm Jane," I reintroduce myself. "Esme's sister."

"Oh, of course." For a moment, she looks flustered, glancing at my name tag.

"I know she's not here," I tell her. "That's actually why I came. Can we talk for a moment?"

"Yes, one sec." She turns to the guy in the brown jacket, then points him toward a nearby table occupied by someone he seems to recognize, assuring him she'll be over soon. When we're alone, she motions us toward two empty stools at the end of the bar, and we sit.

I set down my seltzer and tuck a long strand of hair behind my ear. "I don't know how to say this, so I'm just going to dive in."

She nods, looking concerned.

"Esme's missing. Has she been in touch at all?"

"Missing?" Kiku asks. "What do you mean *missing*?"

"Neither Mark nor I have heard from her since Saturday night. Have you talked to her?" My voice pitches up, eager.

She shakes her head. "I actually haven't heard from her in over a month."

"Oh. Shit."

She frowns. "What happened on Saturday?"

"I don't know. She was in the city, in Midtown. She called asking for a ride, but it was storming. I couldn't get there." I take another sip, swallowing down a fresh twinge of guilt that threatens to steal my voice away. "Then she just never came home."

"I'm sorry, I'm a little lost," she says. "Don't you live in Connecticut?"

"Right. Let me back up." If she hasn't spoken to Esme in over a month, of course she's confused. "Esme left Mark," I tell her.

Her eyebrows fly up. "Really?"

I nod. "She'd spent a couple of nights at a hotel. Then on Saturday, she was trying to make her way to Branby."

"Did she say why she left him?"

"She was bored. Although I'm sure there's more to the story."

Kiku frowns. She picks up her wineglass and takes a small sip.

"I didn't know any of this," she admits, looking around, as if worried someone might be listening in. She drops her voice. "I hadn't talked to her in a while because, well . . . We had a little bit of a falling-out. She quit the salon, actually."

I nod, everything making sense. Mark mentioned as much this afternoon. *Some dustup among the literati.* Surely, drama of my sister's making. I feel bad cornering Kiku at a professional event, stirring up personal issues that obviously have nothing to do with Esme's disappearance. "You don't have to talk about it. I'm just trying to figure out what might have happened, where she could be."

Kiku looks ashen. "I'll ask around. Try to find out who she was still talking to in the last few weeks."

"Thanks." I give her my number, and she texts me with hers. Then Kiku excuses herself to rejoin her author and the others at their table, and I'm left on my own once more, swirling my seltzer. I'm not a detective; what did I really hope to get out of tonight? Kiku did corroborate Mark's story—Esme was clearly going through more than her recent breakup, enough to cut ties with a good friend and probably burn a few more bridges in recent weeks—but it's nothing that sheds any light on Saturday.

I slide my empty glass toward the back of the bar and adjust my purse strap across my shoulder. Time to cut my losses and leave.

"You're not Esme."

My head snaps up. In front of me stands a stout woman of

indeterminate age—sixties or seventies, most likely. Her dark black hair is cut in a shoulder-skimming, Anjelica Huston-style bob, and she wears a tasteful black-and-gray color-block dress—definitely not from Ann Taylor or Banana. She actually looks not unlike a shorter, slightly less severe Anjelica Huston.

"N-no," I stammer. "I'm her sister."

"Ah." She leans against the bar, appraising me.

"I'm here because I'm worried about her. I was hoping to talk to a few people she knows."

"Victoria Shaughnessy." She extends her hand toward me. "Executive editor at Brenner & Reed."

"Jane Connor." I clasp her hand in mine, and her many rings press into my skin.

Victoria selects a glass of red from the bar and beckons for me to follow her. We walk across the room, away from the table where Kiku is now absorbed in conversation with her author and a few others, and toward two empty chairs set up by a tall window.

"I presume Esme has told you about her book deal."

My eyebrows arch toward the ceiling. Maybe I shouldn't be so surprised—my sister is a writer; Victoria Shaughnessy is an editor. But given that Esme hasn't so much as written a new short story since college, the leap to writing—and finishing—a novel seems almost preposterous. And to have sold it to an executive editor at Brenner & Reed?

"No," I splutter. "I'm afraid she hasn't."

"Oh." Now Victoria looks as confused as I feel. "Then what exactly did you wish to talk about, my dear?"

I draw in a deep breath, then give her the abbreviated version of the past few days. When I've wrapped up, I ask her when she and Esme last spoke.

"We met for lunch last week," Victoria says. "Esme had a lot of questions about the publishing process, more than we could get to over one meal. I told her to reach out to my assistant to set up a meeting for this week or next, with Laura—her agent—so we could get everything squared away. Now I see why I haven't heard from her."

The entries from my sister's planner float before my eyes. *Victoria Polo Bar 12:30. Victoria and Laura call, Monday 10 a.m.* Her editor and agent.

Victoria frowns. "No one's heard from her at all? Have you notified the police?"

I sigh and explain the state of the investigation. "They're looking into it, but I get the impression they think she ran away after leaving Mark, perhaps started over somewhere new. Now that I know she had a book deal, that seems even less likely."

"Truly," Victoria says. "She had everything ahead of her."

"I have to be honest, I didn't even know Esme was writing a book, let alone that she'd sold it. My sister has not always been the most forthcoming."

"Mmm." She takes a slow sip of wine. "I am getting that impression."

She glances over my shoulder, and I follow her gaze. A small cluster of young women, probably junior editors, are standing politely at a distance, clearly waiting for Victoria to be free.

"One last thing," I say before she can excuse herself. "Do you know anything about a falling-out between Esme and some of her friends in the publishing world? Kiku Shima, in particular?" It seems like a long shot, but now that I know about Esme's book deal, I have to find out if any of these pieces are connected.

She glances out the tall window beside us, toward the shops and restaurants below. When she meets my gaze again, she lets out a slow breath and settles back in her chair.

"I wouldn't normally share this, but in light of the circumstances . . . After the auction closed, I received an impassioned call from Ms. Shima. As it turns out, she expended considerable time and energy helping your sister develop her story over the past several months. What came to my desk was a fascinating, explosive narrative that my colleagues and I went crazy for. It sold to us in an eight-editor, six-house auction for a major advance. But your sister was not represented by Kiku Shima."

"What do you mean?"

"Esme insists Ms. Shima was doing her a favor, giving her feedback as a friend, not as her literary agent. Ms. Shima says they had a handshake agreement, but the two had a personal falling-out before she could put the manuscript on submission, and Esme took it to another agent."

"Holy shit."

Victoria laughs. "Holy shit is right. I'm sure Ms. Shima has learned her lesson—never develop a project without a formal agreement, even if the writer is a friend. Indeed, especially if the writer is a friend. Perhaps it was a misunderstanding, perhaps not, but either way, Esme cut her out of the deal, and the commission will go to her agent of record, Laura Rosado. Needless to say, I didn't know any of this until after I'd bought the book. I feel badly for Ms. Shima, but there's nothing I can do. She has nothing stating their relationship in writing, Esme has signed with a new agent, and the deal is done."

I sit in silence for a moment, processing everything.

What had Kiku said to me a few moments ago? *I hadn't talked to her in a while because, well . . . We had a little bit of a falling-out.* She definitely downplayed what happened between them, but she was probably trying to spare my feelings about Esme, in light of her disappearance. Besides, we're at a work event, and Kiku strikes me as a professional. Esme's the one who went behind her back. No wonder Kiku—and probably most of their friends—haven't been speaking to my sister. No wonder Esme called me to beg for a ride, feeling like she had nowhere to go.

I thank Victoria and let her get on with her evening. Nothing I gleaned here seems likely to be connected to what happened on Saturday night, to wherever Esme is now, but I did learn something very important. All the time she led me to believe she was doing far more socializing than writing, my sister was working on a novel. And now, she's on the cusp of the kind of success she's dreamed about since college—a contract with a New York publisher, a major advance. My conviction that she wouldn't have skipped town willingly, and certainly wouldn't have taken her own life, is only stronger.

Which means what I've been fearing *has* to be true: Esme is in real danger. Something very bad happened on Saturday night.

5

HOME

Branby's small downtown comprises four attractive blocks of cafés, restaurants, and shops along the aptly if unimaginatively named Main Street. Planter beds brim with colorful arrangements, wrought iron benches line wide sidewalks, and a tall black clock with a round white face keeps time in front of Ruby's, the local florist, family run for four generations. I pull into one of the several open spots a block down from Chez Allard, the Parisian-style bistro Dylan has selected for dinner. It's a charming, intimate restaurant. The kind of place you get a little dressed up for, the kind of place you take a date.

I've changed out of my work clothes and into my favorite sundress, a blue-and-green striped number that brings out the bright flecks in my eyes and cuts an hourglass shape from my flat frame. I pull down the visor mirror and tuck my long brown hair behind my ears, revealing a pair of jade-and-gold chandelier earrings, a gift from Esme a few birthdays ago. The face looking back falls short of gorgeous, but I feel attractive, pretty even, something I haven't felt since my split with Jamie.

My hand travels automatically to my phone, itching to open Instagram, but I pluck it from the passenger's seat and drop it inside my bag instead. Dylan is waiting, and I'm already five minutes late. I am not indulging that habit again tonight.

When I walk through the door, Dylan rises from a bench near the hostess stand and folds me into an easy hug. His arms feel familiar and strange all at once. When we were kids, he was always generous with his affection, even as we reached the age when certain people begin criticizing boys who are too emotional, too soft. Dylan never let that small-minded kind of talk bother him. But it's been fifteen years since we were last in each other's lives in a meaningful way. These aren't the arms of the adolescent boy who once placed me on a pedestal, then broke my heart in two. Dylan is thirty-three now, a year older than me, a man with an impressive résumé for his age and an equally impressive strength to his embrace.

"You have muscles," I blurt out.

We both laugh, and a hint of pink creeps into Dylan's tan cheeks. "Working outside will do that to a guy."

"Don't you have a whole team of, I don't know, engineers and builders and the like?" I don't honestly know that much about the mechanics of what Dylan does, but I imagine that in addition to the on-site work, there's a lot of time spent indoors, hunched over blueprints and fancy design software.

"Yeah, you caught me. I was a scrawny shit when I left for college. You remember. I started going to the gym a while back. I made a few changes in my midtwenties." He plucks at an invisible piece of lint on his shirt collar. "Should we see if our table's ready?"

I nod. There's so much I want to know, so many years for which I have only the haziest picture of Dylan Greer's life, but we have the whole evening ahead of us.

When we're seated at a small table near the back of the restaurant with a tea light flickering between us, he gives me a warm smile. "You look beautiful, Jane. I meant to say that the moment you walked in."

Now I'm the one with pink creeping into my cheeks. So he does want this to be a date. "Thanks. You look really good, too."

Gone are the beanie and white T-shirt from yesterday morning. This evening, Dylan is dressed in dark, slim-fit jeans, a fitted plaid button-down, and brown dress shoes. With the hat off, I can see his mop of blond curls has been cut by someone who knows what they're doing, and carefully styled. I want to reach across the table, touch him again, but instead I pick up my menu and start to read.

Too soon, our server appears to ask if we've had a chance to look at the wine list, and I realize I haven't yet told Dylan that I don't drink. Not anymore.

"Just a seltzer for me," I say, watching for his reaction. "Did you want wine?"

"I'll have a Coke," he says, and our server retreats, wine list in hand.

"I don't drink," I say when he's gone. "With Mom's dementia, and Esme's partying, someone needs to keep a clear head. Besides, after what happened in high school, with the crash . . ." I trail off, unable to finish the sentence. I didn't mean to bring up the accident, or to dance so close to our breakup, especially not this early in the evening.

"No need to explain," he says quickly. "I should apologize, actually. I was such an ass when I left that summer, and then I basically ghosted you once I got to Syracuse. I'm sorry."

I suck the inside of my cheek between my teeth, seventeen again. I can feel the sharp, fiery liquor coursing through my veins, Mom's car keys clutched in one fist, Esme's small hand in the other. My eyes squeeze shut, the memory of the hours after the crash drawing me in—my sister's head wrapped in a thick white bandage, blond wisps sticking out. Our parents crowding her hospital bed, bickering, fretting, bargaining with God, while I hovered inside the doorway, back pressed to the wall, attempting to disappear into the plaster. While Esme slept, a battery of machines seemed to speak for her, beeping and blinking her will to remain in this world. *Stay alive stay alive stay alive.*

Even then, my adolescent brain chafed against the easy aphorisms, that God has a plan or that everything happens for a reason. The truth is I made a choice, first to take those vodka shots, then to get in the car, and from that moment forward, I and everyone around me—Mom, Dad, Esme, even Dylan—were forced to go on in a new reality of my making. There was no firm hand of fate steering the wheel that night. No goddess of destiny descending from the heavens to chart the course of two sisters flying along a slick, dark highway in the rain. There was only me, seventeen and teeming with vodka and conviction, determined to guide my sister out of harm's way. Or so I'd believed. Instead, I replaced one kind of damage with another, a choice I will have to live with, always.

I force my eyes back open, myself back to this moment.

"Apology accepted," I say. I've never questioned why Dylan didn't want to have anything to do with me after the crash, but it means a lot now to know he feels some regret about the way things ended between us. All the years we lost.

Our server arrives and sets our drinks down. We place the rest of our order, and then we're alone again.

"Cheers." I hold my seltzer out to Dylan, and he clinks his glass to mine.

Then I draw in a deep breath. "I have to admit, it hurt when you didn't keep in touch. I understood, but I thought eventually we'd find our way back to each other. I've missed you."

"Shit, Jane." He reaches across the table and slips my hand into his. Involuntarily, I shiver. "I never wanted you to feel like that. The truth is, when I got to Syracuse, I wasn't the caretaker's son anymore, one of the poorest kids in rich Branby. I was getting a lot of praise in school, which felt great, and I was having way too much fun partying. Anyway, I got really good at compartmentalizing, and it was easy to throw myself into my new life. But I never meant to hurt you."

I give his hand a squeeze. It's not what I expected—so much less about *me* than I'd always imagined—but it makes sense. "Thank you for saying that. Now can we leave the past in the past and talk about something else?"

He grins, and my heart stutters in my chest. "Absolutely."

We do not, in fact, leave the past in the past, but the conversation turns further back, to high school, then childhood. All my best memories from growing up involve Dylan, and even the bad times were better because of him. When my parents were splitting up, Esme needed my support, but I needed someone, too. Dylan was there for me with unlimited hugs and funny movies and bike rides through town.

Our food comes, and I tell him I still have the set of wooden Jane figurines he carved for me each year on my birthday, each tracking not only my age but marking his rapidly growing creativity and talent for precision and detail. We talk about Esme's return to Branby, and Dylan laughs and rolls his eyes in all the right places when I describe her slovenly ways, stealing my yogurt, the odd hours she keeps.

"All the same, it's nice having her around," I say. "Even if she is the world's worst houseguest. Sometimes, when she lets her guard down for a second, I think maybe we're not irreparably damaged. Maybe we can be close again, the way we used to be."

"You know she loves you, underneath it all," he says. "But Esme's always been hard to pin down. You did a really stupid thing when you were kids, but you can't let her guilt you about that forever. She loves you, but she's going to take advantage of you until you're old and gray if you let her."

I swallow. He's right, of course he's right, but right now, I don't want to linger on Esme, to think any more about that night, about any of it.

I turn the topic instead to Dylan's dad.

"How's he doing?"

Dylan shrugs. "He's hanging in there, and we're hopeful about the new treatment. But it's been rough. For both of us, to be honest. You know my father, he never wants to ask anything of anyone. It hasn't been easy for him to accept my help, and being back in Branby . . . Well, it's not the city, is it?"

He laughs, and I join him.

"It's most definitely not. Do you hate it?"

He shakes his head. "It's just bringing back a lot of old memories, not all of them good ones. I'm glad I ran into you yesterday, though. I was hoping I might."

My chest fills with a warm glow. By the time our plates have been cleared away and Dylan has pounced on the check, I feel relaxed in a way I haven't felt with another person in a long time. Even Jamie. After all these years, Dylan is still the same kind, compassionate person he always was. The ache of what happened between us lingers, but it was such a long time ago. As adults, we've carved out similar priorities. Family. Work. Home. Maybe, possibly there is something real here.

Out on the sidewalk, Dylan insists on walking me the one block to my car. When we arrive, he leans against the driver's side door and pulls me in to him. Heat radiates through the fabric of his shirt. A frisson of want travels through me, and I let out a slow breath.

"You were always so beautiful, Jane," he whispers into the side of my neck. "Now more than ever."

"Even after you broke my heart," I whisper, "I never thought it would take this long for us to really talk again."

"I regret that," he says, and his voice wavers. "I had my hang-ups, and I let them get the best of me."

I tilt my chin until our lips are so close they're almost touching.

"You're here now," I say. "We're here now."

He reaches one hand up and slides his fingers along my neck and into my hair. For a moment, he cups my face gently, examining every angle. Then he leans forward slowly, until I can feel the air evaporate between us, until his skin is brushing mine, and my lips part to fit his. Heat floods my entire body, and I wonder if he can tell I'm on fire.

"You didn't know how to kiss like that at eighteen," I say when we've finally broken apart, and I'm still tingling. For the first time, I can let the sense memories rush through me, and it doesn't feel like probing an old wound. It feels like sinking into a warm bath after a long, difficult run, the water's welcome caress tickling every inch of my skin. Waking me to a long-dormant desire I'd all but forgotten.

He grins. "Not even close. I promise, thirty-three-year-old Dylan is an improvement in infinite ways."

I kiss him again, deeper this time, then pull back, giddy with the endorphin rush. I want this, everything ahead of us.

"You know what you should do?" I say. "Come to dinner on Friday."

"Jane Connor, are you asking me on a second date?"

"Not exactly," I admit. "I mean yes, I'd like that, too, but Friday is Mom's birthday. We're taking her to Mario's for an early dinner. It'll be like old times."

When we were growing up, Mom and Dad, and then just Mom, would take Esme and me to Mario's for dinner every Sunday. We weren't allowed to bring friends, but Dylan was an occasional exception. At least once a month, I'd twist Mom's arm into letting him join, and Mom would make a show of grumbling about how this was supposed to be *family* dinner while we were getting ready, but as soon as we all piled into the car, she'd give up the pretense, warming to his presence. Mom was as charmed by Dylan as anyone.

He's nodding slowly. "Esme coming?" he asks.

"Apparently. She hasn't been to see Mom at Monte Viso once since she's been back in town, but she's promised to turn up on Friday."

He sighs and leans back against the car door. "I don't know, Jane. We're just getting to know each other again. I might need a little time before I'm ready for Connor family dinner."

My stomach clenches, the cassoulet turning to stone. Of course Dylan isn't ready for Mom and Esme yet. I was thinking only of myself—how good it would be to have him there with me. How I'm eager to make up for lost time. But one look at Dylan's face and I'm hit with the worry I've tamped out the spark starting up between us.

"Of course," I say, backpedaling. "I was caught up in the moment. I wasn't thinking."

He clasps his hands around my waist. "It's incredibly sweet that you invited me. But how about we do dinner again on Saturday instead? Just the two of us."

I smile, relief washing over me. "It's a date."

SIX

GONE

Six days and still no word from Esme. By Friday, the search has begun to seem like the only reality I've ever known. I live and breathe it. It is family and work and love. Each day, it gets easier to let messages from my former life sit unread in my inbox, to allow my colleagues to keep Empire running without me. The surges of guilt over leaving her that night, of pure, unadulterated fear about what may have happened to her since, keep hitting me like a tidal wave, but I bear down and ride them out. This is my job now. I have always been good at what I do. I will find my sister, bring her home safe.

Friday afternoon, I take the train to Grand Central. As I step from the air-conditioned station into the blistering heat and begin the walk uptown toward Hunter College, I try to inhabit her. The click of her heels on the pavement. Raindrops pelting her skin. She left the Monarch before eleven. Was she still looking for a way to Connecticut, or was she headed somewhere new? *Where did you go, Esme? And what happened?*

I'm about to cross East Forty-Eighth when a familiar voice stops me in my tracks.

"If it isn't Jane Connor."

Standing before me, messenger bag slung over his shoulder and file box clutched in both hands, is my childhood best friend and first love, Dylan Greer. He sets the box down on the sidewalk between us to give me an awkward and slightly sweaty hug. He's tall and slim, tan as ever, blond curls sticking out beneath a beanie, despite the heat.

"Fancy meeting you here." I give him a big grin. "I haven't seen you since, what, that Christmas we got a foot and a half of snow?" We've overlapped in Branby at various times over the years—holidays, odd weekends here and there—but we haven't really *talked* in more than a decade.

"Time flies," he says, plucking the box from the sidewalk.

"I hear you're back in Branby? Of course we'd run into each other in the middle of Manhattan."

He laughs. "Got five minutes to walk with me? I'm headed to the copy shop, paperwork for a contract I'm doing with the city."

"Congrats, Dylan."

"Come with." He gestures down the block with his chin. "We're transforming an old industrial lot in the east twenties into green space. I'll tell you all about it."

"I can't," I say, struck by a pang of disappointment. If circumstances were different, there's nothing I'd rather do than spend some time catching up, and more than that, truly getting to know each other again. There's always been so much left unsaid between us, so much I'd like to lay bare. But now is not the time. "I'm dealing with some stuff at the moment. Esme's missing."

"No way." He shakes his head, looking amused, and I bristle.

"Really."

The smile drops from his face. "Oh, you're serious. Since when?"

"Since Saturday. I'm actually headed to an appointment she

had penciled in to her planner. I feel a bit like I'm casting around for clues that aren't there, but I have to do *something*."

"Right, of course. I'm really sorry, Jane." He shifts the box, and his muscles strain against his white T-shirt. "I should let you go, but I'll text you my new number, okay? Let me know if there's anything I can do to help."

I give him a small smile, reluctant to let the conversation end. But we both have places to be. "I appreciate that."

Twenty minutes later, I'm stationed in front of the Hunter College library, peering up at ten or more stories of sandstone and grimy window glass. A fleet of AC units drip steadily onto the sidewalk and steps. I find a dry patch and wait. People stream in and out of the doors—groups of animated undergrads, faculty engaged in intense conversations, bedraggled-looking grad students hefting bulging totes—but no one stands outside looking around, waiting for someone else. I pull Esme's planner from my bag, even though I'm quite sure of what I saw. She had an appointment here at three o'clock last Friday, the day before she vanished. And she was scheduled to be here again at three today. I lean against the railing and wait for her appointment to arrive.

But by three fifteen, the cracks in my Hunter Library plan have begun to show. If Esme somehow gained card access, her appointed meeting spot could be inside the building. She could have canceled. Or, worse, if the person she was meeting had something to do with her disappearance, they would know very well that Esme wasn't coming.

Discouraged, I wait another fifteen minutes, then resign myself to walking back to Grand Central.

At home, I find myself at loose ends, pawing once again through the luggage Esme took care to pack, then left behind. I need a new lead, or maybe I just want to feel close to her after the let-downs of the past couple of days. Mark raises my hackles, but tailing him only revealed he was having dinner with his father. I learned more than I thought I might at Esme's publishing party, but while Kiku Shima has every reason to be angry with my sister, getting burned over a book deal hardly feels like a motive for something as extreme as kidnapping or causing her physical harm. And Hunter Library was a complete bust.

So here I am on Esme's bed, rummaging through her belongings once again. My eyes travel to her passport, almost wishing it wasn't here, that she did skip the country on a lark. Otherwise, it's all the same clothes from earlier this week, the same dresses hanging on the rail, the same shoes in the rack.

Except . . .

In the Instagram post she shared after leaving Mark, she was wearing a pair of gold Balenciaga slingbacks. Presumably the sandals, like the carpet bag in the same photo, went with my sister to the Monarch Hotel that night. I scan the shoe rack again, where I've placed every pair from her suitcase. No slingbacks. It's not much of a clue, but it rounds out her outfit from Saturday night; the gold sandals would pair perfectly with her pink cocktail dress. I make a mental note to update SI Marrone next time we talk.

We last spoke this morning. Since our initial interview, I've handed over her prescription bottles, impressing again how unlikely suicide seems as a possible explanation for Esme's disappearance. To the detective's credit, he's been giving me regular updates, although there hasn't been much. He assured me that my sister's case remains open and active, and that they've verified Mark's presence at Oma from 7:55 to 8:45 p.m., indicating he waited for her forty-five minutes past the time of their reservation. But if Esme lingered at the Monarch until nine or ten, as Jody the bartender indicated, Mark's earlier presence at the restaurant doesn't eliminate him from suspicion.

The days are ticking by. Once again, I'm filled by the urgent need to bring something new to the NYPD, some proof of the suspicious circumstances needed to light a fire under the detectives, change the nature of the investigation.

Frowning, I unzip the interior pockets inside my sister's suitcases, fingers tracing the lining for something I might have missed the first time around. In a pocket inside the lid of the first case, my fingers hit against a slim file folder I hadn't noticed before. I pull it out. It's pale purple, containing several stapled papers. I spread the folder open on the bed.

Inside is a legal document: Esme and Mark's prenup. I've never known the particulars of my sister's financial situation, simply that Mark has scads of money, and the Lloyds insisted on a prenup, of course. It's no surprise that Esme brought it with her when leaving him.

Scanning the document feels like an invasion of privacy; it's truly none of my business what monetary arrangement they came to when they wed. But with Esme missing, the regular rules no longer apply.

On the second page, someone—presumably Esme—has circled a passage rendering the majority of the agreement void if either party produces evidence of adultery.

I let the papers flutter down to the bed, unsure why I feel so surprised. I *knew* there had to be something else going on in their marriage, something both Mark and my sister were reluctant to tell me. The possibility that it was Esme who was cheating flits through my mind—Mark did say she'd been avoiding him and acting aloof for months—but he would have nothing to gain by voiding the prenup. All the money is Mark's.

I snatch up her planner again, flip to last week. A string of seven numbers appears in the box for Wednesday, the day before she left Mark. I'd glossed over it earlier, but it must be a phone number, no area code. I'd meant to look it up before, and now I tap it into Google, first with 203, our local southern Connecticut area code, then with the several possibilities for New York City. On the third try, I come up with a hit—the number for a divorce lawyer in Manhattan named Imani Abebe.

Air hissing through my teeth, I pull my phone from my bag and type it in. I expect a receptionist or answering service, but the voice on the other end says, "Imani speaking."

I introduce myself as the sister of Esme Connor-Lloyd, then say, "I believe she might be your client."

For a moment, there's silence. Then she says, "I'm sorry, Ms. Connor, but I can't discuss privileged matters concerning my clients over the phone, including whether or not they are my clients."

"Of course not." I halt, a deep sigh gathering in my lungs, then decide I may as well barrel on. What do I have to lose? "The thing is, my sister is a missing person. She disappeared last Saturday night, and the NYPD is investigating. And now I'm looking at a copy of the prenuptial agreement with her husband Mark Lloyd, which she took with her when she left him. There's a passage she's circled, about infidelity. If Esme knew about Mark cheating, if Mark knew she'd found out, that's information I really need to bring to the police."

There are literally millions of dollars on the line, which Imani Abebe will know if she was representing my sister. *That's motive for murder.*

There's more silence on the other end, and I hold my breath. She has to understand how this could change everything, how crucial this could be to the investigation.

Finally, Ms. Abebe clears her throat. "As I said, I can't discuss this with you. Attorney-client privilege. But I'm extremely sorry to hear your sister is missing, and frankly, I'm concerned. If you give me the information for the detectives handling her case, I'd like to reach out."

Relief coursing through me, I pull Jay Marrone's card from my wallet and rattle off his name and number. *Attorney-client privilege.* If Esme wasn't her client, she'd simply say so. But by asking for Marrone's contact, Imani Abebe has given me all the confirmation I need. She was working with my sister.

The chain of events is suddenly, dazzlingly clear: Esme found evidence Mark was cheating, hired a divorce lawyer, then left Mark the next day.

I hang up, Imani's assurance she'll reach out to the detectives right away ringing in my ears. Esme was *this close* to cleaning Mark out in a divorce. And then she vanished.

The grim realization settles in: my instincts about Mark have been right all along. Suddenly drained, I fall back against Esme's pillows. I don't feel satisfied with myself, far from it. I feel *terrified*. Because until this moment, my worst fantasies about what might have befallen my sister on Saturday night have been just that: the work of my imagination, perhaps far more likely than Mark's speculation about Esme running off somewhere, but no more grounded in fact. But now, that's changed. Mark has a real, tangible reason to do Esme harm.

If he hasn't already.

6

HOME

Checking Mom out of Monte Viso for the evening is a multistep process. There's the logbook on the sixth floor, which requires contact information for the responsible party (myself) and a secondary emergency contact. For a moment, I consider writing down Dylan, who is without question far more responsible than my sister, but Dylan won't be with us this evening. In the end, I jot down Esme's name and number. Then there's the elevator and the lobby doors, both of which require access codes to allow us to pass through with Mom's ankle monitor. In the lobby, there's a second logbook at the security desk.

Some families think it's a hassle, but I find the process comforting. The layers of security are one of the primary reasons Mom is here in memory support, not banging around Old Boney, where unannounced and unaccompanied excursions from the house, once as far as Main Street, once involving a minor collision with a phone pole, were becoming all too common. Here, there's no chance of Mom rooting out the car keys from their latest hiding spot and taking off. No chance of her wandering down the street in slippers and her favorite evening gown in the middle of a snowstorm, both of which happened last winter.

"Where are we going?" she asks for the third time when I've punched the access code into the keypad and the lobby doors have slid open. I take her elbow and guide her gently outside. She doesn't need help walking, but without a little prompting, we'd be standing in the lobby all evening.

"It's your birthday," I remind her. "Sixty-four. We're meeting Esme at Mario's to celebrate."

"I knew that." She smiles. "Well, what are we waiting for?"

She takes off across the parking lot, striding toward my Subaru—whether by chance or in a flash of recognition, it's hard to say. I hurry to keep up. On the far side of the lot is a little strip of woods, then a creek, then the highway. Danger and more danger. I feel rusty after two and a half months of relying so heavily on the professionals here, but the instinct to keep Mom close takes a mere second to kick back in.

We arrive at Mario's at six on the dot. It's hours earlier than I'd typically go out to eat, but in her time at Monte Viso, Mom has become accustomed to the schedule. The restaurant is located along a charmless professional strip about a mile outside downtown—office park to the left, dollar store and chain hair salon to the right. The sole green space in sight is a small park across the street with a stream emptying into a duck pond. There's no street parking directly in front of the restaurant, and walking any distance with Mom along a four-lane road is to be avoided, so I pull up to Mario's and opt for valet.

Esme is late. The hostess, a woman named Alice who's been here for ages and probably remembers me in pigtails, greets Mom and me with a welcoming smile and shows us to our booth. Mario's does a bustling take-out business, but inside, there's a gesture toward fine-dining destinations of decades past, which has always appealed to Mom's Nutmegger sensibilities. Tall, burgundy leather booths with gold studs. Lighting a touch dimmer than you'd expect in your typical family restaurant. White tablecloths, impressive wine display surrounding the bar. The place is crowded; sometimes I forget how many people eat at six o'clock on a Friday night by choice.

When Esme hasn't showed up by six fifteen, I order a bottle of Perrier and the pan-seared scallops appetizer Mom loves. At six thirty, my sister finally strolls through the door in jeans and a Buzzcocks 1978 tour shirt. It's the most dressed down I've seen her since she arrived on my doorstep, and while Mario's doesn't have a formal dress code, she's definitely the only person in here with *cock* on her shirt.

She reaches over to give Mom a kiss on the cheek, then slides into the booth next to me. Beneath her floral perfume is the distinct waft of pot.

"Thanks for coming," I say, unable to stop myself from glancing at my watch, a gesture not lost on my sister.

"I'm not that late," she quips, as if by saying it she can simply make it so. "Who eats at six anyway?"

"Mom does," I say, and this time, I don't try to hide my annoyance. I left work two hours early to commute home from the city and collect Mom from Monte Viso. If Esme's going to be back in Connecticut, living at Old Boney, she could at least make an effort to be a part of our family again. It's all I've wanted since the moment I picked her up at the Monarch, but so far, she's managed to be little more than a messy, absentee roommate.

She reaches for the Perrier and pours herself a glass. "You look good, Mom. Is that a new top?"

Mom looks down at her royal-blue blouse. "I think so," she says hesitantly. Then, with growing certainty, "Yes."

The inclination toward conviction is a recent feature of Mom's Alzheimer's. When the disease was less advanced, she'd linger in the uncertainty, troubled by her inability to remember but cognizant that she was, in fact, experiencing a memory lapse. Now she is quick to replace doubt with certitude, either because she has tricked herself into believing she remembers or because it's easier to make a choice and move on, for herself and those around her. I suspect it's a little of both.

Our server arrives then, and Esme, who has suddenly decided she's starving despite the early hour, orders pasta, a salad, and a large cheese plate. She asks for Montepulciano, and I suggest a glass instead of a bottle, earning me a glare and a tight "Fine."

When our server has vanished into the back of the house, Mom tilts her head to the side, studying Esme. "Whitney couldn't come?" she asks.

My sister gulps down a mouthful of Perrier. "Whitney lives in Brattleboro now, Mom. With Henri." She pronounces the name of Whitney's cohabitant, presumably a boyfriend or spouse, with an exaggerated French accent.

Mom's face narrows. "Whitney lives in Greenwich Hall with you."

My eyes flicker between them. Dressed in jeans and her Buzzcocks shirt, Esme does look strikingly like her college self. And Mom's not wrong; she and her best friend Whitney did once live together in an NYU dorm in the Village. But that was nearly a decade ago.

Esme squirms uncomfortably in the booth. Over the years, navigating Mom's dementia has become second nature to me. Especially in the recent difficult stretch as her live-in caregiver. But Esme doesn't know how to read Mom. When to play along, when to gently correct, when to change the subject entirely.

I open my mouth, ready to come to my sister's rescue, but what would I say? *Esme lives on Barrow Street with Mark?* That's no longer true. *Esme's back home, with me?* I'm quite certain her reluctance to set foot in Monte Viso has a lot to do with the desire to avoid those precise topics. And it's none of my business what Esme chooses to say or not say to Mom.

"Funny you should mention college," she says after a long pause.

"I have the most talented mentee this semester, a writing student at Sarah Lawrence. He's a senior from Loveland, Colorado. Isn't that the most adorable town name?"

Mom frowns, then plucks the last scallop from the plate and pops it into her mouth.

"Adorable," I agree, mind drifting to the call I overheard earlier this week. Ostensibly, Esme had been on the phone with the afore-mentioned mentee, but the call had sounded a lot more personal than that. Again, the inkling that my sister might be crossing lines with a college student enters my mind. But if so, why go out of her way to mention him?

Before I can find a way to probe for more information, Mom is pushing herself halfway up from the table and looking around the restaurant.

"Where is your father?" she asks, eyes flickering across Esme's face as if the answer is mapped on her skin. "Is he here?"

Christ. If a return to Esme's college years wasn't enough, now we're sprinting down memory lane all the way to my parents' marriage. They divorced when I was fourteen, which means Mom is way back in time. Maybe coming to a restaurant so saturated with Connor family memories was a mistake.

I stand and reach across the table to place my hand firmly on top of Mom's. This is not a time to play along. Mom had some good times with Carl, but those aren't the memories she's likely to access when her brain takes her back there.

"You and Carl divorced—"

But before I can finish, Esme is on her feet, too, cutting me off. "Did you bring him here? What did you talk about?"

I cast her a steely glare. This is not the right tack. Of course Mom and Dad came here—Esme *knows* that. Before the divorce, the four of us came here all the time, which my sister was absolutely old enough to remember. What is she getting at?

Esme meets my glare with her own, and Mom threads her fingers through her hair, looking flustered.

I push past Esme and make my way around to Mom's side of the booth. Gently, I guide her back into her seat. "It's okay, Mom. You and Carl divorced a long time ago. He lives in New Haven now. It's just you, me, and Esme tonight."

Mom is nodding slowly. "Silly me," she says.

Suddenly, I'm glad Dylan didn't come. He was absolutely right: it's far too soon for this, and instead of being comforted by his presence, I would have spent the entire meal worrying about him having a good time, which would have been damn near impossible. Thank god he's not here to witness how fragmented our family has become. Dinner tomorrow—just the two of us—is the preferable option by far.

Somehow, Esme and I make it through the rest of the meal. She gets a box for the majority of her food, but Mom polishes off every bite of her chicken romano and tiramisu, gushing about how she hasn't tasted anything this good in weeks. That's surely true; the kitchen at Monte Viso puts out better-than-average nursing home food, but it's nothing to rave about. Mom is happy. Dinner is, narrowly, a success.

We're on our way out when my phone rings—Nabeel. Shit. It's close to eight, and he's probably still at the office after the rest of us are long gone. I'm hit by another twinge of guilt for cutting out so early.

"I have to take this," I tell Esme. "It's work, but I'll make it quick." I pull the valet ticket from my blazer and accept the call. "Nabeel, hi. Give me one second, okay?"

I press my phone against my shoulder and extend the ticket out to Esme.

"Go take your call," she says, plucking it from my fingers, then shooing me away. "We'll meet you in the car."

"Watch her," I say.

"I've got this. Go." She links her elbow with Mom's.

I nod gratefully and step back inside the restaurant, away from the street noise. From a bench in the now-empty waiting area, I turn my attention back to Nabeel, who opens with an apology for calling me after close of business on a Friday, then segues quickly into the matter at hand: Jason on the West Coast needs to connect right away on a client's homeowner's insurance policy that should have been bound before closing, but, apparently, was not. Unable to reach me, Jason had gone to my boss.

"I'm on it," I assure him. "Thanks for letting me know."

It's almost the end of the day in California. This can't wait. I slide my work laptop out of my bag and pull up the contact for the insurer, then I dial Jason.

I'm inside the restaurant for five minutes, seven at most. But when I walk back outside, Esme gives me a stricken look. She's standing beside my Impreza in the front of the lot, keys dangling from her fingers, alone.

"Is Mom in the car?" I ask.

"I thought she went back inside, with you." She twirls a strand of hair nervously between two fingers, then tucks it behind her ear.

"What?" I twist to look behind me, toward the office park, then across the street, where a steady stream of cars rushes along all four lanes. "Why would you think that?"

"I don't . . ." she splutters. "She was here a second ago. I got a text, and— I'm sorry. Fuck. She can't have gone far."

"Oh my god." She only had to be responsible for five minutes, but Esme has lost Mom. I'm filled with the sudden desire to tear my sister apart, limb by limb, with my bare hands. I dig my nails into my purse strap instead. "There's a crosswalk on the next block. Go over to the other side. Check along the sidewalk, check the park. I'll take the businesses on this side of the road."

Esme's face is flushed. "Jane, I didn't—"

I don't let her finish. My love for my little sister runs deep, but this is unacceptable. "I don't want to hear it. Go find her!"

She nods and rushes down the sidewalk, in the direction of the light. I set off the opposite way, toward the stores on the other side of the lot. Panic rockets through me as the worst-case scenarios unspool: Mom climbing into a stranger's car, a call to the cops when she walks out of a store without paying, Mom wandering into highway traffic . . . The dread sends me back to the not-so-recent past, to the excruciating days before moving her into Monte Viso when Mom's safety always teetered on the blade of a knife. I am horrified to think one hasty decision to trust my sister for a few precious moments may have destroyed everything I've worked to prevent. A heartbeat of carelessness—my own, for putting my faith in Esme when I should have known better; and hers, for failing to step up, as ever—and the universe can split, sending us all hurtling down a terrible new path, no return.

The hair salon is closed for the evening, so I push open the door to the Dollar Tree. Not Mom's kind of place, but I give the aisles a breathless look, then I'm back on the sidewalk and pressing through the door to the tanning salon beside it.

"Has a tall woman come in here, midsixties, wearing black slacks and a royal blue blouse?" I nearly shout.

The young woman at the front desk gives me a startled look. "Nope."

She says something about making an appointment, and I rush back outside before she can finish. The next block is eaten up by a single gray medical building of some sort, then there's another strip of shops beyond. In the opposite direction is the office park, but their security gates must be closed for the evening. I jam my finger into the button for the crosswalk and shift impatiently back and forth in my flats, eager for traffic to stop so I can continue my search. *Where the hell are you, Mom? Please, please be okay.*

My phone chimes when I'm halfway across the street. Esme.

Found her. Watching the ducks.

I force my legs to take me the rest of the way across, and the second I'm on the sidewalk, I collapse against the light pole. My neck and shoulders ache, and it's a struggle to draw in a deep breath.

But it's fine. She's fine. It's all going to be okay.

Two blocks down, I watch Esme attempt to guide Mom across the street. She shakes her arm away from her youngest daughter in annoyance, and Esme jogs to keep up.

The urge to berate myself is overpowering. I should never have asked her to watch Mom, even for five minutes. Responsibility is not a part of her skill set, and even if she was determined to really try, she doesn't know what she's doing. Caring for Mom is a mind trip. Marjorie Connor still looks like our mother, she's in great physical shape, and she has enough lucid moments to trick you into thinking things are as they ever were. But Alzheimer's is cruel. The disease has stripped Mom of far more than her short-term memories; she is easily disoriented, confused, unable to make decisions to keep herself safe. The fact that she made it across a four-lane highway unscathed is nothing short of a miracle.

Back at the car, I snatch the keys from Esme's hand and give Mom a kiss on the cheek.

"You can't wander off like that," I scold her. "Esme or I will go with you. We were so worried."

I open the passenger's side door, and she narrows her eyes at me. "I was just stretching my legs. You worry too much."

"Well, everything's fine now," Esme says brightly, and I fix her with an icy stare. I am not blameless in this, but she's fooling herself if she thinks she's going to get a pass from me, like always. For once in her life, she needs to accept responsibility. She needs to apologize.

When Mom is settled in the car and I've closed the door, I lean over and press my lips against my sister's ear. "Everything's *not* fine. You know nothing about Mom, you never visit. You show up to dinner late—and stoned, I might add. You provoke her by asking about Dad, and then you let her wander off. She could have been killed. *Grow up, Esme.*"

When I draw away, I'm surprised to see tears pricking the corners of her eyes.

"You're the one who treats me like a child," she hisses. "Why do you have to be so fucking mean?"

Her words hit like a slap.

She jerks open the back door and slides inside, leaving me standing in the parking lot alone.

SEVEN

GONE

Hard as I've tried to pack them away, today's revelations won't stop spinning through my brain: Mark cheated, Esme found out, Esme hired a divorce lawyer. She was on the precipice of cleaning him out, and then she was gone. In the space of an afternoon, my suspicions about my brother-in-law have gone from uneasy hunch to bright-red flare: *danger danger danger.*

By six o'clock, I've pulled myself together enough to shower, leave a voice mail for SI Marrone, and drive over to Monte Viso. Now I sit in the parking lot, car turned off, hands shaking against the wheel. The prenup changes everything. Mark had millions to lose, and then on the night she was supposed to meet him, Esme vanished. A thought I'd first had inside their brownstone ricochets back to me now: *Whenever a woman goes missing, or turns up dead, it's always the husband, isn't it?* It's so clear-cut, it's staggering, but that's Occam's razor for you.

I consider the possibility that she broke down and called him back at some point on Saturday night. If they met up, and he abducted her, perhaps now he's keeping her somewhere, trying to convince her to drop the divorce case, unsure how to get out of the bind he's gotten himself into. It would explain his early-morning phone calls on Sunday—covering his tracks. His readiness to bait the police with the story about the other time Esme disappeared for a few days, his hints about the possibility of suicide.

At their home on Tuesday, I'd asked to use the bathroom, and Mark had directed me to the powder room on the first floor, saying something about the plumbing upstairs. I didn't give it much thought at the time, but now, it strikes me as strange. Of course I would use the first-floor bathroom, the one I've always used as a guest in their home. Why would Mark discourage me from going upstairs unless there was something—or someone—he didn't want me to find?

A cold finger of fear shimmies down my spine, and I shudder. Then I suck in a determined breath. Today is Mom's birthday, and rattled as I am, there's no way around putting on a happy face and going inside to celebrate. I pry my hands from the wheel and step out of the car.

I'm just in time to accompany Mom to the little café before it closes. I should have planned something special, a movie or dinner out at Mario's, but with everything that's been going on, I barely had time to wrap her gifts—which I realize, with a groan, I've left at the house. This week of all weeks, I might cut myself some slack, but I'm not in a forgiving mood.

We carry our trays to one of the patio tables, and I shove my deepening suspicion of Mark to the back of my mind, instead prompting Mom to talk about her day. She thinks they watched a movie this afternoon, but she can't tell me which one. The new doctor—presumably Dr. Haruto Yu, who is not new at all—called and was "nasty" with her. I make a mental note to check in with Dr. Yu; I can't imagine he's behaving anything but professionally toward Mom, but I owe it to her to follow up. She tells me all she was served for lunch was dry Raisin Bran, which again seems highly unlikely, but I'll talk to the nurse when I bring her back inside. Even with Mom at Monte Viso, her care is a full-time job.

I remind her that it's her birthday, and she promptly asks after Esme. A thin sweat breaks out across my chest. I haven't told Mom that her youngest is missing, let alone that I have a gnawing suspicion about exactly what happened to her. The lie of omission feels bad, but telling Mom the truth would only upset her, and then two hours later, she'd forget. I apologize for my sister and make up some excuse about an important work event of Mark's.

The lie lands with ease, and I take a small bite of my salad, barely tasting it.

On Saturday morning, a special investigator named Shilpa Bakshi calls. She says she works with Jay Marrone in Missing Persons and asks me to come in first thing Tuesday. I start to tell her about the prenup and my conversation with Imani Abebe, but SI Bakshi cuts me off.

"We spoke to your sister's divorce attorney last night, and while I don't have any news to share with you yet, I expect we will very soon. We're working through Labor Day, Ms. Connor. I appreciate your patience."

I am anything but patient, but I bite my tongue. No news is good news, perhaps. And they're onto Mark now. A fire has been lit.

The rest of the holiday weekend is spent shuttling between the house and Monte Viso. On Saturday morning, Mom accepts her presents with varying levels of interest: The chenille throw is a big hit, as is the box of Jacques Torres chocolates, but the gifts designed to "help the dementia patient in your life express their creativity" are met with general skepticism. The adult coloring book and set of markers are cast summarily aside. She places the gorgeous leather-bound journal and fountain pen on her bedside table but sniffs at my suggestion she actually write down her memories or record the events of her day.

"You bought me my first journal," I remind her.

She gives me a tight smile. "You were a child."

"Lots of people journal. Writing regularly boosts brain health."

She frowns and says she'll think about it.

On Sunday night, I'm driving home from Monte Viso again when Jamie's name flashes across my dashboard. I tap the screen, accepting his call.

"I wanted to check in." His voice is a familiar balm in my ears, and I sink back against the seat. "I'm at the airport, waiting for my red-eye. I've been thinking of you. Of Esme."

"Thanks for calling. It means a lot." I flex my fingers against the wheel and debate how much to tell him. "The NYPD's been keeping in touch; things are starting to happen. This might sound crazy, but I think Mark is involved."

"How so?"

"I found their prenup. Esme stood to gain a lot of money if he was caught cheating. And Esme caught him."

"That's concerning, to say the least." Jamie's voice is heavy. "Have you shared this with the police?"

"Of course. I'm going in first thing Tuesday."

"Good," he says, instilling me with confidence that my suspicions are well founded, that as soon as this interminable holiday weekend is over, things are going to turn a corner.

"I'm so sorry, Jane," he says then. "This is a lot. You're in an unimaginable situation." The kindness in his voice hits me hard, and I press my lips between my teeth. Once upon a time, Jamie would have been by my side for every step of this crisis. Even now, I can feel his sure hands on my shoulders, kneading the stress away, the soft brush of his lips against my skin.

A sob threatens to well in my throat. I'm not sure how much longer I can bear this alone.

"I'll be back and forth between the Manhattan practice and Monte Viso for the rest of the week," Jamie is saying. "Playing catch-up. But let me know if there's anything I can do to help."

I thank him profusely, and when we're off the phone, I ask myself if it's an offer I can truly accept. I don't doubt his sincerity for a minute, but I'm not sure my heart is equipped to distinguish compassion from love right now.

Tuesday morning, I arrive at One Police Plaza to find both SI Marrone and SI Bakshi waiting in the conference room. I pull out the roller chair across from them with a mix of intense anticipation and relief.

Shilpa Bakshi is younger than I am, but there's nothing youthful about how she carries herself. As I settle into my chair, she regards me with sharp, focused eyes from her seat across the table.

"We have a few updates, Ms. Connor," she says, voice serious as her gaze. "Your brother-in-law told us he went directly home after leaving Oma at eight forty-five on Saturday, August twenty-sixth. But we know now that he was not telling the truth."

Her words aren't a surprise, but they nonetheless land with a jolt. I clench my jaw.

"The building next to their residence is equipped with a security camera," Marrone adds. "Fortunately, its view includes a partial capture of the doorway to Mr. Lloyd's brownstone. After speaking with your sister's divorce lawyer on Friday, we were able to obtain the security footage. We can confirm Mr. Lloyd did not go straight home that night. In fact, he did not return home until midday Sunday."

All the air in the room seems to evaporate. I suck in a thin breath.

"We are telling you this in the strictest confidence." SI Bakshi folds her hands on the sleek tabletop; her nails are clipped short and unpolished. "As I'm sure you'll understand, anything you say to your brother-in-law now could seriously compromise the investigation into your sister's disappearance. I know you want to avoid that as much as we do. We are sharing this information with you because we believe Mark Lloyd could be dangerous. We strongly encourage you to avoid all contact with him until we've concluded our investigation."

My head bobs up and down, and I jam my hands beneath my thighs to keep them from shaking. Mark lied. Mark is indeed very, very dangerous.

"And what is the status of the investigation?" I manage to ask.

"We're working as quickly as possible to bring your sister home," Marrone says, scratching at the side of his jaw. Rough red skin is visible where he's shaved too close. "My conversation with Ms. Abebe on Friday was illuminating. She faxed over a copy of the prenup."

"We're working to confirm Mr. Lloyd's whereabouts for the rest of Saturday night," SI Bakshi says. "We have traffic cam footage of him leaving Oma and walking north, but we are only able to follow him for a few blocks."

"It's our working theory," SI Marrone says, "that Mr. Lloyd got into a cab or car service after the cameras lose record of him. We believe he took a car to meet your sister, possibly at the Monarch, possibly elsewhere."

"Unfortunately," SI Bakshi says, "there's no direct footage of the Monarch's bar entrance, so we're unable to verify the time

Ms. Connor-Lloyd left that night, or if your brother-in-law met her there."

I nod slowly, the fear of what Mark's done intermingling with intense relief. *Finally*, the investigators' sense of urgency matches my own.

"What we know for sure," SI Marrone says, "is that Mark Lloyd had motive to harm his wife, and that he lied to us about where he was that night. As SI Bakshi said, we strongly advise you to avoid all contact with your brother-in-law. If he reaches out to you, please let us know immediately."

"Okay," I promise. "So what's next?"

"We are in the process of obtaining a warrant to search your sister and brother-in-law's residence," SI Bakshi says. "The process has been slowed a bit by the holiday, but we expect to make progress by tonight. Please don't go anywhere near the building."

Interview concluded, I find myself walking aimlessly, thinking. A part of me wants to throw their advice out the window and storm over to Barrow Street, demand Mark let me in. But the truth is, I'm as afraid of Mark as the detectives have cautioned me to be. So I leave Park Row's drab municipal buildings behind, then navigate the frenzy of Chinatown before crossing into SoHo. Eventually, I find myself on University Place, headed farther uptown. I don't have a clear destination in mind, but sometimes walking shakes loose what's been stuck inside my head. And I need to work this out.

The new sense of gravity the NYPD has brought to my sister's case should be reassuring, and SI Bakshi seemed to think they'd be able to obtain a search warrant by tonight, so why do I still feel so unsettled?

The brownstone. After I saw the prenup, I too had the thought that Mark might be keeping Esme upstairs, but knowing he didn't come home that night, doesn't that seem a lot less likely? Maybe he really was having plumbing trouble, like he claimed.

I think it through. If he abducted Esme on Saturday and brought her back to their brownstone at a later date, wouldn't that have been captured by the neighboring building's camera? Mark's not stupid, anything but. Even if he managed to sneak her inside, would he really keep Esme hostage in their home, then let me in for the better part of an hour?

The thought that this warrant, once obtained, will very likely turn up nothing gnaws at me as I walk up to Fourteenth Street and through Union Square. Mark is holding Esme somewhere, hopefully alive—but probably not at their brownstone.

Walking briskly, I again replay every facet of my conversation with Mark. We reviewed the planner together, talked about his discussion with the police, and then he made a case for his theory that Esme willingly ran away. I asked him where he believed she was holing up on a shoestring, and he didn't have any ideas.

What about your parents' pied-à-terre in the city?

They sold it when Sean bought the Tribeca loft. There's an attached suite where they can stay.

I'm walking faster now, wheels starting to turn. After leaving the brownstone, I'd followed Mark to Union Square, where he was meeting his dad for dinner. At the time, it had seemed like a dead end. Now I look back, Union Square several blocks behind me.

And then it clicks.

I turn east on Twenty-First, breaking into a run. I'd dismissed my suspicions, but now I know better than to dismiss anything when it comes to Mark. Rupert Lloyd arrived at the restaurant on foot that evening. If he'd been coming from any distance, the senior Mr. Lloyd would have taken a car, but not if he was just walking the few blocks to the restaurant from Gramercy. Mark's claims about his parents selling their city apartment burn hot in my ears, and I'm gripped with the sudden, fierce certainty that Mark was not telling the truth.

I keep running. I don't remember the exact address, but I'll know the building when I see it.

When I arrive on the sidewalk out front, I'm panting and a painful stitch is forming in my side. This is definitely it. I take a moment to recover, then pull up New York City's property records database on my phone and plug the address into the search. The last sale of the penthouse is to Rupert Lloyd, Esq., in 2008. The deed is still listed in his name.

Mark lied to me.

That Rupert frowned on his middle son's union with my sister became clear soon after their marriage. He's never been a great Esme fan. That said, I can't imagine he'd do anything to harm her. But if Mark did something stupid, if he panicked and enlisted his father's help . . .

Heart beating wildly in my chest, I pull up Marrone's number and jab my finger at the call icon.

Family shows up for family. And either my sister is being held inside these walls, or worse yet, something terrible happened here, something she can never come back from.

7

HOME

A lingering unease permeates Old Boney several days after Mom's birthday dinner. Esme exists in brief glimpses—her back retreating into her room, followed by the slamming door; her silhouette in the back seat of a Lyft vanishing down the drive. Resentment frosts the air. I said things I'd rather take back, but I'm far from the only one at fault. I could forgive Esme for being late, or stoned, or out of practice relating to Mom. But she nearly got our mother killed. Let her sulk, keep her secrets, shut me out. I won't go chasing her.

For the first time in a long time, I have my own secret to keep, lovely and thrumming with promise. As the weekend flows into the new week, Dylan fills more and more space inside my brain, and it's a relief to let the new spark glowing between us crowd Esme out. Since that first dinner at Chez Allard, we've gone out again in Branby, and yesterday, the weather was gorgeous and we both had the day off, so we went on a long hike together at Babcock Preserve, something we used to do as kids.

With each new moment we spend together, I can feel us sliding back into our old closeness, but better this time. On days we don't see each other, we check in often. Every time I worry I'm texting too much, he's right there, matching me message for message, his heart keeping pace with mine. The past few days have ended in video calls extending long into the night, neither of us ready to let the day end, let sleep take over. At work, I'm exhausted, but it doesn't matter. I'm running on something more powerful than sleep. *Possibility.*

A tiny part of me says I'm getting ahead of myself, exposing my heart too fast. But this isn't my imagination running wild after a few early dates with a relative stranger. This is Dylan. We were inseparable once. This is us, picking up where we left off, speeding toward the future we were always meant for, making up for an ocean of lost time.

On Tuesday night, I leave Monte Viso and drive toward Main Street. Mom declined dinner, picking instead at a crumbly slice of coffee cake, and Renata, the head nurse, told me that Mom spent the entire day in her room, refusing to join the other residents for activities or a walk through the courtyard. "She's been writing in that notebook you gave her, though," she told me. "We've been happy to see that."

As I drive, I crack the window and drink in the night air. I can't control Esme. I can't fix Mom's mind, can't ensure every moment will be a happy one. But in a few minutes, I am meeting Dylan. After weeks of wallowing over my canceled future with Jamie, I am ready to govern my own happiness.

When I step into Pauly's, Dylan is leaning against the bar, watching the door. He gives me an eager wave, and I hurry over, hungry for the heat of his body against mine, the press of my lips to his.

"I missed you," I say honestly. "Work dragged today."

He tucks a long piece of hair behind my ear, drinking me in. "I had a long day, too. I'm glad you're here now." He orders a Coke for my sake, even though it wouldn't bother me if he had a beer, and I ask for my favorite date-night mocktail, a blueberry mojito minus the rum.

We take our glasses to a table off to the side, and the last thoughts of Mom, of Esme, of work, slip away. It happens a bit faster, a bit more easily each time we're together. I've spent my whole life trying to fix my family, and for what? Dad broke us years ago. Mom isn't getting any better; the most I can do is show up for her and keep her safe. And what has fifteen years spent in my sister's debt gotten either of us? We are as distant as we've ever been, as unprepared to know one another, as quick to sharpen our tongues.

Dylan slips his hand over mine, finds the spaces between my fingers with his. This is the one thing in my life that doesn't need fixing, that requires only my presence. We sip our drinks and talk about our days, and I know that tonight I will go home with him.

When our glasses are empty, a waitress stops by our table to check on us, and we send her away. We don't want a second drink. We want only each other.

We're spilling out of his van and starting up his drive when Dylan snakes his arm around my waist, pulls me close.

"I never stopped wanting you this way, Jane Connor."

A shiver runs down my spine, lodging in the hot space between my thighs. I tilt my head, press my lips to his ear.

"Liar," I whisper.

"I'm not," Dylan insists as he unlatches the front door to the duplex he's renting on Cedarwood. His fingers dance across my shirt, then slide beneath it, grazing my skin, his breath hot on my neck.

"You are," I mumble into his hair, my tongue skimming the outline of his ear, drawing a low moan from his throat until my lips find his, swallowing the sound. We're in the hallway now, Dylan's hand scrabbling against the wall for the light but missing the switch.

"Fuck it," he mutters, drawing me toward the stairs. Our hands find the banister in the dark, and we make our way up.

"I was the one who never wanted to stop," I press, although I know I should leave it alone. "You pumped the brakes."

At the top of the stairs, Dylan lifts my shirt, then kneels before me, his lips making promises against my bare skin. I want to lose myself to this, to shut my mind down, but almost as urgent as what my body wants is the need to set the record straight.

"You can't rewrite history, Dylan."

He lifts his eyes to mine. The yellow flecks in his brown irises catch the moonlight filtering into the hallway through the bedroom window. "Branby taught me how to want what I couldn't have," he says softly. "And how to bury that want away."

I don't fully understand—he could have had me, *did* have me—but it hits that he isn't lying. All those years ago, something got lost in translation, something that was true for Dylan if not for me. Or maybe he's only being kind, maybe after the crash, his feelings about me changed, as I've always suspected. I pull him to his feet, and we stumble into the bedroom, both of us aching for our bodies to finish a story we started years ago.

The week progresses with barely an Esme sighting. Occasionally, when plucking a bra from the back of the couch or rounding up empty wineglasses from the porch furniture (and the library shelves, and the rim of the tub in her bath), the cryptic text I intercepted crosses my mind. *You'll ruin everything. Don't fucking do this.* That was nearly two weeks ago. My sister is scarcely around, but she's fine. I think. Probably, the message was from one of her friends, someone with a similar flair for the dramatic. She doesn't seem to be in any true danger.

I push the text from my mind, but the harder truth creeps in: my frustration with Esme is less about what she's said and done over these past two weeks and more about what she *hasn't*. For our entire adult lives, I've wanted to be the one my little sister comes to with hard problems and angry texts, the person she looks to when things get tough. And I thought, when she left Mark and came to me . . . But nothing's changed, not really. These days, it feels like what we once had means nothing at all.

By Thursday, I'm back to crack-of-dawn visits to Monte Viso now that Jamie has returned from San Francisco and resumed his regular schedule on the floor. I'm tempted by the urge to show up while he's there, rub my happiness in his face, but I swallow it down. This thing between Dylan and me is too special, too new to let my ex in on any part of it. That would only taint something pure and lovely and true.

Thursday evening, I linger at work after most of my colleagues have gone home, catching up on the things I've let slide since Esme's arrival in Branby threw me off my game and, if I'm honest, since I've allowed myself to bask in Dylan's glow, memories of our moments together fuzzing the harsh LED lights inside Empire Lenders, time inside my head slowing down while the hours rush by.

Eight turns to nine, and I am officially the last person left in the office. It's late, but I'm barely tired, fully in the zone, making more progress on my backlog than I have all week. Determined to ride the wave, I order dinner and shoot Dylan a text letting him know I'm still at work, that I'll call when I leave.

At ten to eleven, I shut down my computer and ride the elevator to the first floor, officially tapped. I'm requesting a Lyft to Grand Central when a 212 number flashes across my phone screen. Probably spam. I dismiss the call, but a few seconds later, the same number calls again.

"Hello?"

"Is this Jane Connor?"

I confirm, then ask who's calling.

"Ms. Connor, my name is Maren Testa. I'm an emergency nurse at Bellevue Hospital. Esme Connor-Lloyd was brought in by ambulance earlier tonight. We located your number in the patient's phone. Can you confirm if you are immediate family?"

"Yes, I'm her sister." I slump against the side of the building, legs suddenly wobbly beneath me. Bellevue is here in Manhattan, in Kips Bay. Thank god I stayed late tonight.

"Thank you. We've been having trouble reaching family."

I imagine they've already tried our parents with no success, and possibly Mark.

"I'm glad you called me. Is she okay?"

"Ms. Connor-Lloyd is currently in critical condition following a drug overdose and head trauma."

"Oh my god."

"Dr. Kinnard will talk you through everything when you arrive. How soon can you be here?"

It takes five minutes for my Lyft to arrive, then another fifteen to get to the hospital. The whole ride, my mind is reeling with a million questions about what happened, where she was found, and by who.

Somewhere along the FDR, I text Dylan.

> Esme's in the hospital. I'll call you as
> soon as I know more.

A few minutes later, I've checked in and been met by Esme's doctor. I'm told that they performed gastric suction, but the overdose and subsequent fall triggered serious swelling in her brain. For the time being, she has been placed in a medically induced coma.

"Is she going to be okay?" I ask, heart in my throat.

Dr. Kinnard gives me a tight smile. "It's our hope that the propofol will reduce the swelling, allowing her brain to heal."

She's unconscious, her condition still critical, but I am allowed to go see her. I've never been inside Bellevue before, and it's massive. I take two wrong turns before someone offers to guide me to the right hallway. By the time I arrive at her room, I'm breathing heavily and my hands are trembling.

I stop short in the doorway. My beautiful sister lies in the bed, eyes closed, hair matted and shaved in one patch, some sort of breathing device hooked up to the clear plastic mask covering her nose and mouth. Right beneath the surface lies the same girl, thirteen years old, fighting for her life in a hospital an hour north from this one. My vision blurs, the two Esmes expanding and contracting, the two Janes hovering in the doorway.

Time bends only for a moment. Because standing over her bed, Esme's carnelian red phone clutched in his hand, is my father.

EIGHT

GONE

On Thursday night at eight, I'm on East Twenty-First once again, back pressed against the wrought iron fence surrounding Gramercy Park. From my spot diagonally across the street from the tan brick building housing Rupert and Cynthia Lloyd's pied-à-terre, I have a clear view of the front entrance, its green awning flapping gently in the early-September breeze. It's that liminal time when you can convince yourself that autumn is right around the bend, but summer hangs on tight—the air still warm, the sky still light past dinnertime.

It took two long days for the NYPD to gather the evidence necessary to obtain a search warrant for the penthouse apartment where Mark is, possibly, holding my sister. If she's even alive. But now, the detectives are finally inside.

The metal bars dig into my back, and I'm intimately aware of the damp suction of my T-shirt to my skin, the pink flush across the back of my neck. The knowledge that we've arrived, finally, at the precipice of something big has set every cell in my body on fire.

I peer up to the building's top floor, straining to see in through the windows. It's futile. My sister is inside, or my sister is not inside. The only certainty is that *something* happened here the night she vanished. After my panicked call to SI Marrone on Tuesday evening, Missing Persons got to work, obtaining credit card evidence that Mark paid for an NYC yellow cab at ten p.m., two hours after Esme stood him up for dinner. Then there's about an hour when his whereabouts are unaccounted for, the time after he drops off traffic cam footage and before he put the taxi on his card.

The detectives won't share any working theories with me, but I can see Mark taking the subway to Midtown, meeting Esme at the Monarch, and convincing her to come with him "to talk." If she felt she had nowhere else to go that night—my gut twists once more with the guilt of having left her to her own devices—she may have given in, seeing no better option. But instead of going home, he took her to his parents' Gramercy apartment, a location slightly less conspicuous than the brownstone he and my sister shared. Not a perfect hiding place, but if Mark was trying to buy himself some time, he's succeeded.

At the time the charge on Mark's card went through, the NYPD has footage of a man and woman exiting a yellow cab on East Twenty-First. Bakshi has shared that between the darkness, the rain, and a raised umbrella, it's impossible to confirm the identities of the two individuals entering the Lloyds' building, but it was enough to obtain the necessary warrant.

From the moment the building doors closed behind them, my imagination runs wild, each possibility darker than the next.

I dig my nails into the palms of my hands. I've been here for an hour, waiting. No one explicitly told me not to come watch from across the street, although I'm sure my presence would be strongly discouraged. Fortunately, once four cop cars, two unmarked cruisers, a fire truck, and an ambulance pulled in, the street around me has been a whirlwind of activity. A unit in black body armor put up sawhorses to cordon off the block to vehicle traffic, and I blend right in with the looky-loos crouched on stoops and milling around the sidewalk by the park. Better to ask forgiveness than permission; being anywhere else right now is not an option. Any second now, they'll come out—with or without Esme.

Finally, at eight fifteen, the detectives emerge from the building's front door with their uniformed colleagues. I suck in a sharp breath. With them, under close watch but uncuffed, is Mark. Beside him walks a young woman in dark jeans, an emerald green top, and heels.

Not Esme, but *Kiku.*

Esme's longtime friend. The polite, professional literary agent from the publishing party. The person Esme burned on the book deal. *We had a little bit of a falling-out . . .*

Because Mark's affair was *with Kiku.* My fingers rise to my mouth in surprise, and I imagine how it happened: Esme struggling with the opening of her novel, needing motivation, needing feedback. She'd turned to her friend. Enter Kiku—spending more and more time at their home, helping Esme, then leaving Esme alone once the muse took hold. I picture Esme upstairs on her laptop while Kiku chatted in the living room with Mark, ordered takeout with Mark, stuck around for a nightcap with Mark . . .

Is that all it took? I can't know exactly how it began, but I know how it ended: one thing led to another, until Esme found out about the affair, cut Kiku out of the book deal, and left Mark.

I watch, heart racing, as Mark and Kiku are guided into one of the unmarked cars. The emergency medical crew exits the building a moment later, no stretcher, no evidence they've had anything to do over the past hour. My chest tightens, and I rub at my collarbone with the heel of my hand. My sister is not inside the Lloyds' apartment—and neither is her body.

The car with SIs Marrone and Bakshi, Mark, and Kiku drives off, and I lean hard into the fence behind me. They're presumably not under arrest, given the lack of handcuffs, but they're being taken in for questioning.

For a moment, I'm filled with pure, unfiltered rage. I'd been so quick to cast Kiku as an innocent party in all of this, but now I see that Esme's actions were drastic, but not unwarranted.

I watch a uniformed officer lift the NYPD sawhorse from the end of the block, watch their car disappear into traffic. Kiku is a terrible friend, but even knowing what I know now, it's hard to believe she was involved in whatever happened to my sister. Mark, on the other hand, must have known that Esme had discovered the affair. Kiku would have, of course, told him about Esme's act of retaliation. Burning her friend on the book deal is just my sister's style.

And the fact remains: Mark knew how much he stood to lose in the divorce.

The pied-à-terre may be only a meeting place for my sister's cheating husband and her former best friend, far from the type of crime scene I'd imagined, but that doesn't mean Mark is innocent. He had every reason to feel threatened by Esme, to try to put a stop to her plans to divorce him.

I dig my keys out of my bag and start jogging up the block, over to Third Avenue, where I've left my car. I'm going back to One Police Plaza. I need to be there for whatever comes next, have to know if my brother-in-law's night ends in arrest or walking free.

Ninety minutes later, I'm sitting in a stiff wooden chair, sipping watery coffee from a cardboard cup. The guard won't let me go upstairs, won't let me anywhere near the interview room, but I've been allowed to wait in the lobby.

Beside me is Jamie, identical cardboard cup in hand, which I don't think he's brought to his lips in the twenty minutes he's been here. I went back and forth about calling him the entire drive down to Park Row, but in the end I caved. He'd recently arrived back in Manhattan from his shift at Monte Viso and promised it was no trouble to come downtown for a bit.

And I can use the moral support.

I let my eyes stray to the chair beside me. Jamie's scent, the outline of his tall form, are so familiar. He places one arm gently around my shoulders, and I allow myself to lean into him, press my face into the crook of his shoulder.

In a different reality, he'd lean down for a tender kiss, but I live only in this world. In this world, Esme is still missing and Jamie is here because he's a good person who continues to worry about me, not because he regrets ending our relationship, not because there's any chance this tragedy will bring us back together.

For another half an hour that becomes an hour, we wait. I texted Marrone as soon as I got here, let him know I was downstairs. He didn't respond, but for a moment, three little dots danced across my screen, and I know he saw my message.

Finally, SI Bakshi emerges from the elevators, alone. Every muscle in my body tenses. Did Mark talk? Has he led them toward Esme . . . or her body?

The investigator stalls right outside the elevator, eyes shifting from my face to the man sitting beside me.

Jamie places a hand gently on my knee. "Doubt she's going to speak with you while I'm here. Do you want me to wait outside?"

I shake my head. "It's really late, and I'll be fine. Thank you for coming."

He stands and gives me a small kiss on the top of my head. My entire body floods with heat.

"You can call me," he says. "I'll leave my ringer on."

And then he's gone, and SI Bakshi is crossing through the lobby toward me. She sits in the chair Jamie left vacant.

"You should go home, too, Jane," she says. Her voice is not unkind, but her dark eyes are tired. "We've spoken to your brother-in-law at length."

My eyes lock on hers, waiting.

"He never saw Esme that night," she says. "He was not involved in her disappearance."

I clench the sides of the chair. This can't be right. "How do you know?"

"After Mark Lloyd left Oma, he went to a bar in the West Village, where he was met by a friend around a quarter to ten."

"Kiku Shima," I say.

She nods. "I thought I saw you earlier, across the street from the Lloyds'."

I shift in my chair but don't say anything.

"They took a taxi together to Gramercy, where they stayed in the apartment until the following afternoon. We have confirmation of both Mr. Lloyd's and Ms. Shima's presence at the bar, and we have a restaurant delivery receipt to the East Twenty-First Street address from late that night."

"Since Esme never met Mark for dinner," I say softly, the reality that he did not, in fact, abduct my sister refusing to settle in.

SI Bakshi nods. "Your brother-in-law had the receipt in his wallet, and the restaurant has corroborated the eleven fifteen delivery. At that point, we know your sister had already left the Monarch. Mark's whereabouts are entirely accounted for."

I scrape my hand across my face. The relief that Mark hasn't done something to harm her is overwhelming. But if not Mark, then who is responsible for her disappearance?

"Ms. Shima took a Lyft from the Gramercy address to her own apartment on Sunday afternoon," SI Bakshi continues. "And we know already that Mr. Lloyd arrived home to his residence around three. We did not find any evidence of your sister in the Gramercy apartment, but we did find plenty to suggest that Mr. Lloyd and Ms. Shima have been frequenting the space for weeks, as they've both attested. I'm afraid what we've uncovered is the affair you believed him to be having, but no direct ties to your sister's case."

"So we're back to square one," I say, voice small.

She gives me a tight smile. "I wouldn't say square one. In any missing-persons investigation, most leads prove to be dead ends. But it has been twelve days since your sister's disappearance, which concerns me. We're going to do everything in our power to bring her home."

She pauses for a moment, then places her hand gently on my forearm. "I know this is hard to hear, but in the meantime, I think you should begin to prepare for the possibility that we may not find Esme alive."

8

HOME

"What the hell are you doing here?" I ask from the doorway to Esme's hospital room, eyes locked on my father. He looks like a giant looming over her bed, tall and broad shouldered. His hair is still blond in places, but grayer than the last time I saw him.

"Jane." He clears his throat, and my sister's phone drops from his hand down to the sheets. Beneath him, her chest rises and falls, and the machine she's hooked up to beeps gently as she sleeps.

"She had my office line saved in her contacts," he says after a moment. "I came as soon as I picked up the message."

I narrow my eyebrows. If he had time to commute in from Yale, he had time to call me. I could have been here an hour ago.

"You shouldn't have left it to some nurse to track me down."

"Sorry." He frowns, then glances sheepishly at Esme's phone, which rests face down where he dropped it on her bed. "I was trying to look up Mark's number, but I don't know how they got into this thing. Do you have her password?"

"I have Mark's number," I tell him. "But they're not together."

"What?" Carl's eyebrows crease, and he takes a step around the bed, toward me. There is something immensely satisfying about holding the news of my sister's separation over his head. As distant as Esme and I have become, the gap between us is nothing compared to the galaxy separating us from our father.

"She's been living with me for the past two weeks," I continue. "In Branby."

"I had no idea."

"Of course not," I snap. His office line lights up my phone once or twice a year, usually Christmas Eve when he's alone on campus, avoiding his empty house, and on my birthday. But the last time I actually saw Carl in person was Esme's wedding, four years ago.

A memory. Mark and Esme tied the knot in the Terrace Room at the Plaza Hotel on a picture-perfect Saturday in May. The affair was lovely, if rather more formal than I imagined Esme would have chosen without the Lloyds' money and influence, but Dad was a dark spot on the gorgeous spring day. Esme put off telling him until the rehearsal that Mom—and Mom alone—would be walking her down the aisle. He arrived the morning of the wedding in a shitty mood and hit the bar before the ceremony even started. By the time passed hors d'oeuvres were going around, he had had a few too many bourbons. For the next hour, he relentlessly hounded Esme to join him on the empty dance floor, an invitation she gracefully sidestepped. From my station beside Mom I could see the anger building behind his eyes, one of his tirades swelling, threatening to ruin the whole day. But Rupert Lloyd swooped in as dinner was being served, and perhaps shocked into submission by the firm hand of the father of the groom, Carl allowed himself to be steered into a cab.

When we were growing up, Dad wore two different faces: esteemed professor by day, emotionally abusive husband and father by night. On all matters professional and personal, Dad always found a way to feel slighted, always wanted *more*. I thought for a time that he'd managed to keep Mr. Hyde hidden from his Yale colleagues, but stories have filtered back to me over the years. Sometimes, his grad students would get an earful of what Mom, Esme, and I experienced at home. The angry flare-ups were only part of the bad behavior with his protégés, although he swore the affairs stopped after the divorce, and I have to assume he would have been fired by now if they hadn't.

Or maybe not. Dad is tenured, but it's more than that: Professor Carl R. Connor is a much-lauded member of the academic elite, the kind of wealthy white man shielded by the impervious halo of career eminence. While I'm sure his superiors at Yale are aware of his ethically uncouth behavior, it takes more than a few stories of lost tempers, more than a few relationships with consenting graduate students, for men like my father to lose their posts.

But he lost us years ago—Mom, Esme, and me. In the divorce settlement, Mom got the house and the guarantee of ample alimony payments until Esme turned eighteen. Dad got two weekends a month and two weeks over the summer, more than Mom wanted given his volatility, but he never got physical, and she was never able to prove he was a danger to us in the eyes of the court. We did our time in New Haven, but Esme and I both stopped trying to have a real relationship with him long before we aged out of the custody arrangement.

"They're keeping her under for the night at least," he says finally when I've divulged no further information about Esme's separation. "Her doctor was here a bit ago. They're monitoring the swelling in her brain."

"Do you know who brought her in? Was she with anyone when she overdosed?"

He shakes his head, looking flustered. "I don't think so. I didn't think to ask."

"Jesus, Dad." I pull the room's single chair up to Esme's bedside and slip my hand into hers. "You can go now. I'll stay with her tonight."

For a moment, I think he's going to protest, but then he picks up his aging leather satchel from the windowsill and slides it over his shoulder. "Good, right. I'll come back in the morning."

"You don't have to drive all the way back into the city."

He walks toward the door, then turns back around to face me. "I know I was a terrible husband to your mother. But I never stopped caring about you girls. Truly. Despite what you may think of me."

Liar.

I turn, giving my full attention to Esme so he can't see the tears spring to my eyes.

At a quarter after midnight, my second attempt to call Dylan goes to voice mail, and I settle for leaving a message. He hasn't responded to my texts either, which is very unlike him. That said, it was already after nine the first time I reached out. He'll see my messages in the morning.

Earlier, I gritted my teeth and left a message for Mark as well. I've never been a big fan of Mark Lloyd, even less so now that Esme has left him. Nonetheless, I figure he should know what's going on, but I say a tiny prayer that if he comes to visit, he does it while I'm not around.

Over the past hour, I've squeezed as much information out of the hospital staff as they seem to know. Esme was found slumped on the sidewalk outside a closed storefront on the LES. The person who called 911 either didn't leave a name or the hospital failed to record it. She was unconscious, covered in vomit, and bleeding badly where her head had struck the pavement. Fortunately, she collapsed in a busy area with a robust nightlife scene, and the paramedics said she hadn't been out for long when they arrived. She came to just long enough to express confusion about where she was and how she'd gotten there.

At the hospital, they pumped her stomach and treated her head wound, but the swelling—a product of both the head trauma and the overdose—was severe enough for them to put her back under.

The toxicology report hasn't come back yet, but they suspect some mix of hallucinogens, alcohol, and the benzodiazepines they found in her purse. Dr. Kinnard says she could be out for a few hours or a few days, depending on how long it takes the swelling to go down.

As I half-doze in the hard hospital chair, fingers interlaced with Esme's, I try to work out what the hell happened. In one scenario, my sister was partying downtown, and when she collapsed, whoever she was with got spooked and left her there. In another, she went outside alone and intentionally OD'd. In either case, I don't have any idea who she might have been out with tonight. And the head trauma—did she really just hit her head when she fell? Or did someone do this to her?

The thought sends a chill racing through me.

Around four a.m., I give up on sleep and give myself over fully to the mire of questions clogging my brain. I need answers the hospital can't provide. With Esme out indefinitely, and faced with the uncertainty she'll be able to remember what happened when she is awake, I can't wait for the anesthesiologist to bring her around. I switch on the light and reach for her phone. After three failed attempts to get the facial recognition to comply, I finally lift Esme's mask gently from her face and raise her phone screen again. The ventilator gives three quick beeps and my heart nearly explodes with the certainty I'm harming my sister, but then the phone unlocks, and I slip the mask back into place. The machine's steady rhythm resumes.

Going through my sister's phone is a clear invasion of privacy. I know this. But I've also known that something troubling was going on with Esme since the moment I brought her home nearly two weeks ago. And instead of demanding a real conversation, I let my hang-ups about our relationship get in the way. I allowed this to happen. The guilt overpowers any reservations I have about snooping; the regular rules no longer apply. Someone either maliciously harmed her or drove her to attempt suicide. Either way, a lot is on the line.

I start with Instagram. She wiped her account the day she broke up with Mark, a discovery I made a few days into her residence in Branby, but the app is everything to her. Surely she has something saved in her drafts.

A quick poke around gives me access to all her old archived posts, but the few saved drafts from the last two weeks are photos with no captions. Esme's feet in ruffled knee socks crossed beside her open laptop, staged on a wicker table I recognize from the three-season porch. The reflection of her pensive face in the window glass of a Metro-North train, the Cos Cob station whipping by outside. A chipped coffee mug beside a composed stack of library books on a marred wooden table: *The Glass Castle*, *The Liar's Club*, *Inheritance*, *Wild*.

Her DMs are filled with notes from her followers asking for details about her fresh start and if she can give any hints about what she has in store. She hasn't responded to any of them.

I move over to her texts, hopeful I'll find something to shed light on who she was meeting tonight, but I see nothing about making plans. A search reveals she's deleted her entire message history with Mark. In fact, Mark's been deleted from her contacts altogether, which explains why the hospital called Dad, then me, when attempting to contact her family. I make a mental note to show Esme how to set up her emergency contacts when she wakes up from this.

I scroll through a list of texts from her spin studio, American Express, AT&T, and names of friends I haven't met, searching now for the unsaved number I'm not sure I'll recognize, the sender of the threatening text I intercepted two Sundays ago.

Several days back in her text history, I'm rewarded by a conversation with someone now saved to Esme's phone as "Fucker." My breath catches, and I tap it open.

Sun, August 27, 7:03 PM

You'll ruin everything. Don't fucking do this.

Mon, August 28, 6:48 AM

You know, it took me all night to figure
out who this was.

9:12 AM

I'm sorry. I was upset last night. But
we need to talk.

9:15 AM

We really don't.

9:16 AM

I'm serious, Esme.

11:02 AM

Let me guess, Kiku called you.

11:08 AM

And I'm glad she did.

Wed, August 30, 11:23 PM

You need to cut it out. You have no
idea what's at stake.

11:51 PM

Or maybe you do and you don't fucking care.

11:52 PM

Do you realize how incredibly selfish
you're being? I'm calling you. You
need to pick up.

Thurs, August 31, 11:08 AM

Do you even hear yourself? STOP
THREATENING ME!

11:12 AM

That's truly rich. Me threatening you.

Fri, Sept 1, 8:09 PM

You can't avoid me forever.

8:11 PM

We need to talk. Face to face.

Then there's nothing. The texts stopped nearly a week ago, but
I move over to Esme's call log. Since that time, she's had a dozen
missed calls from "Fucker." The most recent was Thursday night. I
tap open the contact info and cross-reference it against the numbers

in my own phone. A suburban Connecticut area code, but there's no match. So, a mutual friend of Esme's and Kiku's, but not someone I know.

I type the number into Google to see what comes up. The search reveals little more than I already knew: it's a mobile phone registered to a Verizon customer. A handful of sites offer to give me private customer information for a fee, which feels like a scam.

Why pay when I can just call? Using Esme's phone, I tap dial. It rings three times, then a recorded voice clicks on. *You've reached an automated voice mail messaging system for Verizon customer two-oh-three-eight-nine-one—*

I hang up. Then I take screenshots of the texts and missed calls and send them to myself. Her last contact with the mystery number was an incoming call lasting six minutes, which came in at shortly before eight tonight. This time, Esme picked up. What were they talking about for six minutes? Did she give in, were they making arrangements to meet?

In Esme's settings, I change the autolock to never, to keep it from going to sleep and locking me back out. Then I lift her bag from the bedside table and start rummaging through. The benzos the paramedics found are gone, presumably confiscated for Esme's safety, but I do find something strange: another phone.

It's a basic flip phone, the kind people on TV use for drugs, affairs, or the lack of tracking capability. A burner. Given the circumstances, my money's on drugs. I open it up, and it prompts me for my password. There's no facial recognition on this phone, no thumbprint sensor either. I try Esme's birthday, just in case, then Mark's. No luck. Her password could be literally anything.

Discouraged, I drop the burner back into her bag and return to her regular phone. Instagram was a bust, and the person sending her threats is an enigma for now, but there's got to be something else on here. I skim a bunch of her recent texts, but there are surprisingly few exchanges with friends. Kiku seems to have been deleted along with Mark, although Esme claimed to have been meeting her in the city only last week.

I keep reading. Nothing that reveals the truth behind the reason for her separation from Mark, or the identity of "Fucker," or who she was meeting on the LES.

After a while, I find myself back on her call log, scrolling. Two names I don't know—Laura Rosado and Victoria Shaughnessy—pop up several times, but the majority of her recent outgoing calls are to someone named Hunter. I tap open his contact. Colorado area code, no last name, no company listed. Over the past couple of weeks, she's had three incoming calls from him, and she's placed more than a dozen. I flash back to the private conversation I overheard last week. *Do we have to do the whole library thing again? I want to get to know you—really get to know you.*

That was Tuesday evening, right before my date with Dylan. I consult the call log. *6:37 PM, outgoing call to Hunter, 4 minutes.* Bingo. Esme claimed to have been talking to her new creative writing mentee, and her comments at Mom's birthday dinner seem to support that claim—*I have the most talented mentee this semester, a writing student at Sarah Lawrence. He's a senior from Loveland, Colorado*—but no student mentorship program warrants this many phone calls. There's something else going on here, something she didn't want me to uncover. Something that possibly resulted in this: Esme in the hospital, fighting her way back from an overdose, and me scouring her phone for answers.

My gaze flickers between my sister and her phone screen. The most recent Hunter call was around eight, just three minutes after the call with the mystery number ended.

Just two hours before she was found unconscious and bleeding.

NINE

GONE

Late Friday morning, I drag myself out of bed and down to the three-season porch, mug of tea and Esme's planner in hand. It's nearly noon, but I'm achy and exhausted. All night, I drifted in and out of sleep, all-too-real dreams jolting me awake: NYPD officers storming the Lloyds' Gramercy penthouse, then SI Bakshi breaking the news that Mark was not, in fact, responsible for my sister's disappearance. In the morning light, what happened to Esme is still as much a mystery as it was before last night's search.

I sip my tea, feeling absolutely defeated. I found the prenup, found Esme's divorce lawyer, found out about Esme's book deal and how she cut Kiku out. And for what? None of it has provided a single useful answer when it comes to my sister's case. SI Bakshi's words ring loud in my ears: *I know this is hard to hear, but I think you should begin to prepare for the possibility that we may not find Esme alive.*

My chest grows tight, and hot tears stream down my cheeks. I swipe angrily at my face as the now-familiar cocktail of guilt and fear floods my system, demanding my absolute submission to its punishing hold until it's good and ready to let me go.

Finally, I breathe, nudging my mind to recenter on something positive.

The one part of last night that wasn't entirely horrible was Jamie. In spite of myself, I smile remembering his warm, comforting presence beside me in the lobby, the heat of his lips against the top of my head.

I place my sister's planner on the wicker table in front of me and flip it open to August for the hundredth time, not sure what I hope to find. Just then, my phone chimes, and Dad's number flashes across my screen.

My finger hovers, and I debate sending the call to voice mail. His office line lights up my phone once or twice a year, usually Christmas Eve, when he's alone on campus, avoiding his empty house, and on my birthday. Today, there's no such special occasion, but I've known it would be only a matter of time before Esme's disappearance drew him out of the woodwork. I did send him an email directly following my first interview with Marrone, letting him know what was going on and that they'd likely be reaching out, but in typical Carl style, it's been well over a week, and he hasn't so much as checked in. Growing up, even when Esme and I were staying with him, his mind was with his work. We always felt like an afterthought.

"Dad."

"Jane, I'm so glad I caught you. I'm in Manhattan."

"Okay . . ." I say slowly. "I'm in Branby."

"Well. I was called in to speak to the detectives working on your sister's case. Honestly, when I didn't hear anything after your one email, I assumed she'd turned up."

My jaw drops slowly open. Is he seriously suggesting that *I* should have kept him better informed when he couldn't make the time to hit Reply?

Before I can say something I'll surely regret, he barrels on. "But it seems she hasn't. I answered their questions to the best of my ability, but there's not much I can contribute."

"Because you haven't seen her recently," I say, voice flat. The last time I actually saw my father in person was Esme's wedding, four years ago. It was messy and awkward, and I have no reason to believe things have been any different between the two of them.

"No, not recently," he confirms.

"Have you talked to her? Anything?"

He sighs. "You know how your sister feels about me, Jane. I truly don't have any idea where she could have gone, or what might have happened to her. I'm sorry."

Of course not. I raise my eyes to the ceiling, blinking back the tears that threaten to spill over once again. I knew Dad wouldn't have any useful information to contribute; it's why I didn't try harder to track him down when he didn't respond to my email. As always, talking to him dredges up ugly memories from childhood—Dad screaming at Mom, rumors of Dad cheating with his graduate students, all of which turned out to be true.

"I have to go," I tell him. "I'm glad the NYPD contacted you. They're still working to find her, but I think they're running out of leads. If you think of anything else, you should call them."

"I'm sure I won't," he says, "but Jane, if there's anything I can do to help . . ."

I scrub at my eyes and clear my throat. When has Dad ever shown up for us, ever done anything that required putting his family first? He'll get off this call and go back to New Haven and bury himself in work like always.

"Thanks," I say tightly. "I'll let you know."

Phone face down on the wicker table once more, I return to Esme's planner. I'm a workaholic like my father, but I am *not* like him where it counts. I have my priorities straight. I'm poorly rested and emotionally tapped, but I can't let last night's set-back at the Gramercy apartment destroy my resolve. As SI Bak-shi said, most leads in a missing persons' investigation turn out to be dead ends. I was so sure Mark's affair was the answer to all of this, but just because I was wrong about that doesn't mean I can't uncover the piece of information that will crack this whole thing open. I know my sister as well as anyone, and I have the time because I am choosing to make the time—unlike Dad. I have to keep trying.

I raise my mug to my face, inhale a cloud of steam. Then I focus on the planner, my one conduit to my sister. Surely there's something I overlooked, a previously meaningless ap-pointment that, after nearly two weeks of searching, will finally click into place. The calls and meetings with Laura and Victoria now make sense—Esme's agent and editor, both acquired after she learned about Kiku's betrayal. The calendar appointments *do* now paint a clearer picture of the days and weeks before she disappeared: finding out about the affair, the subsequent falling-out with Kiku, the book deal, preparing to divorce Mark. But given Mark's and Kiku's confirmed alibis, none of that sheds any light on what happened in the hours after she called me, before she vanished.

Determined not to wallow in defeat, I return once more to the Hunter Library appointment listed on the day before her disap-pearance, then again the following week.

Hunter Library 3 p.m.

That's still a mystery. I stood outside for half an hour, and no one showed.

Then there's the Saturday-morning coffee date at Café Lisse in mid-June. The coffee shop is located not far from the Lloyds' pied-à-terre, but I know better than to read too much into that now. Unless Esme was onto Mark and Kiku all the way back in

June and trailed her husband over to the East Side that morning? Equally as likely, her coffee date had nothing to do with them.

I flip back in the planner, then ahead, but nothing else stands out. Eventually, I land once more on the blank rectangle for Saturday, August 26, the day she disappeared, and the Hunter Library appointment the afternoon before.

Unless . . .

With a sharp inhale, I grab my notepad and pen. I'd been so sure *Hunter Library* was Hunter College, but what if I was waiting in the wrong spot? Just as easily, Hunter could be a person. I try it out.

Hunter,

Library,

3 p.m.

When I went to see Mark, he was cagey about the contents of Esme's planner, but I've uncovered his big secret now. He has nothing left to hide.

I pick up my phone and dial. On the fifth ring, he answers.

"Jane."

"Mark. I heard . . . about last night." I'm nearly certain he didn't see me waiting on East Twenty-First, and with any luck, Marrone and Bakshi didn't bring me directly into the conversation when they were questioning him.

On the other end of the line, he sighs. "I don't know what you heard exactly, but the detectives were way off base. I want Esme back safely as much as anyone."

I stifle a snort. Given his affair, that's a little hard to believe. I know I need to move on from my suspicions of Mark, but one lingering question needles at me.

"The other day, when I was over, you didn't want me going upstairs. Why?"

There's a brief pause, and he clears his throat. "Your sister packed a good number of boxes before she left; I assume she was planning to come back for them at some point. I thought all the boxes cluttering the hallway might make it seem like I didn't want her to return. I knew you had your doubts about me, and I didn't want your imagination running wild."

I let that sit for a moment. The boxes may have struck me as evidence Mark was trying to vanquish Esme entirely from his life, although that pales in comparison to the prenup and his affair. Even so, I have to trust the detectives on this: Mark is a liar and a cheat, but he didn't harm Esme. And right now, much as it pains me to admit it, I need his help.

"Look," I say. "It's been almost two weeks. You can't still believe Esme is perfectly fine, lying low somewhere."

His voice softens a bit. "I admit, it's looking less likely."

"The day before she went missing, there's an appointment in her planner for 'Hunter Library' at three p.m."

"Hunter College?"

"That's what I thought. But it could be Hunter, at the library. Who does Esme know named Hunter?"

"No one I know of."

"Think, Mark. Hunter. Friday, August twenty-fifth at three o'clock."

For a long moment, Mark is silent. Then he says, "I don't know a Hunter. But she's involved with a mentorship program for college seniors. Career advice, writing feedback, that sort of thing. Typically starts with an orientation in late August."

"At NYU?" I ask.

"All over the tristate. Her mentee is at Sarah Lawrence this year."

I suck my lower lip between my teeth and pull up the Sarah Lawrence College calendar online. Their year began on Monday, August 21.

"That could be it. Thanks, Mark."

I hang up and search around the college website for anything about the program, but there's only a general description of opportunities for mentorship. Nothing useful like a list of participating students or meeting locations. On the one hand, if Hunter is Esme's mentee, it's hard to imagine an appointment with a student at the Sarah Lawrence College library has anything to do with her disappearance. On the other, he would have been one of the last people to see Esme. It's possible she told him something important. For instance, if she canceled that second appointment, that might indicate she left willingly or knew something was going to happen to her. Maybe they talked about their plans for the weekend. Maybe Hunter knows something that could help.

A few minutes of searching for Hunters who are students at Sarah Lawrence takes me to the website for a small public high school in Loveland, Colorado. A PDF of an old school newsletter archived on its site displays the names of its graduating seniors from three years back and their college or career plans for the fall.

Hunter Mendez, Sarah Lawrence College.

If Hunter's a senior now like Mark thought, this could be him. I pull up the main Sarah Lawrence office number and dial.

Five minutes later, a squeaky-voiced student worker has read me the Family Education Rights and Privacy Act, verbatim. After some wheedling, she reluctantly confirms that a Hunter Mendez is a current undergraduate student, but nothing else. When I ask if she can give me his contact info, she holds firm.

"My sister is missing," I say finally, desperate to get something out of this adamant rule-follower. "I think she might have been mentoring Hunter Mendez, and that they met the day before she disappeared. I need to verify that the student she met with was him."

"Oh," she says. "I'm sorry."

"Thanks. I just . . . Can you tell me if he's part of a writing mentorship program? Or his major, anything?"

She giggles. "Students here don't declare majors. But I am authorized to disclose honors and awards information. As a first year, Hunter came in under the Lux Creative Writing Award."

"Perfect." Sarah Lawrence is a small school. The website tells me there are fewer than four hundred students in a typical graduating class, and historically over seventy-five percent of the student body is female. It's not impossible that there are two seniors named Hunter studying creative writing, but odds are, I've identified my sister's mentee. Now I need to find him.

It takes me a solid hour of sorting through search results and profile pages, but by one thirty, I have located the correct Hunter Mendez on Instagram. In a stroke of luck, he posted a story an hour ago.

> the best sugar rush on campus is at
> the Teahaus! @nora_aura's vegan
> blondies are out of this world

I throw on clean clothes and race down to the garage. It's a forty-minute drive between Branby and Bronxville. I park in the visitor lot and make my way across the lawn separating several lovely old Tudor buildings from the decidedly less charming dorms. In the center is the Teahaus, a cozy stone hut that could have been plucked straight out of *The Hobbit*.

The doors are flung open to let in the warm September air. I pause on the path, peering inside. In the back of the tiny one-room building, a student is sprawled across a sagging armchair and two others occupy cushions on the floor, quietly reading or listening to music. A large array of teas and a platter of blondies and blueberry bars rest on a table toward the front. Behind it, a young man with light brown skin, green eyes, and dark brown shoulder-skimming hair perches on a window seat. I'd guess he's biracial, Mexican maybe, and white. He may not be tall, but he's strikingly handsome, and I'd wager he knows it.

He gives me a slight nod as I step inside. "Welcome."

Without a doubt, this is the same Hunter Mendez from Instagram. I glance toward the students in the back, but despite the close proximity, no one is paying us any attention.

I draw in a deep breath and flash him my most winning smile. "Hunter? I'm Jane Connor, Esme Connor-Lloyd's sister?"

"Ah. Hello, Jane."

He regards me calmly, eyes meeting mine for an uncomfortably long time. For a barely adult, he's supremely confident in his own skin.

"Listen," I say, breaking his gaze, "I know this is a little weird, but I'm looking for Esme, and I think she was mentoring you?"

A knowing smile stretches across Hunter's face, one I've seen on more than a few men interested in Esme before, and I wonder if—more like *what*—he's thinking about my sister. His eyes are intense and expressive, and despite his probably being only twenty-one, his self-assured demeanor radiates more man than boy. He reminds me of Dad's literature students at Yale—attractive, overprivileged, confident the world will stand up and deliver everything they're owed. He leans back against the window frame.

"Yes, I know Esme. We only met once, though."

"Can you tell me about that?"

He steeples his fingers together, debating what to make of this impromptu interrogation.

157

"Can I interest you in a baked good? Sales benefit the Students for Students Scholarship Fund."

"Oh, sure." I select one of the vegan blondies and hand Hunter a five. "Keep the change."

He flashes me a smile. "Thanks."

"About Esme," I try again. "The thing is, she's missing, and I'm talking to everyone she knows."

His wide brows arch. "Missing?"

"Can you tell me when you met with her? What you talked about?"

He nods, all business now. "It was a couple Fridays ago. We talked about various publishing internships in the city, and she wanted to introduce me to a writer she knows who runs a lit mag in Williamsburg."

"You met here on campus?"

"There are a few of us doing the mentorship program. We all met in the library."

"Did she say anything about future plans, or your next meeting?"

Hunter nods again, and his long hair swings forward. "We were supposed to meet again, the next week. I was very much looking forward to it. But she didn't show."

"And you didn't hear from her otherwise?"

"We'd been emailing for a while, over the summer. She was very invested in my writing and getting to know me. I wasn't sure what changed, but now . . ."

"I'm sorry," I say. "It definitely wasn't personal. She's been missing since the day after you two met."

He agrees to exchange numbers, just in case, but by the time I leave the Teahaus, vegan blondie clutched inside a paper napkin, it's pretty clear that Hunter Mendez is just a student—attractive, confident, and probably talented—who met my sister only once. *Hunter Library 3 p.m.* is yet another dead end.

On the drive home, Jamie's name flashes across the dash, and my heart squeezes. I'm glad he can't see my flushed face as he asks how I am, and I thank him again for coming into the city to sit with me last night.

"It's fine," he assures me.

"It meant a lot. I haven't been okay since Esme disappeared. Really, since before then."

For a moment, he's silent, and it hits that I've said too much. Before he can say something that will break my heart all over again, I barrel on.

"I struck out again today. I followed up on an appointment in Esme's planner from the day before she went missing, which turned out to be with her mentee at Sarah Lawrence. They'd only met the one time, and of course he didn't know anything." I laugh, and it comes out dry and raspy. "I don't know what I'm doing, Jamie. I should have been there for her, and I let this happen. I'm at a total loss."

He sighs. "I'm worried about you. I don't think you're being very kind to yourself right now."

"Maybe not. But Esme's been gone for nearly two weeks. What am I supposed to do?"

There's a long pause, and I'm about to check if the call has dropped, when he says, "I'm in the city at the moment, but I'll be at Monte Viso on Sunday. Can I bring you dinner after my shift? I'd like to see you. To catch up."

My breath catches, and for a moment, I can't speak. For weeks, all I wanted was to hear Jamie say those words. The thought that my sister's disappearance might bring us back together sends my stomach into knots, equal parts horror and eager anticipation.

"Jane? You still there?"

"I'm here," I choke out. "I'd like that."

9

HOME

At eight, I extract myself from the stiff chair in Esme's hospital room to stretch and search for a café. While I wander the halls, I leave a message for Nabeel, letting him know I need to take a personal day.

When I return to the room, tea in hand, I review what I've learned about Hunter, Esme's supposed mentee (although I have my doubts about that). Her call log indicates they've been talking a lot over the past two weeks, and their last conversation was just two hours before she was found unconscious and bleeding.

I'm itching to call, but if he really is a college student, I'll have a better chance of making contact if I hold off until the sun is a little higher in the sky. While I sip my tea and wait, Dr. Kinnard comes by twice. The swelling has decreased slightly, enough to downgrade Esme's condition from critical to serious, but she stresses that she's still acutely unwell and not even close to out of the woods.

When I'm alone in my sister's room again, I pull up Hunter's contact on her phone and dial. The voice on the other end is young, and despite the very reasonable hour of ten a.m., the mumbling and throat-clearing suggests I've woken him up.

"Esme?"

"Not Esme. This is Jane, her sister."

"Ah. Hello, Jane."

I put on my most authoritative voice and explain that Esme is in the hospital and I need to see him urgently. He starts to ask why, but I cut him off.

"Where can we meet? I'll come to you."

There's a slight pause, then he says, "I'm starting my shift soon, but come to campus at three. I'll be on the South Lawn, in front of the Pub."

A few hours later, I've left Bellevue, returned home to collect my car, and driven out to Westchester. I walk onto the Sarah Lawrence campus from the visitors' lot, taking in the groups of students camped out on brightly colored sarongs in the grass and sipping coffee at little tables in front of the redbrick-and-stone building known as the Pub. A young man with light brown skin, green eyes, and dark brown shoulder-skimming hair gives me a chin tilt from his spot on the grass, then raises a cardboard coffee cup to his lips.

"Jane Connor." I stick out my hand, and he stands to greet me. He isn't tall, but he has a firm shake.

"Hunter Mendez."

I sit down beside him in the grass, taking him in. I'd guess he's biracial, Mexican maybe, and white. He's wearing dark-wash jeans, a threadbare tee, and a brown jacket with worn plaid patches on the elbows. Very Oxbridge chic. He's strikingly handsome with his bright smile and high cheekbones, and I'd wager he knows it. I feel out of place on this college campus in my black slacks and work blouse, now badly wrinkled after a night spent in a hospital chair.

"You don't look like Esme," he observes, a curious smile stretching across his face. It's a look I've seen before on more than a few men interested in Esme, and I wonder if—more like *what*—he's thinking about my sister. His eyes are intense and expressive, and his self-assured demeanor radiates more man than boy despite the fact that he's probably only twenty-one. Not for the first time, I wonder if my sister has gotten herself involved with a student.

"No, not really," I agree. "I take after our mother."

His wide eyebrows crease together as he leans back and shamelessly takes me in. The level of scrutiny I'm presently receiving is a little disconcerting, but then again, he's probably smart to be wary of a thirtysomething woman showing up out of nowhere, claiming to be Esme Connor-Lloyd's sister. Especially if he knows what went down last night. He probably thinks I'm a cop.

"Look." I pull out my phone, pull up photos from last Thanksgiving, the two of us with our mother. "All the Connor women."

"Huh, I see it." He regards me calmly, eyes meeting mine for an uncomfortably long time. For a barely adult, he's supremely confident in his own skin. "I take after my mom, too, mostly. Brown skin, dark hair."

I smile politely, trying to figure out how to steer this conversation toward my sister's overdose without instantly scaring him off.

"Right, well. As I mentioned on the phone, Esme's in the hospital, and it's pretty serious."

"I'm really sorry to hear that," he says, face creasing with concern.

"The doctors are very worried. So we need to figure out what happened last night. Okay?"

He nods but doesn't offer anything up. I ease off a bit.

"How did you two meet?"

"Esme's my mentor. Creative writing." The answer comes quickly. A little too quickly.

I tuck my legs beneath me on the grass, lean toward him. "You know I got your number from her phone, right? She's called you a lot over the past couple weeks. That was all about creative writing?"

He sets his coffee down in the grass and steeples his fingers together, debating what to make of this impromptu interrogation. "No, not entirely. Esme *has* been very invested in my writing. But after that first meeting, we started talking regularly. You might think it's strange, because she's older—"

"And married."

"Separated, I believe? But it's not like that. We have a lot in common."

I press my lips between my teeth, not sure I can trust him. Esme is beautiful and enigmatic, and when she shines her light on you, she can make you feel like you've won the lottery. It's hard to believe Hunter *wouldn't* fall for my sister. Why she, in turn, would invest so much time in a college senior—even a handsome, confident one—is more of a puzzle, but maybe he really is a brilliant writer. Undoubtedly, she's been feeling vulnerable these past couple of weeks, unmoored. Hunter's playing it cool, but I'd bet good money he worships her. When she's talking to him, she probably feels like she's won the lottery, too. I don't know the full details of what happened between her and Mark, but allowing Hunter to fall for her is precisely the kind of confidence boost Esme would seek out.

"I get it," I say, sensing it's better not to press the issue. Instead, my mind travels to last Friday night, Mom's birthday dinner at Mario's. Esme arrived late, dressed in jeans and a band T-shirt, reeking of pot. It now seems highly likely she was coming from Sarah Lawrence, and I bet Hunter has access to a whole buffet of drugs.

"You guys what, get stoned and read poetry?" I ask, trying to keep my voice light.

His shoulders lift, body tensing. Clearly I've hit a nerve. "She's working through some personal stuff right now, and she likes it here. She says being on campus makes her feel a million miles from everything she knows, everything she's trying to escape."

That sounds exactly like something my sister would say.

"Fine. But, Hunter, she overdosed last night. That's why she's in the hospital."

"Oh. Well, shit."

I scan his face for signs of recognition or surprise. We've been talking for a while now. Is it strange that he didn't ask me what happened?

"Do you know where she got the drugs?" I ask.

He shakes his head, long hair whipping back and forth. "We've smoked together, but that's it. I don't know what she got into last night." He won't meet my eyes.

"I know she called you a couple hours before she OD'd."

He tucks his hair behind his ears, frowning. "Esme did call, but we didn't meet up, okay? My buddy opened for Swiss Maiden at Remy last night. I was helping him set up."

"Remy?"

"Yeah, it's an outdoor venue." He gestures toward the other side of campus. "Look, I only spoke to Esme for a few minutes. She was upset about something, but I couldn't really talk. I was in the middle of stuff."

"So you had no idea she OD'd."

He shreds a strip of cardboard from his empty cup and lets it fall to the grass. "Not until you told me."

I sigh. Maybe Hunter is hiding something, or maybe being questioned has set him on edge. My gut says he provided at least some of the drugs in Esme's system, but he didn't force her to take anything. If Esme wakes up and remembers what happened, if it turns out he supplied the drugs, he'll be in plenty of trouble, but retribution's not really what I'm after. I want to know *why* Esme got so out of control last night, and much as I suspect Hunter isn't telling me the whole truth, I don't think he has the answers I'm looking for.

"Is she going to be okay?" His face is impassive, his voice warbles. Even if he was responsible, in part, for what happened, it's clear he cares about my sister. Something real must've developed between them over the past couple of weeks.

"I don't know yet," I say softly. "Right now, they're keeping her in a medically induced coma. But I'll call you when I know something, okay?"

He looks up, and his eyes are shiny. "Yeah, thanks."

On my drive home, I call the hospital. The nurse tells me Carl stopped in for a bit, but nothing has changed with Esme since I left earlier this afternoon. They'll be keeping her under overnight, and I'm told she's stable. I think about driving back into the city, but I need to go home sometime, take a shower, get some sleep.

First, I join Mom for a quiet dinner at Monte Viso. As we pick at our salads, I debate telling her about Esme. When the meal ends and I still haven't said anything, I know I won't. The lie of omission feels bad, but telling Mom the truth would only upset her, and then two hours later, she'd forget.

As I'm walking across the parking lot, Dylan texts that he's coming over, and I smile for the first time all day. He finally texted me back this morning, apologizing for missing my calls last night. We texted back and forth a bit more this afternoon, but his messages were the brief, preoccupied kind he sends when he's busy at work. On the drive home, my body hums with the anticipation of seeing him, and not until I remember Esme lying alone in the hospital do I feel a little guilty.

"I am so happy to see you," I tell Dylan when I pull into the drive and find him waiting on Old Boney's wide front steps, "but I haven't been home, and I'm still wearing yesterday's clothes. Keep me company while I take a shower?"

A grin spreads across his face. "Is that an invitation?"

"To hang out in the bathroom while I take a very utilitarian shower? Yes."

He laughs, and I open the garage door and wave him inside.

Ten minutes later, I'm scrubbing two days of filth from my skin and Dylan is leaning against the doorframe separating my bedroom from the en suite bath.

"I'm sorry I missed your messages last night," he says, although he's already apologized over text.

"It's okay." I squeeze more bodywash onto the loofah and inhale the scent of mango and brown sugar.

"I feel bad. I would have driven down to the hospital."

"Were you out in Branby?"

"Something like that. My buddy Joe was down from Syracuse. I must have had my ringer off and didn't realize."

"Huh, okay." Is it strange that I've never heard of Joe, or that Dylan didn't mention earlier that he had a friend in from out of town? I let the hot water stream down my skin and decide that it isn't. It does seem like we've been telling each other everything lately, but there's still a big gap in our history. What we have is so new, the rules so undefined. He's hardly obligated to inform me of who he's hanging out with or every little plan. Yes, Dylan ghosted me fifteen years ago, and the sting of that is harder to forget than I'd like. But we've both grown up.

"It's better that you didn't come, honestly. There was nothing to do, and you had to be up early this morning."

"So early. Seven a.m. on-sites are a killer. Anyway, tell me more. Did you get anything out of that Hunter kid?"

I fill Dylan in on everything that was too complicated for text, from my excavation of Esme's phone to my conversation with Hunter Mendez.

"He wasn't telling me everything," I wrap up, rinsing conditioner from my hair. "They spoke earlier that night, and he clearly has access to drugs."

"Or maybe he was nervous," Dylan says. "Being questioned by a beautiful older woman."

"Ha ha." I switch off the water and crack open the shower door. Dylan smiles and hands me my towel.

"Seriously, though. I'm glad you spoke with him. If he does know something, maybe he'll come around."

I step out of the shower, tucking the towel around my body, and reach for a second towel for my hair.

"Do you think she's going to pull through?" I ask, needing to voice the unanswerable question.

Dylan takes a step toward me, then folds me into his arms. "I want to say yes. She's lucky someone called nine-one-one as soon as they did."

I nest my face in his shoulder and breathe in the clean fabric smell of his shirt, the slightly woodsy scent of his deodorant.

"If I wasn't so worried about her, I'd be furious."

Dylan leans in, and his lips brush my forehead, then find my lips. "I know."

Gently, he pulls me out of the bathroom, into the bedroom. My towel comes untucked, and I let it fall to the floor.

He sits on the edge of my bed and places his hands on my bare hips, anchoring me between his knees. Then he nibbles at the sensitive skin beneath my breasts, making his way down my stomach, and a soft moan slips through my lips.

"For now, you've done everything you can." Dylan's voice is soft. "For the next few minutes, let's forget about Esme."

That sounds like an excellent idea. "Okay," I mumble.

And then we stop talking.

TEN

GONE

By the time we've filled the dining table with cartons of spring rolls and drunken noodles and basil chicken, the initial awkwardness of Jamie's presence in the house after all these weeks has dissolved into a tentative kind of familiarity. Jamie in his usual spot at the foot of the table, me catty-corner in the chair closest to the kitchen. A contemporary folk mix piping from the speakers while Jamie spoons rice onto his plate, then onto mine. For tiny moments, when I allow myself to forget that Esme's disappearance has brought us together, it feels just like old times. It feels nice.

"Tell me about San Francisco. It was good seeing your family?"

Jamie nods. He's wearing jeans and a soft, old T-shirt, and it hits me that this is the first time since the breakup that I've seen him in anything but the professional slacks and button-downs he wears to Monte Viso. I've missed this Jamie. Weekend Jamie. The Jamie who used to be mine.

"Martha and Jim definitely monopolized my time," he says. "But that's always the way when I go home. You'd think I was their only child."

"Maybe because you *are* their only child." I give him a wink, and Jamie matches it with a playful grin.

"Oh, that's right," he says.

We'd been together for about three months when I first met Jamie's mom over a video call. She brought up someone named Ralph, and Jamie instantly changed the subject. After the call ended, further prodding revealed Ralph to be an imaginary hippo that had followed Jamie around as a little kid. I'd found it adorable, of course, and teased him about being "such an only child," a jab he returned with the equivalent any time I exhibited bossy big-sister traits, which was admittedly often.

Now the old joke triggers a pang of longing so intense I have to take a big gulp of water to keep myself from crying out. When Jamie ended things between us, I lost not only the people we used to be to each other but also the promise of the future we'd newly started to plan. It felt like losing *everything*, and now, eating Thai takeout at my dining room table and making easy conversation, I'm overcome by a tidal wave of emotion.

I smile wide, determined to keep the mood light and my feelings tamped down. "You see anyone else back home?"

"A couple friends from high school." He glances at my plate. "More noodles?"

I shake my head. "This is nice. Dinner, talking. I've missed this."

"I have too." He sits back in his chair. "I'm sorry about, well, everything. I truly am."

It's far from *I think I still love you* or *Ending things was a mistake*, but it's something.

"Thank you. I appreciate that." I bite back the rest, determined to take this slow. This is good, the two of us, tonight. Surely I can't be the only one in the room thinking about the way things used to be.

"But enough about my trip," he says after a moment. "Is Mark angry about Thursday night?"

My mind travels to the scene on East Twenty-First, Mark and Kiku being guided out of the Lloyds' penthouse and into a black police cruiser.

"He'll get over it. I spoke to him this weekend, actually. He helped me track down Hunter Mendez, the guy from Esme's planner."

I tell Jamie more about my trip to see my sister's mentee at the Sarah Lawrence Teahaus. "He'd only met her that one time. But I'm not giving up. I can't."

"I know." Jamie reaches across the table and closes my hand in his. I draw in a sharp breath.

For a moment, we stay that way, frozen. Then he lifts his hand from mine and pushes back from the table. "Let me help you clean up. Then we can get to it?"

Ten minutes later, we're back at the dining room table, two mugs of tea steaming before us and Esme's planner spread open to August.

"Nothing in these calendar squares has led to my sister," I tell him, "but it's become a bit of a ritual. Every time I open it up, there's a chance I might uncover something I've missed."

It feels impossibly good to let it all spill out. He nods, listening intently, as I take him through everything I know. During these two trying weeks, I've had no one aside from the detectives to talk to, no one who understands. Through no fault of her own, Mom's not a support network. Dad ceased to be someone I could rely on when I was a kid. And if I hadn't given up so much to be there for Mom, maybe I'd still have close friends I could lean on, but the reality is, I don't.

"Why are you here?" I ask when I've finished walking Jamie through the calendar appointments. "You don't have to be."

"I know," he says, placing his hand lightly on my shoulder. "I never stopped caring about you, Jane. I don't want you to have to go through this alone."

Our eyes lock, and for a moment, I can barely breathe. His eyes drop to my lips. His hand lingers on my shoulder, and his face is so close to mine, I can feel the heat radiating between us. My lips part, inviting him to come back to me, to give in to the heady, magnetic tug of possibility. But then he clears his throat and lifts his hand, reaching instead for his tea.

"Besides, you know I'm good in a crisis." He cracks a smile, raising the mug. "Professional hazard."

I exhale, not sure if we almost kissed or if it was my imagination.

"I've always loved that about you," I manage to say.

Jamie's free hand flexes on the table, and I think he wants to touch me again. Instead, he reaches for the planner, flips back to June. "It sounds like you've pieced most of this together. Except for this coffee date?" He taps the calendar square.

Café Lisse, 7:30 a.m.

"That's right."

He picks up his phone, pulls up the coffee shop on Google Maps.

"It's near Gramercy," he muses, and I shake my head, about to explain how I've already considered that, and dismissed it as a coincidence, when something else occurs to me.

"And also near Dylan's jobsite."

The first time I looked up the café, I hadn't run into him, didn't know what he was working on. But now . . .

"Who's Dylan?" Jamie asks.

While I crack open my laptop and pull up Dylan's website, I explain that he's a childhood friend I recently ran into in the city.

Under current projects, I find the NYC green space he'd mentioned and turn the screen toward Jamie. "Looks like the project started back in May. And the industrial space he's converting is just two blocks from the café."

"That could be something," he says. "Dylan knows your sister well?"

"We all grew up together. The Greers lived in the stone cottage on the back of our property; Dylan's dad was the caretaker, back when Mom could still afford a caretaker. Anyway, Esme was five years younger than Dylan, so she was never as close to him as I was, but five years means a lot less now. They've both been living in the city, until recently. They might have reconnected."

Was Esme meeting Dylan that morning? I take a sip of my tea and sit with the possibility. She'd spent a long weekend in Branby, helping me move Mom into Monte Viso, right before the Café Lisse appointment. She could have run into Dylan in the city, or she could have run into him that weekend. Maybe they planned to get coffee the following week. It's not a sure thing, but it feels promising.

"I need to talk to him," I say. "Just in case."

Jamie nods. "I think that makes sense."

When I ran into Dylan outside Grand Central, he promised to text me his new number, but it hits me now that he never did. I have no idea where in Branby he's living, but I do know the location of his jobsite. "I'll go find him at work tomorrow," I say.

Jamie frowns. "Do you want me to go with you?"

For a moment, I'm tempted to take him up on his offer. I want all of Jamie's time I can get. But he'd be missing work, and besides, I'm just going to ask Dylan about the coffee date, to find out if he saw her back in June, if she told him something useful. Dylan's a good guy. He broke my heart fifteen years ago, but he'd never hurt my sister. If I truly thought I had any reason to be worried, I'd call Marrone and Bakshi.

I shake my head. "It's *Dylan*. I'll be fine."

10

HOME

I spend most of Saturday at the hospital, sitting in Esme's room while she sleeps. Sunday afternoon, I'm at Bellevue again, waiting. A nurse tells me I've missed the physician on call today, someone named Dr. Price, but that he may come back through later this evening. No one has an update for me about when my sister will be woken up, when she can come home. I'm assured that tomorrow, Dr. Kinnard will be back; tomorrow, I will know more.

In the meantime, the unanswered questions churn through my brain: What brought Esme to the LES on Thursday night? Who called in her OD? Was it an accident, or was Esme trying to harm herself? Worse, even, was someone trying to harm her—perhaps the person labeled "Fucker" in her phone?

My thoughts rove back across the two weeks since Esme returned to Branby. The truth is, I have very little idea what my sister was doing during that time. She was out a lot. She met up with Kiku once, supposedly, but Kiku has been deleted from her phone. She came to Mom's birthday dinner. And sometimes, she was hanging out with a handsome young writer at Sarah Lawrence. Beyond that, my knowledge of her whereabouts runs dry. I thought I was giving her the privacy she so clearly craved, that I was mitigating the tension always crackling between us, but I should have tried harder to find out who she was seeing, where she was going. If I had, maybe I would know what she was doing that night. Maybe I could have stopped this from happening.

Eventually, I crack open my laptop, start searching through online police blotters and NYC news sites for Thursday. Maybe I'll find something about a drug bust or a woman found in an alley on the Lower East, anything to shed some light on what happened. *Minor stabbed in Sunnyside laundromat robbery; chaos caught on camera. DA reports Manhattan lawyer stole $1.6 million from three clients. Woman in wheelchair assaulted crossing NYC street, police say.* If Esme had been found in Branby, it would be one thing, but there are far too many results to be useful. I'm about to give up when something on the Channel 4 blog catches my eye: *Two Swiss Maiden band members found in possession of firearms at Washington Heights bar; Thursday and Friday tour dates canceled.*

I flash back to my conversation with Hunter on Friday afternoon, his claim he couldn't get together with Esme the night before. *My buddy opened for Swiss Maiden at Remy last night.*

Hunter wasn't helping his friend set up for the concert, because the concert didn't happen.

Before I can explore all the possible implications of Hunter's lie, there's a light rap on the door. I crane my neck to look behind me.

"Dad."

"Hi, Janie. I . . . Can I come in?"

I swivel back around in my chair. "You're here, aren't you?"

There's a slight pause, then I register the sound of his loafers against the vinyl floor. He slips off his shoulder bag and places it on the windowsill.

"I came by on Friday," he says.

"I know. The nurse told me."

"I must have missed you."

I sigh and pull my knees up to my chin in the hospital room's one chair. "It's been years, Dad. Why are you here?"

He gestures weakly toward Esme.

"Don't say because of Esme. She doesn't know you're here, and please. She's not going to give you a gold star for good behavior when she wakes up."

He crosses his arms defensively over his chest and leans back against the wall. "Fine. On Thursday, I came because the hospital called me. But I came back because I was hoping I'd see you."

"Okay," I say cautiously.

He walks around and perches on the corner of Esme's bed, right across from me. He looks hulking beside her, has never been a person who can look small, even when he tries to take up less space. "I failed your mother completely. I can admit that now. At the time, I was angry with you girls for taking her side, blaming me for the divorce when she'd been unfaithful too, but you were right. I betrayed Marjorie, again and again, and I couldn't control my temper. What happened between your mother and me was one hundred percent my fault."

I blanch. The last thing I want to talk about is the assignation of blame between my parents, how their feuding didn't end with the divorce. "That was eighteen years ago, Dad."

"I know. And I waited entirely too long to have this conversation with you. With either of you." He glances regretfully down at Esme, both of us registering the machine's soft beeping beside her head.

"So why now?"

His shoulders lift and fall. "Life is short. Your sister's in the hospital. I wasn't the best dad, or even a good one. Before the divorce I was a mess, and after, I was bitter. I let my anger taint my relationship with both of you. I'm truly sorry, Jane."

I squirm uncomfortably in the chair. *Taint my relationship* hardly captures Carl's behavior three years after my parents' split, the summer of the crash. I'm the one who nearly killed Esme, but I never would have grabbed Mom's keys, dragged my sister into the car if not for Dad. I made that choice—but I was driven by the fear of what he was about to do.

I compose my face into a placid mask. If Carl suspects how much I know about that weekend, he's never brought it up. After the accident, after Esme nearly died, the Connors came together one last time, focusing the full force of our attention on Esme's recovery. Dad stood down in his feud with Mom, and we all moved on with our lives. I got what I wanted, but at a cost far greater than I'd meant to pay.

"Thanks," I say, his apology hanging in the air between us. I'm not sure I can trust it, but I'd rather smooth things over than dig up the past. "I appreciate that."

"I know it's been too long. But can we try this again? Just coffee, whenever you'd like."

My eyes stray back to my sister. Her pale, sleeping face is a reminder that life can end in a blink—hers, mine, his. If Carl died tomorrow, would I regret not getting that coffee?

Alzheimer's has no cure; in some ways, Mom is already lost to me. Maybe Esme will be fine, but maybe not. I can't know the person she'll be when she wakes up. I wrote Dad off years ago, and for very good reason. Part of me says he doesn't deserve another chance. But what if he really has changed? What if he's the only family I have left?

"Coffee. I'll call you after things settle down a bit. When Esme's home."

He smiles and pulls out his phone. "I got a new one of these a few weeks ago. I'll text you my number."

"Okay."

He reaches across the space between us and places his hand lightly on my knee. "I'll get out of your hair then. Take care, Janie."

A few minutes later, Carl is gone, but instead of the usual anxiety and anger, a tentative calm has settled in his wake. *Possibility.*

I open my phone to save his new number to my contacts, and my breath catches. There is something incredibly familiar about the digits on my screen. Local 203 area code, followed by an 891 exchange.

Fingers trembling, I close out of Dad's text and pull up the screenshots I sent myself from my sister's phone. My gaze shifts to Esme, the breathing tubes, the mask strapped to her face, the bandage patching her forehead, and my stomach clenches into a hard knot.

He says he cares about keeping her safe, but Carl is the person labeled "Fucker" in my sister's phone.

Dad has been threatening Esme.

ELEVEN

GONE

When I arrive at Dylan's jobsite on Monday morning, I'm greeted by a redbrick warehouse spanning an entire city block. This lead—a coffee date with my sister more than two months before her disappearance—feels even more tenuous than the others I've followed, but it's something, and I need to find out what Dylan remembers.

The ground level of the warehouse is enveloped in the forest-green paneling the city uses to keep trespassers out of construction sites. Above that are two or three levels of scaffolding. I begin walking around the building. The first door I encounter is padlocked; maybe there's no one here today. But around the corner, I'm rewarded by a second door, this one unlocked and slightly ajar.

Now that I'm here, I'm caught off guard by the prickle of regret at the base of my spine. Once upon a time, Dylan was a constant in my life, my rock. Now we work in the same city, live in the same small town, and we haven't really talked in years. We are two people who were close once, who have become strangers.

And now I'm here to ask if he knows anything about my sister's disappearance.

I nudge the door open and peer into the murky semidark. I feel a little weird about showing up unannounced like this, but I don't have Dylan's number, and I suppose I could have sent an email to the "info at" address on his website, but I doubt Dylan is personally responsible for managing the company inbox. It might have taken him days to see my message, if at all, and I don't have days.

"Hello?" If there's anyone else here, they haven't bothered to switch on the lights. Carefully, I step inside, leaving the door open behind me. It's dangerous to wander around a construction site without a hard hat or the proper boots, but I glance at my sneakers and decide to risk it. In the center of the warehouse, an angular streamer of daylight pierces the darkness where a large rectangular stairwell has been erected, or retained. Otherwise, what I can make out of the vast space around me appears mostly barren. I make my way over and peer up; three stories of steel stairs ladder to the sky where the roof has been removed, exposing the staircase to the elements. The effect is a little eerie, not unlike sunlight penetrating a cavern from a single escape hole above. The base of the stairs is ringed by several wide planters, and an array of foliage I can't identify by name seems to be thriving in the open air and sunlight.

"Hello?" I repeat. My voice echoes back at me.

With the exception of the stairwell, the ground floor is protected by a high ceiling, and the wood paneling around the building's exterior blocks out the windows. I take two steps away from the stairs, and I'm again swallowed into the misty dark.

This may have been a mistake. There's no one working, and despite the unlocked entrance, I feel like I'm trespassing. I take two steps back toward the thin rail of light where I left the door cracked open, eyes struggling to adjust after staring into the daylight. Just then, a loud clatter rings out above my head, metal striking something hard.

I jump, the sudden shock of the sound knifing through me, and suck in a gasp of air. Then there's silence.

"Dylan?"

Nothing.

This should be my cue to leave, I know it should, but there's someone on one of the floors above me. I spin around and hurry back toward the stairs, making quick work of the darkness until the side of my sneaker lands on something uneven, a piece of brick or stone, and my hands fly out, grasping for something to steady myself. My ankle rolls, and I go down, hip meeting the concrete floor with a painful thud.

"Shit," I whimper. Above me, the sound of heavy footsteps—someone wearing the proper footwear. "Dylan? It's Jane!" I call up.

There's no response. I stretch my ankle to the right, then the left. It's sore, but I don't think it's sprained. I'm going to have a nasty bruise where my hip kissed the ground, but I seem to have escaped any serious harm. I shove myself to my feet and test out my ankle—it's fine, a little tender—then make my way to the staircase and find the path between the planters.

"I'm coming up," I shout, and my voice ricochets into a dozen hollow clinks.

Daylight speeds the climb. I pause on the landing to the second floor and squint into the fuzzy dark beyond, softly calling out Dylan's name. Then I continue up.

The third floor is bathed in light. Surrounding the cutout above the stairwell, the building's roof has been replaced with greenhouse glass, so this floor, unlike the two below, is brightly lit. Dylan stands alone by the wall facing the sidewalk, his back to me. At his feet is a long metal ruler, which must be what fell. He's jotting something onto a notepad and—ah. On top of a gray beanie sits a pair of over-ear headphones.

I walk into the center of the room and angle myself so that, if he turned his head, he could catch me in his peripheral vision. "Dylan," I call out again, louder this time. Then I stamp my foot, and he wheels around.

"Jane!" His eyes are wide. He snatches the headphones from his ears.

"I'm sorry." I laugh. "I didn't mean to sneak up on you."

"What are you doing here?" He doesn't sound amused. He takes two steps toward me.

"I'm sorry for just showing up. I didn't have your new number . . ." There's something chilly in Dylan's expression. I take a step backward, then another.

"No, Jane, wait."

I freeze.

"Here, step into my office." He gestures to two beat-up khaki folding chairs in one corner. "And you're right, I never texted you. Let me fix that."

A second later, my phone chimes, his new number flashing across my home screen.

We sit, and I apologize again for startling him.

"These things are noise canceling," he explains, tapping his headphones. "Living in Branby again has been a distraction in some unexpected ways. Working alone, listening to music, they both help me focus."

I nod. "Got it. Where's everyone else today?"

"A few on the team had first responders in the family. A couple Blue."

I narrow my eyes and press my lips together. I'm clearly missing something.

"Nine-eleven?" he says. "If I'm working with an NYC team, I always give them the day off."

"Oh, right." It's amazing how easy it is to forget the date when you're not in front of your computer all day.

Dylan gives me a kind smile. "Still no news?"

I shake my head. "Nothing. It's . . ." My throat tightens, unbidden, and I have to stop and breathe for a second. "Sorry, the stress is catching up to me. Esme's actually why I'm here. Before she went missing, did you see her at all?"

He shakes his head. "No, sorry. If I knew anything I would have told you right away."

"Of course. I thought maybe you'd gotten together at some point. To catch up?"

He frowns. "Esme and I never really hung out one-on-one. You know that."

"Sure. It's just, there was this Saturday in June, right after we moved Mom into Monte Viso. You didn't happen to meet Esme at Café Lisse over on First Ave.?"

"Oh." Dylan runs his hand across the back of his neck. "She told you about that?"

I sit up straight. My eyes snap to Dylan's. "It was in her planner."

He lets out a long, raspy sigh. "Okay, yes. I did meet Esme for coffee, but that was nearly three months ago. I thought you meant in the past few weeks."

"Sorry, I should have been clearer."

Dylan's brows crease together. "It was just coffee. I can't even remember what we talked about, but I promise it had nothing to do with her disappearance."

"No, I'm sure it didn't. I mean, not directly." I lean forward. "But if you can remember anything she told you that day, it could really help."

I want to keep talking, tell him how little I knew about Esme's life two weeks ago, how much I never would have uncovered without asking a lot of questions about things people swore had nothing to do with my sister's disappearance. The book deal, Mark and Kiku's affair, breaking up with her best friend. None of that has led me to her, but I have to keep digging, keep asking questions until I get to the truth.

I want to say all that, but Dylan shifts uncomfortably in his chair, and I'm reminded of how awkward a silence like this can be. If I wait long enough, he will fill it.

When we ran into each other outside Grand Central less than two weeks ago, Dylan seemed delighted to see me, eager to catch up. Now he seems different. Preoccupied, almost abrupt. From the moment I brought up Café Lisse, he's seemed on edge. Or maybe it's my imagination; I did interrupt his workday. His mind is probably on other things.

"We talked shop," he says finally. "Mark's brother, the older one, has a summer house on the Cape."

"Sean."

"That's it. Esme wanted a recommendation, someone who could do some work for Sean Lloyd and his wife. But I don't really know anyone doing garden-variety landscaping in eastern Mass. I'm afraid I wasn't much help."

"That's it?"

Dylan looks up, squinting into the sun piercing the glass roof. "Honestly? We mostly talked about you."

"About me?"

"Esme thought, with your mom moving into long-term care, that you might, I don't know, move back to the city or change jobs."

"Change jobs?"

"I didn't quite follow, to be honest. She was gushing about wanting the best for you. She kept saying, 'I've always wanted the best for my sister, the absolute best.'"

I sink back against the hard metal chair, and my pants chafe against the bruise forming on my hip. "That's weird," is all I can think to say.

And it is. We spent the whole weekend together when we moved Mom into Monte Viso, and Esme never once asked if I planned to move back to Brooklyn or pursue a new career path. While my sister has been known to lavish compliments on me from time to time, I can't remember the last time she expressed any interest in what I was doing with my life or asked after my happiness.

"And there was no additional context for the outpouring of sisterly love?"

Dylan shakes his head. "Esme being Esme."

He shoves up from his chair and walks across the room to retrieve his notebook and pencil. "I'm actually just about done here. I like the quiet time, when the team's off, to think. But I have an appointment at noon. Can we catch up more some other time?"

I take the hint and show myself out, shifting my weight off my rolled ankle as I take the stairs down.

Esme being Esme. Dylan's words rattle around inside my skull. On the one hand, I know exactly what he means. Ever since we were little, Esme has been mercurial and aloof. On the other hand, I can't shake the sense that there's a subtext to their conversation I'm failing to grasp—either because Dylan himself doesn't know what Esme meant, or because he's decided not to share it with me.

Back on the ground floor, I wade carefully into the semidarkness, which swallows me whole after the bright light of the top floor. When I've made my way across the large open space, I grope along the warehouse wall for a door handle and shove it wide.

Instantly, I recognize my mistake. The door leads not outside but to a part of the site that seems to be a kind of dumping ground. Light filters in from a small window cut out above, illuminating old tools, a collection of cinder blocks, and a giant blue tarp covering what looks like a heap of dirt along the far wall. I turn to resume my search for the correct door, but a glint of gold at the base of the tarp catches my eye, and my hand pauses on the door handle. Small hairs on the back of my neck tingling, I draw closer until I'm shifting the tarp aside and digging through dirt like a woman possessed.

Because in this deserted corner of Dylan's jobsite, underneath a pile of debris, is one of Esme's gold slingbacks, a dark red stain marring the satin.

11

HOME

On Monday, I pick Dylan up at his duplex and we drive into the city. The hospital called at the crack of dawn with very welcome news: The swelling in Esme's brain reduced significantly overnight. She's been brought out of her coma, and while she's still being closely monitored, she's remained in stable condition. If all goes well, she'll be released in a few hours.

I'm missing work again, but it doesn't matter. I'm exhausted from the weekend and so on edge that even if Esme weren't awake, I'd never be able to focus. Thankfully, Nabeel was sympathetic, encouraging me to take as much time as I need to get my sister settled back in at home.

Dylan rides in the passenger's seat, his hand resting gently on my knee. The last time we were together, I was fresh out of the shower, his lips fluttering across my skin. This morning, he radiates compassion and support, and I'm struck by how lucky I am to have him back in my life. Even sitting in silence, his presence is a comfort, and I breathe easier than I have all morning.

"Thanks for coming with me. I really appreciate you taking the day off on such short notice."

He looks over and smiles. "I'm happy to. The team is off for nine-eleven, so it's not a bad day to miss."

"Right, nine-eleven." I hardly slept last night, after yesterday's pair of unnerving discoveries—Hunter, who lied about the night of my sister's OD; then Carl, the mysterious number in Esme's phone. All night, my thoughts ping-ponged between the two until I gave up and tossed the covers back.

"Do you want to talk more about your dad?" Dylan asks, and I know the stress of it is written all over my face.

"He's always been a shit to us, so I don't know why I was expecting anything better this time."

"Because he's your dad. Because he sounded like he was trying to make amends. Don't beat yourself up."

"I know, I know. But he flat-out threatened Esme."

"You have any idea what that's about?"

I shake my head. "I could hazard a guess, but I don't know what Esme has up her sleeve because she never fucking talks to me." I slap my palm against the wheel, then flinch, surprised by the force of my outburst. "Sorry."

"Jane." Dylan twists around in his seat. I meet his eyes, then look back to the road. "I'm going to say something that might sound crazy, but I want you to hear me out, okay?"

I give him a tiny nod, eyes fixed ahead and hands tightening on the wheel.

"Have you considered that it doesn't matter what your dad and Esme are feuding about?"

"What?"

"Hear me out. If it turns out he drugged her and left her on the street, I'll take it all back, but I highly doubt he was involved in her overdose."

"But he called her that night. He—"

"I know. And maybe it means something, but it's probably a coincidence. Honestly, I think it's far more likely this Hunter kid gave her some bad shit, and he freaked out. Maybe Esme didn't tell you about what was going on with your dad because she didn't want to drag you into their mess. And maybe it should stay that way."

I shake my head so hard my hair whips back and forth. There is no world in which I'm going to let Esme and Carl go toe-to-toe without intervening. Whether or not he was directly involved in what happened on Thursday, he's been harassing her for weeks. And exasperating and evasive as she may be, she's my sister. I'm on her side, and I'm not going to let her deal with this alone.

Dylan squeezes my knee, and I swipe my arm across my eyes, wiping away tears.

"I'm worried about you. You're so deeply mired in your family's dirt, and you're an incredible sister, don't get me wrong. I admire the hell out of you." He shoots me a warm grin, and I sniffle.

"Thanks."

"Truly, you amaze me. But you've been the rock of the Connors for your entire life. Caring for your mom, moving back in, maintaining the house, coming to your sister's rescue over and over when you were kids."

I swallow, but my throat is dry. "It's not as simple as all that."

"Isn't it, though? Marjorie's at Monte Viso now, getting excellent care that you're paying for. And Esme is a grown woman. She's had a terrible few days, and I'm not suggesting you abandon her, of course not, but as soon as she's back on her feet, don't you think it's time you focus on yourself for a change?"

I catch Dylan's face out of the corner of my eye. He looks pained.

"What are you suggesting?" I ask.

"Give Esme her walking papers. She's never going to stop taking advantage of you as long as you keep letting her."

"I know, but—"

"Then sell the house, move back to the city."

It's not like I haven't had that thought before, more and more often since we moved Mom out in June. It would be such a relief to unburden myself from the substantial monthly payments. Selling would be the logical thing to do. But I love Old Boney. I grew up there. Am I ready to give it up now? Will I ever be ready?

But I don't say any of that. "Mom needs me," I say instead.

"See her three times a week. Allow yourself that freedom."

I open my mouth to protest, but then I close it. Would Mom's quality of life diminish if I didn't visit every single day? The truth of the matter is, she doesn't remember my visits from one day to the next, and depending on her mood, she doesn't always enjoy them while they're happening.

"I know it's very early, but . . . what about us?" I ask, trying out Dylan's proposition. Is he being selfless, putting my interests first, or is he subtly pushing me away? "You here, me in the city."

He gives my knee another squeeze. "I'm not here permanently. Truthfully, I'm far more worried about the strain you're under than I am about you living a little farther away. If you're happy, we're going to be fine, whatever comes next for us."

"Okay," I say, my resolve wavering ever so slightly. Maybe I could sell the house. I have a good job, and it would sell for a lot. Practically, we don't need it like we once did. Maybe, for Dylan, I could allow myself to let go of the past.

"But I can't make those choices for you. And I want this to work, I do." He lifts his hand from my leg to gesture between the two of us.

What he doesn't say is that my life is messy, because of my family, exactly as it's always been.

Tears well in my eyes again. "It's not always like this," I manage. "This is an especially bad week."

"I know. Of course not."

Underneath Dylan's kindness, there's a hard truth: If I can't make the two of us a priority, we're not going to survive. And I want us to, badly. But how can I choose between us and my sister? There will always be a new crisis with Esme, a new way she needs me. How can I say no?

I bury those thoughts. "Mom doesn't have anyone else," I say. "It's not so easy to step back."

He sighs and leans into the headrest. We're getting close to the hospital now. I take exit seven, then turn onto East Twenty-Fifth.

"There's something I need to tell you, about your mom," he says. "I've wanted to bring it up since our first dinner at Chez Allard. But it's uncomfortable. I wasn't sure how."

My chest tightens, and I steer us into the hospital lot. "What are you talking about?"

"She never approved of us. Of me."

"What do you mean?" Dylan was like part of the family growing up. Wasn't he?

I pull into a space, barely breathing, and shift into park.

His cheeks fill with air, then he exhales. "Marjorie didn't think I was good enough. Not for you. She made it absolutely clear that I could be your friend, but nothing more. Of course I ignored her, but it was hard to shake how she looked at me after we got together."

I unclasp my belt and twist around to face him. "What the fuck?"

"She didn't want you messing around with the caretaker's son. She wanted you to marry rich."

"Oh my god. She *said* that to you?" It's not like my mother made it a secret that she wanted Esme and me to "secure our family's future," but Mom has always traded in staid euphemisms when it comes to sex and money. That she said something so blatant to Dylan is frankly shocking.

"I believe her specific words were, 'Don't go getting my daughter in trouble.'"

"Oh." That sounds more like Mom—and naturally she'd worry about an unplanned pregnancy. How rich.

"I didn't say anything when we were kids. It was too embarrassing. But it's why I waited until I was graduating to make a move." He lets out a dry laugh. "I knew I was leaving for Syracuse in a few weeks, that we could never last. It felt safer that way, somehow. I'm sure your mom was pissed off, but she didn't try to intervene."

"I don't know what to say. There's no excuse for how she acted, how she must have made you feel."

"Esme didn't like us getting together either, you know. Thirteen-year-olds can be brutal."

The shock burns through me, turning quickly to anger. At my family. At myself. "How did I miss that?" I ask.

"It wasn't a big deal," Dylan says, shrugging it off. "Some jabs and nasty looks. She was jealous, you know? I imagine she always felt like a bit of a third wheel, with the age difference and all, and when you and I became a couple . . ."

"She felt left out," I say, the understanding settling uncomfortably in my gut. It's obvious, looking back, but I'd been so wrapped up in my romance with Dylan that summer, I'd completely failed to notice how it must have made Esme feel. Or how she lashed out at Dylan.

"I had no idea," I say. "I'm sorry she took it out on you."

"Jane, don't blame yourself. And—shit. I'm not trying to turn you against Marjorie, or Esme. It's not some bitter grudge I've been carrying around all these years, promise. I'm only telling you now because I don't want any secrets between us." He cups the side of my face in his hand and draws me in to him. "I don't want to lose this."

I kiss him gently, but my mind travels back to Mom's birthday dinner, which Dylan swiftly declined to attend. No wonder he didn't want to be around my mom and sister. And the other night, when Esme OD'd and Dylan didn't answer his phone. He swore he had his ringer turned off, that he was out with a friend from college, but something about the excuse has been nagging at me. Would he really not see two texts, two missed calls, or my voice mail until the next morning? More likely, he didn't want to get sucked into my family's drama again, and I can hardly blame him.

He says he doesn't want any secrets between us, but as we climb out of the car and start toward the front entrance, it's hard to shake the sense that Dylan's not being entirely honest.

That evening, I watch my sister like a hawk, pinching myself that she's here at home, walking and talking, wearing her normal clothes and helping herself to my yogurt once again. While she seems to have escaped severe physical damage or memory loss—"very lucky" was the extremely scientific term used by Dr. Kinnard earlier today— she's weak on her feet and in need of close supervision.

Around eight, Esme retreats to her bedroom, and when I follow her inside, she doesn't kick me out. The memory of our fight in the Mario's parking lot hasn't faded, but my anger toward her cooled over the weekend, while she lay in a coma, fighting for her life. Yes, she still has a lot of growing up to do, and no, she can't be trusted to supervise Mom, but now the whole thing feels somehow less significant in light of the overdose and her return to Old Boney.

"I don't need rehab." She flops down on her bed and brushes the stack of pamphlets given to us by the hospital onto the floor. "I went overboard on Thursday. It was stupid. But I don't have a drug problem."

"You sure about that?" I frown and lean down to scoop up the pamphlets. "You scared the shit out of me."

I try to shake Dylan's voice from my ears. Yes, I need to face my family issues and make some hard choices. And I'm not pleased about how Esme acted toward him the summer we got together. But that was a million years ago, and right now, my sister has been home for a mere hour, and I need to focus on getting her settled back in, on feeling a little bit settled myself.

"And I'm sorry," Esme continues, "but we've been living on top of each other for the past two weeks. If I had a problem, you'd know."

What I know is I've seen Esme consume an astonishing quantity of wine since she moved back here. And the pills they found in her purse said expressly not to mix with alcohol. But I don't want to argue about that now.

"Can we talk more about what happened on Thursday, please?"

Esme leans back against her pillows and pats the mattress beside her. Gratefully, I slip into bed and draw my arm around her shoulders. For a moment, it's like we're children again, before the accident tore a gaping rift between us, and I hold her tight, breathing her in.

"I was in a bad place," she begins. "There's been a lot going on."

"Care to tell me what?"

She ignores my question. "I wanted to stop feeling so fucking messed up, you know? I'm usually responsible about my meds, but I took a couple antianxiety pills and started drinking. It wasn't enough. So I called this guy I know, looking for something with a bit more edge."

"Hunter."

Her head snaps toward me. "Yeah, Hunter."

"He took you into the city?"

"His friend's show got canceled, some dumb stuff the headliners pulled the night before. Anyway, his friends were partying at a bar on the LES, and Hunter said there would be mushrooms, maybe some other stuff. I ate some shrooms, I drank more, I took some more pills. I felt fucking fantastic. After a while, I was tripping pretty hard, and I wandered outside. Hunter came with me, I remember he tried to get me to come back in. I wasn't listening. I broke away from him, kept walking for a block or two, but I couldn't really see straight and I went down. Then I woke up in the hospital."

"So Hunter left you there?"

She shakes her head gingerly back and forth. On one side, a patch of her beautiful hair is shaved and bandaged where they had to give her stitches. "No, he was with me the whole time. After I blacked out, he called nine-one-one. He made sure the paramedics came."

"You're certain he's the one who called?"

"Absolutely. I talked to him earlier today." She turns to me. "He said you went to see him."

"He lied to me, Esme."

She sighs and leans her head against my shoulder. "Don't be too hard on him, Janie. He was scared he'd get kicked out of school if people found out he gave me the mushrooms. But I fucked up all on my own, okay? Let him be."

I sigh. "Fine. But you need to tell me what else has been going on with you. I know you deleted Mark from your phone. And Kiku."

For a moment, Esme is quiet. Then, she says, "The thing about almost dying is, it puts a lot of stuff into perspective."

I clasp her hand in mine and give it a gentle squeeze. She looks at me hard, then leans back into the pillows.

"Okay. Over the summer, a few things happened. First, I found out Mark's been having an affair . . . with *Kiku*."

"Oh my god."

"Then, I sold a book. A memoir."

My eyebrows fly up. "You wrote a memoir?"

Esme has long fancied herself a novelist, but the label has always been aspirational. She's never expressed any interest in writing nonfiction, at least not to me, but my surprise is less about the genre and more about the elbow grease. Her creativity and talent have never been in question, but any major writing project takes more stamina, more discipline, more unswerving commitment than I thought my sister had in her. I'm surprised—and impressed.

She nods. "The first half of it anyway. It sold on proposal."

"Congratulations?" It seems like the right thing to say, but it comes out more like a question.

"Dad found out," she continues. "Kiku was pissed as hell because I cut her out of the deal, which she absolutely deserved, but she called him and told him everything that was going to come out."

I press my lips between my teeth, everything locking into place. That explains Carl's threatening texts, and his connection to Kiku.

"You're writing about his affairs?"

She nods. "Damn right I am. That was a huge part of my childhood. He broke up our family, and worse, how many young women did he seduce? As far as we know, they were all over twenty-one, but that doesn't mean he didn't mess up their lives, their careers. I've talked to two of them. They want to go on the record now, and being addicted to Instagram has its perks. I have a platform."

"Have they reported him to the school?"

"One has, one hasn't. But it was so many years ago, and there's no proof. Yale isn't pursuing a case, but when this goes public, people will finally know the truth. His shiny reputation will be tarnished. All these years, he's been sailing by with no consequences. That fucker deserves what's coming."

"Wow." My head bobs slowly up and down. "This is a lot."

"You don't agree?" She purses her lips together, a challenge.

"I do. I'm just processing." I reach for my phone. "While you were sleeping, he came poking around the hospital, making noise about going out for coffee, turning over a new leaf. I almost fell for it."

"Are you going?" Her eyes are wide. A lock of blond hair falls in her face, and she tucks it behind her ear.

I shake my head. "I don't want a fresh start with Dad. You're what matters to me."

Esme finds my eyes with hers, locks in. "No more secrets. Right, Janie?"

A lump rises in my throat. This is the second time today someone's made that promise. It feels like the fresh start I've been longing for.

"I'm deleting his number," I say. "And if Dad comes after you about the memoir, we'll handle it together."

A slow smile stretches across my sister's face, and when I've erased Carl from my phone, she slips her hand into mine.

TWELVE

GONE

It's been nearly two hours since I fled Dylan's jobsite and placed the 911 call, then a second to SI Marrone directly. Now back at home, I pace the grounds, the desperate desire to call Dylan and scream angry questions through the phone clawing at my throat. *What have you done?*

But Marrone's stern advice keeps me tethered to Old Boney: *Stay home and wait for my call.* I clench my phone, check for the third time that the ringer is cranked all the way up.

It stays stubbornly silent.

Finally, at half past two, a black police cruiser pulls into the drive.

"What happened?" The words are out of my mouth before SIs Marrone and Bakshi can close their doors. The fact that they're here in person can't be good. "Did you find my sister?"

"Let's all go inside, Ms. Connor." Marrone gestures to the front door. "I'd like to sit down with you for a few minutes."

They've found her. They've found *her body.*

Legs wobbling beneath me, I get the door open and point them toward the living room.

"Just spit it out," I say when they've settled into chairs behind the coffee table and I am alone on the living room couch, jelly legs drawn to my chest. "If you've found her body, please just tell me."

"We haven't," SI Bakshi says kindly.

I sink into the cushions with a small moan, and hot tears flood my cheeks. The investigators exchange glances.

"We've conducted a preliminary search of Mr. Greer's jobsite," she continues. "We've recovered the shoe you located, and we have reason to believe Esme Connor-Lloyd may have been there recently, but I'm afraid your sister is still missing."

I exhale. *Missing* means alive. Possibly, still alive.

"Both the shoe and the dress will be sent for forensic analysis," she continues.

"The dress—" I start to ask, and Bakshi pulls up a photo on her phone.

"Do you recognize this?"

I freeze, all the air rushing from my lungs. It's a pale pink cocktail dress like the one Esme was wearing the night she vanished, now bloodied and split up one side. "It's hers." I can barely get the words out. "That has to be Esme's."

"It was also recovered at the jobsite this afternoon," Marrone says. "We hope to know more soon. Please keep your phone on and be prepared to answer when we call."

Then they're gone, and I'm alone again in the empty house, reverberating with the shock that Dylan has harmed my sister— Dylan, whom I've known since we were babies, who once upon a time, I knew inside and out.

No light presses against the seams of the blackout curtains, but I can't fall back to sleep. I went to bed hours ago, exhausted, but now I lie here, listening to the house shift and moan, forecasting the coming autumn chill. Jamie has taken the day off, will be here at eight, but that's hours away. I need to rest, but my mind has other ideas.

Dylan is in custody. I have learned that much since the investigators left. While they hold him, a lab is analyzing my sister's clothing for prints. I toss to my right side, then my left. I can't get comfortable, can't switch off my brain. *Dylan kidnapped Esme. Dylan hurt her.*

Finally, I sit up in bed, switch on the light, and give in to the flood of memories, questions, and fear. We were together for only two weeks as teens, but I spent my entire adolescence in love with Dylan, most of my childhood, too. And we were all three thick as thieves then, weren't we? Esme was younger, but she was still part of our trio. I can't imagine what could have caused him to hurt her now. True, it's been years since we were close like that, but how much do people truly change? Could I have been that wrong about someone I knew so well, someone I once loved?

I reach for the glass of water on my nightstand and take a sip, forcing myself to acknowledge that yes, I have been that wrong, because while the reason behind what happened remains a complete mystery, the fact of the matter is, Dylan abducted Esme. He must have taken her to his worksite that night, where they struggled. He ditched her bloody clothes there, and then . . .

Then it's a complete blank.

I force my mind away from the darkest possibilities and return to the *why* of it all. What reason could Dylan possibly have to hurt Esme?

I remember hearing somewhere that crimes where the victim knows the perpetrator are often motivated by love or money. Esme had access to plenty of money, but Dylan runs a successful business. I doubt that's what he was after.

Which leaves love.

I suck in a sharp breath. Maybe my detective work into Mark's affair wasn't for nothing after all. Esme took her revenge on Kiku by cutting her out of a major book deal. But what about Mark? Before Esme disappeared, she was planning to divorce him. Maybe voiding the prenup wasn't enough. Mark's betrayal was so personal, cheating with Esme's *best friend*. And my sister has never been one to leave a revenge card unplayed. Yesterday morning, Dylan was strangely reluctant to tell me the details of their coffee date in June. What if, after Esme learned about Mark's affair, one coffee led to something more?

It's not hard to imagine. Esme is beautiful, elusive, anointed with the golden sheen of wealth and society that plenty of men find impossible to resist. Why should Dylan be immune? As a kid, he was never interested in my baby sister that way, but five years is nothing as adults. If Esme hooked up with Dylan to get back at Mark, and Dylan thought it meant something more than it did . . . I can imagine Esme callously casting him aside once she was through with him, how badly it would have hurt.

Badly enough for him to snap? It's not who I thought Dylan was, but I have to admit that it's possible.

Or what if it *was* money?

Yesterday, Dylan said Esme had wanted a recommendation for Sean Lloyd, Mark's brother. He'd claimed he hadn't known anyone to suggest, then quickly changed the subject, but what if there was more to it that Dylan didn't want to reveal? I met Sean and his wife, Cora, only once, at Esme's wedding. He's a tech CFO, and like all the men in Mark's family, he gives off a brisk, chilly vibe. Could he have taken advantage of someone in Dylan's network, stiffed him on work or belittled him in some way?

When we were growing up, I always wanted Dylan to feel welcome around Old Boney, but Hank Greer was our employee, and

Dylan his son, a power dynamic it strikes me now was probably a lot less easy for Dylan to ignore than it had been for me. We never talked about it in depth, but it now seems nearly impossible that the disparity in wealth between our two families didn't affect him. It stands to reason that a recent financial slight could have stirred up bad old feelings from the past.

And then I remember something. It was a few months after the accident, and Esme was fourteen. One Saturday, she'd slept past noon and was upstairs taking a midday shower. The water stopped, and a minute later she started screaming bloody murder. When Mom and I got to the top of the stairs, Esme proclaimed that Hank—who had been up on a ladder, clearing out the gutters—had peeked in on her through the bathroom window.

"You need to fire him," Esme had hissed while Mom made a weak attempt to calm her down and I stood in the hallway, eyes darting between them. "He's a creep. He did it on purpose."

It was clear Mom didn't trust Esme's accounting of events, but she knew enough about being a mom, and a woman, to understand that calling her youngest daughter a liar would only worsen an already bad situation. So she made a show of taking Esme seriously, and then did nothing.

It was part of a developing pattern between them. In the weeks and months following the crash, as Esme slowly regained her physical health, she had become increasingly angry, obstinate, defiant. Mom was like a deer in headlights, unsure what to do with this sweet, sensitive child who had transformed into a troubled teen, seemingly overnight.

I remember feeling torn myself. I suspected Hank's appearance at the window in the moment Esme had been exiting the shower was most likely accidental. Hank had been our employee for years, and he'd proved himself to be trustworthy, honest, and never inappropriate with Esme or me. But Esme felt violated, and that deserved attention.

Mom should have gone to talk to Hank about it, but she took a back seat, probably hoping it would all fade into the background. It didn't. Whether or not Hank was innocent, Esme had gone to our mom with a problem, and Mom didn't act.

The incident ate at Esme. Dylan came home from college for Thanksgiving break, and she spent the whole time making snide comments about his father the pervert. Ultimately, I sat down with Hank like our mom should have done. Hank apologized profusely, swearing it had been entirely unintentional, a moment of terrible timing. And as time passed and nothing similar ever occurred, I felt sure he was telling the truth, but Esme remained unconvinced, and the tension never really dissipated between them. I can't help thinking it might have, if our mom had handled the situation better.

I'm sure Dylan isn't still stewing over it fourteen years later, nursing the old memory like a bitter grudge, but if some recent occurrence with Esme stirred up old feelings, could that have triggered him?

I slouch back down in bed, wondering if Dylan will confess, if I'll ever get to know what caused him to snap. But soon, my spiraling thoughts about potential motives are overtaken by the more pressing, immediate worry: What did Dylan do to my sister after he abducted her? Could she still be alive?

At eight on the dot, Jamie's black Audi pulls into the drive. I rush to the front door, fling it wide, and in a moment he's stepping into the foyer and folding me into his arms. I'm unshowered, wearing the sweats I slept in, and my face is puffy with tears that have come and gone throughout the night. I don't care. I sink into his strong embrace and begin to sob.

"Let me fix you a tea," he says when I've recovered enough to disentangle myself from him and blot my face with a tissue. He guides me gently into the living room, settling me on the couch and tucking the blanket around my feet. I nearly begin sobbing again in gratitude.

Jamie moves around my kitchen with ease, filling the kettle and pulling the box of my favorite tea from the cabinet. While he works, I fill him in on what I know: local law enforcement has teamed up with the NYPD to search several locations, including Hank Greer's home in Branby, Dylan's jobsite in the east twenties, and the duplex Dylan is renting somewhere in town. So far, aside from her dress and shoe, I'm not aware that they've found anything.

He places my tea on the coffee table, and I burrow deeper into the blanket. Right then, my phone rings, and SI Bakshi's contact flashes across the screen.

I put it on speaker. "Have you found her?"

"Good morning, Jane," she says, voice calm where mine is frantic. "We have not yet found your sister, but I'm calling to give you an update from the lab. The forensics team has determined that the blood on her clothing was fresh—they think not older than a day."

All the air rushes from my lungs, and it's a moment before I can speak.

"They think she's still alive," I choke out.

"That is our hope," she says.

Jamie's hovering over me, nodding encouragingly. I motion for him to join me on the couch.

"I promise to keep you informed as soon as we learn anything more," she says. And then she's gone.

Jamie settles in on the cushion beside me and places his hand on top of mine.

"Last night," I tell him, "as I was not sleeping, trying to work out what could have happened between them, and why, I assumed Dylan must have taken her to the construction site after she left the Monarch, that the blood was from a struggle the night she disappeared. But if it's still fresh . . ."

"It's promising news," he says. "Really promising. Have you heard anything further about Dylan?"

"Only that he's in custody. Apparently it can take some time to formally bring charges against him. But they will."

"Don't give up hope," Jamie murmurs gently. "I know it's scary, but this is progress. They're going to find her." Then he squeezes my shoulder. It's such a small gesture, but I allow myself to close my eyes and melt into the comfort of his touch.

12

HOME

The morning after Esme's return from the hospital, I wander into the kitchen to find her making breakfast.

"You should be resting," I scold, but she ushers me over to the island and pulls out a stool.

"I'm fine. Truly. I've been sleeping for days. Moving around is good for me."

"Okay," I say cautiously, allowing her to fill two plates with watery eggs and slightly burned toast. "I thought we'd do a movie marathon, all the stupid comedies we can find on streaming. But we could take a walk after breakfast, get some fresh air."

She pulls out the stool next to me and lifts her fork. "Don't you have work?"

"I'm taking the day off."

She shakes her head. "Not because of me you're not."

I open my mouth to protest, but she cuts me off. "I'm serious. We're good, right? You and me? Let's not ruin it now."

I pile a forkful of eggs onto my toast and take a bite. It's not as bad as it looks. "You promise you'll take it easy, stay around the house today?"

She rolls her eyes. "Yes, Mom."

When I hesitate, pushing eggs around my plate, she says, "I know you hate getting behind at work. And I don't need a babysitter."

"Fine, I'll go in," I relent. "I have plans tonight, but I'll stop home first, in case you need anything."

Esme hops up from the island and makes a show of sashaying over to the sink with her plate. "Not necessary. I'm good as new."

After work, I catch the 5:46 to Branby. I'm not going out before I check on Esme, and I need to change anyway. Dylan and I have dinner reservations at Adelaide's Supper Club, followed by tickets to see Charlotte Prew, a local singer-songwriter we've both liked since high school, at a tiny venue nearby. I let my forehead rest against the window glass, feeling relaxed for the first time in days. This is the night away from my family drama we both need.

I climb into my car in the park and ride and let Dylan's words from yesterday wash over me. *Don't you think it's time you focus on yourself for a change?* I still went to see Mom before heading into work this morning. How much anger does she deserve for something she said to Dylan all those years ago, something she almost certainly doesn't remember? Wouldn't I want to be forgiven for a bad decision so far in the past?

But I'm thinking about everything Dylan said. An apartment in the city. The sale of the house would pay for Monte Viso for the rest of Mom's life. I could change jobs, do something more creative, something I've never even let myself contemplate. Make time for Alisha and Claire, if they'll have me. Three trips a week to Branby is a lot less commuting than I do now. And Dylan's right, his rental here is a temporary setup. Sooner or later, he'll be back in the city, too. This could be good for us, for me. Maybe, possibly, this could work.

I come up through the garage and tiptoe into the living room, careful not to disturb Esme if she's sleeping on the couch. But the living room is empty, and when I step into the kitchen, I'm stunned to see clean counters and the spatula and pan drying in the rack. Upstairs, I tap lightly on her door. No response. Gently, I turn the knob and peek inside. Her bed is made up, and the pile of laundry that's been accumulating beside it is gone.

"Esme?" I call out, knocking on the bathroom door—also empty—then hurrying back down the hall. I call her name again, louder this time, then dig out my phone.

My call goes straight to voice mail.

Worry pricking between my shoulder blades, I open up our chat from earlier today. I'd texted her sparingly, careful not to smother, and she'd responded. She was back from a walk, chilling on the couch. She was going to take a nap. But that was hours ago.

> Just got home and you're not here.
> Everything OK?

When three minutes have ticked by and she hasn't responded, I force myself to set my phone down and get in the shower. I tell myself if I haven't heard back by the time I get out, I can text her again.

Ten more minutes. I stand in the bathroom, hair dripping down the back of my robe, and glare at the silent screen.

> Where are you? Starting to worry!

Then I cross into the bedroom and pull out clothes for tonight, a skirt and boots and three possible tops. Typical Esme. We *just* got through her overdose, and already she's testing me, sending me into yet another panic. She was so insistent I go into work today—because she wanted me out of her hair.

My throat tightens with the realization. I'd thought we were in a good place. She opened up to me about Mark and Kiku, her memoir, the threats from Carl. I thought she'd put our fight behind her, as I had. But this is the same old Esme, nursing her secrets, doing whatever she wants no matter how much I'll worry. Perhaps, even, *because* I'll worry.

I pull up Hunter's contact and dial.

"Is my sister with you?"

"Jane, hello. And no, she's not."

"You'd better not be lying," I snap. "She needs to rest. You are the last thing she needs right now."

"I swear to god," he says. "She's not here. I haven't heard from her since yesterday."

"Fine. If she calls or texts or anything, you need to tell me."

"Of course. And Jane? I'm really sorry about Thursday night. I never meant for anything bad to happen."

He sounds genuinely remorseful. And underneath all that inflated confidence, a little scared. I sink down onto my bed and draw in a deep breath.

"I know you didn't. Please call me if she shows up, okay?"

"I will."

She's not with Hunter. I think about calling Mark, but there's no chance she's gone to see her cheating husband. I turn my phone over and over in my hand. She's not with him, or Kiku for that matter. I rack my brain, replaying every scrap of our conversations since she was released from the hospital. *No more secrets. Right, Janie?*

Tears spring to my eyes. I was so desperate for her to be serious, but Esme's claim was yet another move in whatever game she's playing. I rush down the hall, back into her bedroom. Her books are on the shelf. Her dirty clothes, gone from the floor, are now piled in the hamper. Both of her suitcases still sit on the closet floor. I draw in a deep breath. She didn't go far. She's coming back. But something is nagging at me . . .

Carl. He didn't come to the hospital yesterday, but he's probably learned of Esme's release. I know he didn't have anything to do with her overdose, at least not directly, but armed now with the context for his threats, I'm sure he's not going to let anything go. Esme seemed certain he wouldn't lose his job, but I'm not so sure. Only two of his students spoke with her, but more will come out of the woodwork after publication. Her book will get buzz: *Manhattan socialite, daughter of prominent academic, writes scathing memoir accusing father of inappropriate conduct—and Ivy League institution of sweeping it under the rug*. One of his former students must have kept emails, texts, the kind of proof the university, and the public, won't be able to ignore. Dad knows it. His career is on the line— reputation, livelihood, academic future. There's more at stake than Esme probably realizes, and Carl is terrified.

And seriously, fuck him. Esme's right, he does deserve to go up in flames. But the more I think it through, the more uneasy I become. I don't trust Dad, not at all. Especially not when he's been provoked. He kept it together at the hospital this weekend, but he hasn't changed. He's always been able to turn on the charm to impress judges, colleagues, Esme and me when we were young enough to believe his temper would never flare in our direction. But if Esme agreed to that face-to-face meeting he's been after, if they're together now . . . I dial her one more time, and once again, my call goes straight to voice mail. She doesn't want to talk.

Or someone else has made sure she's unreachable.

I collapse onto her bed, panic coursing through me. I deleted Dad's number, but I still have it saved in the screenshots from my sister's phone. I meant what I said to her last night, I wasn't planning to use it, but the situation has changed. Should I call him? Or should I get in the car, drive over to his house?

Before I can decide, my phone rings, and I yelp. But it's not Esme, or Carl.

Dylan. "Oh my god. What time is it?"

"Are you okay?"

"Yes. No. Esme's missing."

When I've finished bringing him up to speed, I draw in a jagged breath. "I have to go find her. Carl's unpredictable, and he's mad. She could be in real danger."

"Don't go anywhere," he says. "I'm coming over."

Dylan arrives ten minutes later, and I register with a guilty twinge that he's dressed for our night out. I've changed into jeans and a sweatshirt and pulled my damp hair back into a ponytail.

"We'll go to his house first," I say, tugging him toward the stairs leading down to the garage. "Then try campus."

"Jane."

"If he's home, if he has Esme there with him, I'm calling nine-one-one."

"Jane." Dylan stops in the middle of the kitchen floor and drops his hand from mine.

"What?"

"Can we sit for a minute? Please?"

We need to get in the car, we need to *go*, but his face is creased with worry.

"Okay. One minute."

He pulls out two stools from the island where Esme and I sat this morning, eating eggs and toast, and reluctantly, I sit.

"Do you know what time she left the house?" he asks.

"The last text I have from her was at two something. She said she was taking a nap. But I don't even know if that's true."

"Okay. But she didn't say anything about going to see your dad, right? And she's been dodging him the whole time she's been staying with you?"

"Yes, but—"

"And your house wasn't broken into? There's no sign she did anything but leave here willingly?"

"You don't understand Carl," I start to say. "You don't—"

"I *do* understand," Dylan cuts in. "I grew up with your dad, too. The man has an outsized ego and a nasty temper. But Esme wouldn't get into a car with him. She wouldn't go over to his house. She's smarter than that."

I sit for a minute, letting that digest.

"I truly don't think she's in danger," he says gently. He reaches for my hand, and I let him cover it with his. "There's a real possibility she went into the city. She's at a movie, or with her friends. She could have let her phone die or turned it off. She knows she's supposed to be home resting, but she's *Esme*. She's going to do whatever she wants. And she doesn't want her big sister watching over her shoulder."

"I'm not—"

"I know. But put yourself in her shoes. By the time we get home tonight, she's going to be back here. I promise you."

My eyes go wide. "You still want to go out?"

Dylan's eyes shift to the stove clock. "There's time, we can make our reservation. Come on, get changed. Let's go eat. We need this."

"No. No, no, no." I shake my head slowly back and forth. "I'm sorry, but I'd be a mess the whole time. I hope you're right, okay? I hope she's ignoring me and hanging with her friends in the city. But what if she's not?"

Dylan lifts his hand from mine and drops it down to his side. "Okay. We'll cancel. But Jane, there's something I need to tell you."

"Can we talk on the way?"

He shakes his head. "I need to get this off my chest. That night in high school, the night of the crash."

I nod, slowly, the old guilt creeping in. Of course the current Esme crisis would take Dylan back there. I was a disaster that night too, so scared for my sister, so intent on saving her . . .

"I never should have poured those shots for us. You were so upset, and I wanted to help, but I went about it all wrong. For years, I've felt guilty about what happened."

My jaw hinges slowly open. I got in Mom's car drunk, not Dylan. I caused that crash.

"It's not—" I start to protest, but he holds up his hand.

"It's why I ended things," he says. "There were a lot of factors. Your mom's disapproval and my upcoming move. But mainly, it's because I was drinking, a lot, those last months of high school. After your car crash, I felt so guilty. I'd dragged you into my shit."

The revelation sends a jolt up my spine.

"I had no idea," I say. "After I put Esme in the car that night, I thought you hated me."

He shakes his head. "That wasn't it at all. I hid my drinking from everyone, especially you, but I was a mess. Being poor here takes its toll. And when I got to college, I started partying even more. Then there was the incident over Thanksgiving break, with Esme and my dad, the shower thing. It really chafed at me, more than I let on. I couldn't wait to get back to school, where I could get blackout drunk and no one would bat an eye. By the end of freshman year, I'd almost lost my scholarship, the drinking got that bad. But I've been sober for a decade now. Until recently."

"You're an alcoholic?" My mind retraces the last couple of weeks. I'd assumed it was for my sake that Dylan's never ordered alcohol when we'd been out.

"I should have told you right away. It's not a secret; I'm proud of my recovery, what I've done with my life. Until a couple months ago, I was in a really good place. But being back in Branby hasn't been easy. It's dredged up a lot of the old insecurities I felt growing up here, and right before I ran into you the other week, I slipped. It was just the one time, but at dinner that first night, when you said you didn't drink, I couldn't honestly say I was sober. I was too embarrassed to tell you the whole truth, so I didn't say anything.

"Then on the night Esme overdosed, I was out with a friend from Syracuse, like I mentioned. Joe's an old drinking buddy, and I thought what the hell, I can have one drink with him, for old times' sake. But I can't stop after one."

"That's why you didn't pick up your phone?" I ask.

"I honestly didn't see your texts at first," he says. "I was in a bar, it was loud, I was catching up with Joe. By the time you called, I was wasted. I couldn't talk to you like that, not when your sister had *overdosed*, for Christ's sake. So I lied about having my ringer off. I'm sorry."

I don't know what to say. This is a lot to process, and I want to give Dylan my full attention, but I need to go look for Esme. I fidget on the stool.

"I freaked myself out," he says. "I got in touch with my sponsor right away, and I'm not going to let it happen again. But Jane, being back in Branby, back in the thick of your family's problems . . . it's a lot."

I nod, concerned.

Dylan draws in a deep breath, and my stomach clenches. Whatever he's about to say next, I'm not going to like it.

"You need to be there for your sister, and I understand that. But I'm not sure I can handle this right now."

My throat starts to close up, and blood rushes to my face. "What are you saying?"

"I want to be with you. I want this." He gestures between the two of us. "But I need to sort myself out right now. And what I asked yesterday, for you to focus on yourself, I think what I really meant was focus on *us*—not on Esme, not your mom. And that's not fair, I know it isn't."

Explicitly or not, Dylan is asking me to choose. Him or Esme. My relationship or my family.

"I'm sorry," I choke out. "But I need to go. I have to look for my sister."

He nods, looking defeated. "I understand," he says, and what he means is goodbye.

For a moment, we're both silent. Then I sit frozen at the kitchen island while Dylan Greer stands, shoves his hands in his pockets, and walks away from me, history repeating.

THIRTEEN

GONE

When my phone rings at ten minutes to one, I'm still wide awake, staring at the ceiling. There's some saying about a phone call after midnight, and my mind gropes for it in the dark. I toss back the covers and switch the lamp on. *Something, something, never good news.* It's a local number. I don't recognize it, but I know. Branby police. My throat clogs with thick, musty dread as I wait for the voice on the other end to tell me the worst.

She identifies herself as Officer Jacquie Larson. "Have I reached Jane Connor?"

"Yes, speaking," I manage.

This is the call. The one that informs me the search efforts have been successful. Somewhere in Branby—Hank Greer's house, perhaps, or Dylan's rental—they've located my sister.

Or my sister's body.

"Have you found her?" The question bursts through my lips before Officer Larson can tell me the purpose of her call. "Is she alive?"

I shove out of bed, needing to move, and start down the hall toward Esme's room.

"We have found her, yes." There's a pause, and I freeze at the threshold, willing her to seal Esme's fate. *Dead* or *alive*. *Dead* or *alive*. For more than two weeks now, I've thought I might be the one to find her myself, or that it would be SI Marrone delivering the news. Not some local cop I've never met.

"I'm afraid Ms. Connor was pronounced dead on arrival to Branby General at twelve forty-seven a.m. Did you know she was missing?"

I stumble into the room and sink to my sister's bedroom floor. The hard wood is cold against my bare legs. *Dead on arrival.*

"Ms. Connor-Lloyd," I correct her, not that it matters. This cop doesn't know anything, doesn't have any idea how deeply I've been involved in the search. "Tell me what happened," I manage to choke out.

"I'm so sorry," she says. "Monte Viso is cooperating with the investigation, and we are working to get answers as quickly as possible."

The phone slips from my fingers and clatters to the wood slats. I stab my finger at the screen, putting it on speaker. "Monte Viso?"

"What we know so far is that she exited the facility sometime between eleven thirty and midnight. She was struck by a car about a quarter mile from the premises. It appears she was confused and wandered into traffic."

I gape into the darkness of Esme's bedroom. Officer Larson's words are slippery shapes in the dark, and I strain to focus, latch on.

"You've found my mother," I say finally. "Marjorie Connor. My *mother* is dead."

"Yes."

"But she wears an ankle monitor." I say it as if that will turn back time, make this untrue. "She couldn't possibly have wandered off."

"The department has submitted a request for security footage. Monte Viso alleges the cameras have been on the fritz since a power outage knocked the system offline a couple weeks back, but please know we are viewing this case as possible negligence. I'm hopeful we'll have more information soon."

The room is spinning. Esme is still missing, and my mother is dead. The power outage was the night of the storm, the night Esme vanished. Why haven't they gotten the cameras fixed? My brain wants to draw a neat line, connect the dots between these two horrible events, but there's no link, is there? It's nothing more than a terrible coincidence.

No matter how it happened, my mother is gone.

"We're very certain the deceased is Marjorie Connor," Officer Larson is saying. "But we'd be grateful if you could come to the hospital to formally identify her, as her next of kin."

I say I'll do it. Of course I'll go. What else could I possibly do?

But when I'm off the phone, I sit on the floor of Esme's bedroom, paralyzed. My *mother* is dead. My mother is *dead*. It's not possible—not with her monitor, the nurses, the guards, the cameras. All the reasons she lives at Monte Viso now. To keep her safe. But somehow, the worst has happened.

I stare numbly at my phone. I want to call Jamie, but it's so late, and besides, he's not in Branby tonight. He would have to drive here from Manhattan, and much as I want his reassuring presence, he was just here with me this morning. To call him again so soon feels like too big an ask, too much for who we are to each other in this moment.

A low sob starts in the back of my throat, and soon I'm howling, hot tears streaking down my face. My mother—dead. My sister—gone. My father—out of my life. Dylan—behind bars. And Jamie—no longer mine. Not in the way I need him to be. The self-pity wells in my throat, and I give in to a fresh wave of sobs.

Their faces float across the backs of my eyelids, Esme's and Mom's. No one asked me to choose, but I feel wrung out, cheated somehow. A bait and switch of the cruelest kind, this eviscerating news for that. And no promise that any second now, the other shoe won't drop. I slam my fist against the floor, and my phone skitters toward the dresser.

"Bring her back!" I scream into the empty house, and I am crying for Esme, and I am crying for my mother. My voice splinters against the cold plaster walls.

After some time, I stumble into the bathroom and splash water on my face. Then I climb into my car and drive to Branby General to identify my mother's body.

13

HOME

Tuesday night, I don't sleep. Every twenty minutes, I check my phone, as if I might have missed it ringing. Every hour, I throw back the covers, pad downstairs to check the front door, the back door, the garage. As if Esme might be locked out, as if I could have missed her knocking. I don't want to be right, not about this, but as the hours crawl by, I grow more and more certain. It's been too long, and she hasn't called, and she hasn't returned. Something has happened to my sister.

After Dylan left, I drove to New Haven. For an hour, I parked on the street outside my father's dark house and waited. Around nine, his car pulled into the driveway, and my breath caught. Through the passenger's side window, a woman. A glimpse of blond hair. When the house lights flickered on, when two figures appeared in the panorama of the living room window, I raised my binoculars to get a closer look. The woman was young, tall and curvy, didn't resemble Esme at all. I watched while Dad disappeared, then reappeared with a bottle of wine and two glasses. He was on a date. Probably the grad student of the semester; I'd been a fool to think his habits had changed.

Esme wasn't there.

I was wrong about Carl, but not about my sister. Things were so good between us the night she came home from the hospital. If she went out with her friends, maybe she'd avoid my calls for a little while, but eventually she'd send me a text, tell me she's fine and to fuck off. But all my texts have gone unanswered. Her phone still goes straight to voice mail. This is something else, something bad.

When the first traces of daylight brighten the sky, I pull out my laptop and google *how long do you have to wait to report a missing person in Connecticut?*

The results take me to a CT.gov site, some manual for cops. I skim down to a bullet titled "Reporting Myth": *It is an incorrect assumption that 24 hours, or any other time frame, must pass before a law enforcement unit will accept a missing person report. There is NO waiting period for reporting a missing person.*

I dial the Branby police.

An officer named Jacquie Larson takes my report. She sounds serious, sympathetic, and I wonder how often people are reported missing in quaint Branby. "She could have gone into the city," I tell her. "Or anywhere, really. Her phone's turned off, and she hasn't responded since two p.m. yesterday."

I tell her about Esme's overdose, her recent release from the hospital. She assures me they take all missing-person reports quite seriously, but when I admit there's been no break-in, that she took her purse with her, there is an unmistakable dip in her level of concern. She asks me to please call back right away if Esme calls or returns home.

When Officer Larson is done with me, I call in to work, leave a message for Nabeel letting him know that Esme is missing, that I'll be taking yet another personal day.

That done, I stare at the wall across from me, at a loss for what to do next. I want to call Dylan, badly. *You were wrong*, I want to scream, but also, *You were right*. Because Esme really is missing, I'm sure of it, but there was truth to what he said. I'll never stop chasing her, never stop trying to protect her.

Surely anything is better than this. Esme—missing. Dylan—over and done. The unfairness of it wells inside me, a gnawing, childish pain so strong, so visceral, I can't hold back the tears. I smash my fist into the mattress, cursing Dylan for abandoning me, even if he has every right to focus on himself right now, cursing Esme for coming between us, even if she had no way of knowing what she was doing. Cursing myself for letting it happen.

Eventually, the self-pity and anger leech out of me and worry sets back in. I wasn't able to give the police much to go on, and with her phone turned off, I doubt they'll be able to track it. I need to think. Need to find Esme myself.

It's still very early, but I grit my teeth and call Mark, who hasn't heard from her in days, not since before the overdose, and assures me she and Kiku are not in touch. I want to ream him out for cheating on her, for setting this all in motion, but I tell myself he's not worth my energy.

After I've hung up, my finger hovers over Hunter's number once again.

Yesterday, he swore he hadn't seen her. But—Hunter's lied to me before. He lied about being with Esme the night of the overdose, and about the drugs. Even with her explanation, something keeps needling at me. Over these past two weeks, my sister has spent more time with a college senior, as slick a liar as he is handsome, than anyone else. There's something going on there, something both Esme and Hunter are hiding. A layer I haven't peeled back yet.

I'm coming to campus. Need to talk.

Hunter leads me across the lawn to some fancy new student center. He's freshly showered, dressed in worn corduroys and a plaid button-down, but he still looks half asleep. Nine a.m. must be hours before he's typically up.

"There's something you're not telling me," I say as soon as we're standing at the urns, filling our cups with Colombian roast and hot water, respectively. I select a tea bag from a bin on the counter.

His mouth begins to open in protest, but I cut him off. "Esme's not well. You get that, right? She overdosed six days ago, to the point they had to put her in a medically induced coma. Then less than twenty-four hours after she comes home, she's missing. She should be resting, but she's god knows where. Do you have any idea how serious this is?"

He nods vigorously, then tucks a thick strand of hair behind his ear. "I get it," he says softly.

At the register, I reach for my wallet, but Hunter hands the cashier his student ID and insists the drinks are on him. I let him lead me to a window table far away from anyone else.

"I want to help," he says. "But I don't know anything useful."

I sigh and blow across my tea. "Tell me about Thursday."

He grimaces, and his eyes skate around the room.

I lower my voice. "I'm not going to get you in trouble, promise. Frankly, I don't give a shit that you gave her some magic mushrooms. She was going to self-destruct one way or another. I care about what was going on with her that night, beyond the broad strokes. My sister has never been particularly forthcoming, but I bet you know more than she would give me."

"Fine." He leans back in his chair, studying me. "First of all, I didn't know she was popping benzos. That shit doesn't mix with shrooms and booze."

"What did you talk about, Hunter?" I redirect. "What did she tell you?"

"Okay, okay. She mostly talked about her ex, how their whole relationship was a sham."

I nod, encouraging him to keep going.

"You know he was cheating? Sounded like it wasn't the first time. She said she felt stupid. Like he never really cared the way she did, in the beginning."

I take a long sip of tea, guilt knotting my stomach. I always had a bad feeling about Mark, should have warned Esme off him the second I knew they were together. Then again, she wouldn't have listened.

"So you talked about Mark. What else?"

He shrugs. "Honestly, she was more interested in getting fucked up than talking. She needed a distraction."

I eye Hunter carefully. Drugs are a distraction, but so is sex. He may be a college kid, but he looks older. He has that tortured-artist look Esme's always been drawn to, Mark notwithstanding. The very first time I overheard them on the phone, I thought Esme was having an affair. When I met Hunter, he insisted they were no more than friends, but was I too quick to believe him?

My sister has never been confrontational, but not because she's meek. The way Esme sees it, why fight when you can get revenge? That's precisely what she's been doing with Carl, and Kiku. Avoid confrontation, hit them where it hurts. It stands to reason she'd be doing the same thing to Mark.

I bore holes into Hunter's forehead until he meets my gaze.

"Be real with me. No matter what kind of shit she was going through, no writing mentor would spend this much time with the mentee she's just met—partying, talking on the phone. Are you sleeping with her?"

"No!" Hunter looks stricken. We get a few glances, and he lowers his voice. "I swear to *god* that's not it."

And suddenly, I believe him. He looks horrified by the thought, repulsed even. And there's something else. His short stature, green eyes, the high cheekbones. The way he tucks his hair behind his ear. I can't believe I didn't see it before. But now that it's clicked, the resemblance is unmistakable. He looks a lot like Esme.

"Where are you from again?" I ask.

Hunter frowns. "Colorado. But originally, Carson City, Nevada."

I nod, all the pieces locking into place, creating a diorama that shouldn't shock me as much as it does. Because while I didn't know Esme had a half brother, I've known about Esme's father—her biological father—since the summer I was seventeen.

Esme doesn't know the truth. Except that somehow, she does.

"You're his kid, too, aren't you?" I ask. "Nolan Bristow's."

Relief washes across Hunter's face, the secret he's been keeping for Esme finally out. "That's right. Esme's my half sister."

Growing up, Dad had affair after affair, but to the best of my knowledge, Mom had only the one, a several-months-long dalliance when I was pretty little, after which she recommitted to her marriage, flawed as it was, and Mom and Dad welcomed their second child, Esme, into the Connor fold. Marjorie's one spate of retaliatory cheating was no secret around the house—Dad brought it up often, whenever his own faithfulness was called into question—but I didn't doubt that my sister and I shared a father.

Everything changed the summer Esme was thirteen, and I was seventeen. The summer of Dylan, the summer of the crash. It's possible that Carl had always suspected, a little, that Esme wasn't his. He knew about the affair, must have clocked the timing of Marjorie's second pregnancy, but she'd assured him that he was the father, and for years, he'd believed her. His youngest daughter did, after all, share a lucky number of his attributes—blond, slim, undeniably attractive—but as Esme entered early adolescence, it became clear that she shared just as many with the man Mom had once been seeing. Green eyes; petite frame; high, delicate cheekbones. Once I learned Nolan Bristow's name and looked him up, the resemblance was unmistakable.

We'd been at Dad's house the weekend he called to have it out with Mom, the weekend I learned everything. In a highly uncharacteristic move on Dad's part, he'd allowed Esme to return to Branby early for a sleepover, one of her best friend's birthday parties, so Dad and I were alone in New Haven that Sunday night in June.

It was late, after eleven. I'd been reading in bed and had just switched off the light when the yelling started. At first I thought someone else was in the house, but I soon realized Dad was in his library downstairs, shouting into the landline. I heard Esme's name, and Mom's, and that of someone named Nolan Bristow. I crept into Dad's bedroom, picked up the second receiver, and listened in.

Mom was on the other end. As I listened, it became instantly clear why Dad hadn't wanted Esme in the house that night. He laid his suspicions bare, then threatened to "track Nolan down in Carson City" and demand a paternity test.

I sat there on Dad's bed, receiver cradled to my ear, and googled *Nolan Bristow + Carson City, Nevada*. What I found was the professional profile for a man who could only be described as "pretty." Fine blond hair graying ever so slightly, delicate features, slight build, bright green eyes. He was the head of the cardiac unit at some hospital in the desert. Nolan Bristow didn't look like what I assumed a high-profile surgeon would look like, but he did, unmistakably, look like Esme.

Mom broke down almost immediately, admitting the truth. While I listened in, mouth gaping wide, Dad told Mom he was not going to continue paying child support for Esme, under any circumstances. On top of that, unless she agreed to tell Nolan the truth and demand he assume his share of the financial responsibility going forward, Dad would sue for years of back payments Mom didn't have.

It would bankrupt us.

My mind spiraled from there. Because once Esme's biological father learned about her, what if he wanted custody? I imagined my baby sister shipped off to live all the way across the country for half the year, until she turned eighteen. It was unthinkable.

As Mom sobbed into the phone, my shock turned to churning dread, the truth about Esme's parentage soon overtaken by fear. It would not be beyond my father to punish Mom for her deceit by encouraging Nolan to sue for joint custody, just to be cruel. His motivations were often egotistical, selfish, mean. Taking Esme away from us—from me—to live with a complete stranger was emphatically *not* in her best interest. But Carl wasn't known for putting others' interests before his own.

By the end of the phone call, Mom had tearfully agreed to Dad's terms. The very next night, Dad would come over to Old Boney, and our parents would sit Esme and me down in the living room and tell us everything. Then they would contact Nolan and tell him the truth about the daughter he didn't know he had, and Dad would bring in his lawyer to put his financial demands in motion. Mom was a wreck, but no amount of pleading would change Dad's mind, and with the threat of the lawsuit hanging over her, she was backed into a corner.

That night, I didn't sleep. I spent the dark hours racking my brain, trying to figure out what I could do to stop this bomb from detonating, potentially tearing Esme away from me. I was deeply concerned for my sister's well-being. But also, I was scared of being left alone with my parents and their mess. What if Esme grew to love Nolan more than any of us? What if she never came back? I didn't know the legal ins and outs, but surely whatever the outcome, this would split us apart.

Selfishly, I couldn't bear the thought of life in Branby without her. I *had* to stop Carl. But by the morning light, I had come up blank.

Now Hunter peers at me, looking for a reaction, and I shiver, mind flashing to the puffy pink scar running down Esme's arm from her shoulder to her elbow. Then to thirteen-year-old Esme in a hospital bed, barely clinging to life, the machines breathing for her. My fault.

Dad was scheduled to come over the next night at six, but there were storms in the area, and he was delayed in New Haven dealing with a faulty sump pump and a rapidly flooding basement. As the minutes ticked by, and six became seven, the perfect plan of how to stop this family meeting still failed to materialize. My nerves ratcheted up and up until Dylan saw me pacing around the grounds, getting soaked despite my boots and raincoat, and pulled me inside the stone cottage.

I was spiraling, but I couldn't risk telling Dylan the truth, risk anyone else harboring this terrible secret that could explode any moment to destroy our family. So I made up some not-so-far-fetched story about Carl lashing out at Esme and me to explain why I was in such a state, and Dylan poured us shots of his dad's booze.

Three shots later, it was completely dark and the storm was raging on, but I was feeling a thousand pounds lighter. The solution was simple: All I had to do was get Esme out of the house, take her away for the night. Dad's cabin in the Catskills—once our family's vacation home, now rarely used except for Dad's writing retreats—would be the perfect spot. We'd hole up overnight, let Mom and Dad stew.

I'd get in trouble when it was all over, but so what? All I needed was to buy myself time to reason with Dad, alone. To tell him that I knew everything, to talk him out of this plan that could result in all of us losing Esme. He'd been in a rage on the phone the night before, would still be in a rage when he came to Old Boney, but after a night worrying about his missing daughters, he'd cool down. And I'd do what I always did—step up like the only true adult in my family, make him see reason. Esme may not have been his biologically, but for thirteen years, he'd raised her as his own. He'd never been a great father, but deep down, I knew my dad loved us both, and that if he really thought about it, he'd acknowledge that child support wasn't a financial strain for him, and he wouldn't want to risk giving up his rights to his youngest just to punish Mom.

I said good night to Dylan and ran through the downpour back across the lawn to the house. Mom was in the kitchen, anxiously scrubbing the counters for the third time. I sneaked up the stairs, into Esme's room.

What exactly I said to get her to follow me out of the house is lost to the recesses of memory, but knowing my sister, it probably didn't take much convincing for her to agree to an adventure. Vodka-fueled confidence surging through my veins, I got a wad of cash from Mom's wallet and her keys from the bowl in the hall and we waited until she had stepped into the bathroom to slip down to the garage and into her car.

I'd had my license for a few months, had been allowed to borrow the car a handful of times, but only in broad daylight. The moment I eased us out of the garage and into the drive, rain pelted the car roof, and a huge clap of thunder bellowed overhead. It was pitch black out, but I switched on the headlights, then the wipers, confident I knew what I was doing. Besides, I didn't even feel drunk anymore. I was perfectly equipped to drive us through some rain.

"Where are we going?" Esme asked from the passenger's seat.

"I told you, it's a surprise. An adventure."

She flashed me a grin.

I drove around the leaky old fountain, down the drive, and onto the street. Every few seconds, I glanced back at the house, but Mom hadn't heard the garage door in the storm. We were safe.

Soon, Dad would arrive. They'd be scared when they discovered we were missing, furious when they realized what I'd done, but then, they'd both see I was the adult here, the one thinking things through, keeping an irreversible family disaster at bay. Someday, my parents would thank me.

We never got as far as Dad's cabin in the Catskills. I'd barely merged onto I-95 when a battering gust of wind slammed into the side of the car, and I lost control. The tires skidded on the rain-slick road, and then we were spinning, spinning, our voices rising in one piercing scream.

They say your life flashes before your eyes when you're about to die, the function of a profound shift in your neurocognitive processing. But for me, time stood still. Maybe that's how I knew I was going to live, would be fated to face the consequences of my actions, however dire. It was probably a matter of seconds, but we seemed to spin forever, tires hydroplaning on the asphalt, and I remember thinking very clearly that somewhere outside the car existed another Jane who never took those shots, never took Mom's keys, never hustled Esme out of the house in the storm, never steered us onto the highway. Somewhere, another story was unspooling, Carl arriving to Old Boney to tear the rug out from beneath us all, rip Esme's fragile thirteen-year-old world apart. As we spun toward impact, I saw the two paths branching out into darkness, destruction at either end.

I don't remember the moment we crashed, just a rush of relief we weren't moving anymore. That I was still breathing, and somehow, nothing hurt. For a moment, I thought everything was going to be fine. But when I clawed myself free from the airbag, Esme was unconscious beside me. The passenger's side door was crumpled inward, crushing her, and there was blood everywhere.

I must have found my phone, dialed 911. I don't remember much of what happened next. We were rushed to the hospital. At some point, Mom and Dad came. No one mentioned paternity or Nolan Bristow's name.

Esme was rushed into surgery, and we all held our breaths. No one yelled at me for taking the car without permission. For days, no one even asked what I'd been thinking, where I was going. Perhaps because the storm seemed the obvious cause of the crash, no one checked my blood alcohol level. Only Dylan and I knew the truth, that I'd driven drunk.

Only I knew why.

Esme made it through surgery, but her injuries were serious. Head trauma, concussion, broken arm, broken leg, deep cuts on her scalp and arm. She was in the hospital for three weeks, then inpatient rehabilitation for three more. Our lives reduced to Esme's recovery, and there was no more mention of Nolan Bristow or a lawsuit for back alimony payments.

Ultimately, the accident shook Dad up enough to make him stand down. Nearly losing Esme must have shocked Dad into realizing what I'd hoped to make him see through diplomacy and reason: despite the facts of her DNA, he loved his daughter more than he cared about making Marjorie suffer for deceiving him. Probably, it had also hit him that exposing the truth, and the reality that he'd been duped by Mom for thirteen years, might be a ding on his image. Perhaps that's why he never told Esme the truth. He hardly turned around to become an amazing father to his girls, but he did drop his revenge plot against Mom.

In the end, my plan worked, but at far greater cost than I'd ever imagined.

Now I train my focus on the handsome young man sitting across from me, tracing one slender finger around the rim of a cardboard coffee cup. Hunter Mendez, Nolan's son. Esme's half brother.

"Nolan's dead," he says after a minute. "I wasn't sure if you knew."

"I'm sorry to hear that." Many times, I've thought about googling Nolan Bristow again, but doing so seemed to be tempting fate—that Dad might change his mind, or Nolan might develop suspicions of his own and emerge from the woodwork.

Hunter nods. "Colon cancer, ten years ago. After he died, Mom moved us to Loveland, Colorado, the town where both she and Dad grew up. We had family there, and she needed the help."

"Your mom's last name is Mendez?"

He nods. "I've never felt like a Bristow. Esme and I have that in common. We have a lot in common, actually. During our first meeting, she acted like a normal mentor. But the second time, she told me why she'd picked me as her mentee. She knew exactly who I was."

My mind reels, trying to make all the pieces fit. Esme has always believed that what happened on the night of the crash was the result of a reckless, adolescent whim. It's bad enough that way. She'd never understand how I bargained with the devil to stop her from learning the truth about her biological father and all the terrible consequences that would have followed. How I was motivated, in part, by my own selfish desire to keep her close.

But I always thought that one day, I'd tell her about Nolan. She deserved to know, and it wasn't my place to hide the truth forever. At first, I thought I'd do it once she turned eighteen, once alimony and custody would no longer be part of the equation. But by that time, Mom's dementia had begun to set in, and Esme was starting college, and then it never seemed to be the right time. Somehow, though, she's learned about the affair, has unearthed Nolan. And in doing so, has found Hunter.

"So where is Esme?" I ask.

Hunter glances around, then his eyes settle on me. "On Thursday night, she was a mess. On top of the stuff with her ex, and deadlines for the book she's working on, she was feeling a lot of guilt about this guy she's been seeing. Did she tell you anything about that?"

I shake my head, although the thought that Esme might take revenge on Mark by seeking out her own affair has certainly crossed my mind. The affair just wasn't with Hunter.

"Once we were at the bar," he continues, "she wanted to go outside, take a walk. I went with her. While she was still lucid, she told me a few things she made me swear I'd never repeat."

I grip the edge of the table. "Such as?"

He stares down into his cup. "I think I know where she went."

FOURTEEN

GONE

I haven't slept in the hours since Officer Larson's phone call, informing me of Mom's death, but even now that I'm home from the hospital, I can't make myself rest. While I wait for the Branby police to call with more information, and for Marrone to update me on my sister's case, I spend the hours at the kitchen island, making arrangements: The memorial service, the funeral, the burial. Contracting the right kind of lawyer to file civil litigation against Monte Viso.

By the afternoon, the shock has begun to fade into true grief, and I've run out of things to keep me occupied. Between crying jags, my mind wanders. I want Esme. If my sister were here, I'd still be the one handling everything, but she'd fix me tea. She'd know the right way to share the news on social media. She'd annoy the crap out of me, but even that would be a welcome distraction. Jamie has offered to come over again tonight, and while I'm looking forward to the comfort of his presence around the house, he's not family. In this moment, Esme is the one person who could come close to understanding, and she's not here.

There have been no further updates from the NYPD, but now

that there's evidence of wrongdoing, her case has finally made the news. I keep the TV on mute in the background, refresh my browser every twenty minutes, hungry for any little scrap. Dylan's face appears again and again on the screen, a professional photo they've pulled from his website. He looks handsome, eager to please. He does not look like a killer. One site wrongly identifies him as Esme's childhood boyfriend. Over and over, I watch a clip from an interview with Dr. Andre Hubenthal, a striking older man who identifies himself as a former professor of Dylan's. He speaks in soft, concerned tones about his prize student's struggle to overcome a serious substance abuse problem in his early twenties and his rise to professional acclaim. "Even at his lowest point, Dylan Greer would only ever harm himself," Dr. Hubenthal says into the camera. "This isn't the Dylan I know."

This isn't the Dylan I know either, but then again, we haven't been close for fifteen years. That he ever struggled with addiction is news to me. And until I put him on the spot, he lied to me about meeting Esme at Café Lisse, too. I don't want the perpetrator we've been searching for to be Dylan, but Dylan hasn't been the eighteen-year-old boy I knew and loved for a very long time. And the evidence is hard to dispute. The blood they found was fresh; two days ago, my sister was alive. But now? With each passing hour, my hope flickers.

At one, I go in to Monte Viso for a meeting with the president and CEO, the head of nursing, and the head of memory support. I am assured time and again that they are cooperating fully with police, that they are as eager for answers as I am, but the stench of bullshit hangs heavy in the air. No one seated in this tastefully decorated office is eager for answers except me, because answers are sure to point toward criminal negligence. They are *desperately* trying to recover camera footage from last night, were *horrified* to learn from security about the persisting intermittent outages, are in touch with the service provider *hourly* to follow up on their inquiry into possible data-recovery options.

I am not reassured by anything that spills from their gravely concerned and deeply apologetic lips. These are three panicked people, desperate to avoid a lawsuit. What I know is this: Somehow, Mom exited both the sixth floor and the building between eleven thirty and midnight, which means either her bracelet was deactivated or someone keyed her out. Either way, the people who were supposed to keep my mother safe are to blame. After enduring fifteen minutes of their groveling, I've heard enough. I push back my chair.

Renata, the head of nursing, trails me down the hall to Mom's room, making noise about how Monte Viso will arrange to have her personal effects, even the furniture we brought, packed and shipped home, free of charge.

"Could I have a few minutes?" I snap. "I want to be left alone."

Cowed, she steps back into the hallway, leaving me in Mom's room. The bed has been stripped, but otherwise, everything looks untouched. I close the door and sit on the bare mattress, breathing in the smell that is not quite Mom and not quite antiseptic. Monte Viso is the highest-rated private nursing facility in the state, the best of the best. She was only sixty-four. She was supposed to be here for decades, comfortable, safe. I want to cry, but I feel scraped out, able only to *do*.

I open Mom's closet and find one of her large, luxe handbags. I'll let Monte Viso ship her furniture, her clothes, but I'm taking a few things with me. I select her favorite pieces of jewelry from the box on her dresser, the bottle of her perfume, the album of family photos I put together for her back in June. Then I walk over to her nightstand, eyes landing on the beautiful leather-bound journal I gave her for her birthday. It's in the same exact spot she placed it that night, and I pick it up and crack open the spine without much hope.

To my surprise, it's been written in. Quite a lot, actually. During the past two weeks, Mom has filled nearly half the pages. I sink back down to the mattress and begin to read, starting from the last entry, dated the afternoon before she wandered into traffic, and work back. I'm eager for any clues that might be buried inside these pages, anything that might shed some light on what the hell happened.

Mostly, Mom has been writing about the past. Memories from the time she was married to Carl, from when Esme and I were small. For a while, I get lost in the past along with her, and the more I read, the more I realize she's not recounting memories. For Mom, the past and present were ever-blending. *This morning, Carl was too ill to take Jane to daycare. Last night, we made it through Esme's dance recital without incident. On Friday, I discovered a half-smoked joint and two bottles of gin beneath Esme's bed.* I feel the usual stomach drop that accompanies a reminder of Mom's dementia. Then I realize it doesn't matter anymore, and grief knifes through me again.

Last night, my mother was alive, and now her life is over. The path I thought would continue for thousands upon thousands of miles abruptly severed, replaced by a sucking black ocean of unmapped space. The decision to move her to Monte Viso was all mine. I did the research, conducted the interviews, handled the accounting. Now it seems like the worst choice I've ever made, but when I rack my brain, searching for the red flags I missed, I come up blank.

I keep flipping pages, skimming entries, but there's nothing revealing about the day she died. Sometimes, Mom is squarely located in the present. There are the typical gripes about Monte Viso—the bland food, her neighbor with the very loud grandchildren that come to visit on weekends. I'm pleased to find a complimentary entry about a resident who lives down the hall, someone named Monica, whom I didn't know Mom was friendly with. I'm momentarily comforted by the knowledge she was making friends here before the crushing reality of her death hits me square in the chest once more, knocking the wind out of me.

In one entry, Mom writes at length about my relationship with Jamie, past again merging with present, which comes as a bit of a surprise since when we were actually together, Jamie never stuck in Mom's mind as anything other than her neurologist, and that, too, faded once she began seeing Dr. Yu. But Mom's mind is slippery, which is a constant struggle for me. Was a constant struggle.

Often, she's confused Esme and me in her entries, using our names interchangeably, and it's possible she's confused Dr. Yu with another staff member as well, complaining, as she has to me several times lately, that the new doctor is "a bad man" and that he was "nasty with her again." I had meant to write to the social worker on staff about her complaints, but with a guilty twinge, I realize the email is sitting in my drafts folder. There's been so much on my mind, I'd forgotten, and frankly, it's been hard to imagine gentle Dr. Yu saying anything unkind to Mom. But there must have been tension with someone on staff, and now I wonder if my failure to follow up on Mom's grievances somehow led to the events of last night.

Cringing, I slip the journal into her handbag along with her perfume and jewelry, and then I leave the sixth floor and take the elevator downstairs.

In the lobby, I give Harold at the security desk a smile and ask to see the logbook. I brace myself for some pushback, but he smiles sympathetically and nudges it toward me. The higher-ups have already provided the police with a list of every staff member who was working last night, all of whom are being interviewed by the Branby police, but the security log will capture everyone else who entered and exited the building. I scan through names of visitors here to see residents, all of whom checked out well before the time Mom went missing. The solitary late-night entry marks the arrival of a PPO shipment for the second floor.

"No one else signed in after ten o'clock?" I ask. *Someone* removed Mom's ankle bracelet or keyed her out. Someone who knew their way around Monte Viso's safety protocols.

Harold shakes his head. "Could have been some Grubhub drivers, but they don't leave the lobby. Staff come down to pick up their food."

"What about employees who weren't on the schedule? Would they have to sign in?"

Harold's eyes travel to the top of the sliding glass doors at the front of the lobby. "Staff don't use the books, but that's why we have a camera."

My heart sinks. "And the camera was out."

"There's no *recorded* footage after around ten thirty, but the system wasn't entirely down. We still have the database."

I raise my eyebrows, surprised. "Database?"

He nods. "Facial recognition. Camera wasn't recording, but the system kept logging staff comings and goings."

I suck in a sharp breath. "Do the police know about this?"

"Requests we've gotten have been for camera footage, which we've provided up until it went out." He frowns. "I'm not sure if the boss would have sent over the database."

"Who else knows about the facial recognition?"

"Besides security?" His brows pinch together. "We offer annual refreshers down here for anyone who wants to attend. Some of the admins come, maybe a tech or a nurse. Everyone *should* know how the system works, but I can't tell you the last time I saw a doctor at one of those things."

He pulls up something on his computer, then swivels the monitor toward me. On the screen is a simple spreadsheet showing employee names, ID numbers, dates, and times.

"Don't go memorizing any of those IDs," he quips, but my eyes are locked on a single entry.

11:01 p.m. arrival: Paulson, James.

14

HOME

I leave my car double-parked in the street and station myself outside
the twelve-story high-rise on Lex, the place my conversation with
Hunter has led me. I shift my weight from one foot to the other, willing someone to leave. The first resident out the door is a tiny woman
in her seventies who definitely isn't letting me in. But after a string
of eternally long minutes pass, a young mom pushing a double-wide
stroller crosses the lobby, and I reach to help with the door.

"How old are they?" I coo.

"Five months tomorrow. But sometimes it feels like five years."

I give her a warm smile. "I can only imagine. They're cuties,
though."

She beams, and I step across the threshold as she pilots the
stroller down the sidewalk.

In. The lobby is as I remember it—a clutter of packages strewn
across the unoccupied security desk, the wide bank of mailboxes
behind, lush greenery sprouting from several tall planters. Nice but
not ostentatious, especially for this neighborhood. I start down the
short hallway leading to the elevators, which is lined on one side
with floor-to-ceiling windows looking out on a small stone court-

yard. I used to love going out there for a drink on warm Manhattan evenings, making chitchat with Jamie's neighbors.

But it's eleven thirty on a Wednesday, and this morning the courtyard is empty. I hurry past the side door and down to the elevator, throat dry. For weeks, I longed to be back here. Now that it's happening, I feel ill.

The elevator dings, and I step out onto his floor. Jaw ticking, I walk past a row of doors and round the hall to 8L, the corner apartment Jamie has owned since cofounding his Manhattan practice. I press the bell and wait.

Every fiber in my being wants Hunter to have been wrong. I think back to what he told me at the student center—*On Thursday night, she was a mess. On top of the stuff with her ex, and deadlines for the book she's working on, she was feeling a lot of guilt about this guy she's been seeing. She said she regretted it now, that she wanted to end things. But she wasn't feeling guilty because she was married; she told me she'd started the affair because of* you.

I hear her before I see her—the unhurried *clack, clack, clack* of Esme's sandals against the white tile floor. My breath catches. Hunter was right. *I* was right. There's a long moment in which I can feel her eyes on me through the peephole, and I wonder if she's going to send Jamie to open the door, try to hide somewhere in his charming but small one-bedroom.

I clear my throat. "I know you're in there, Esme. Open up."

Her sigh is audible through the door. The dead bolt unhinges, and then she is stepping back, wearing nothing but one of Jamie's button-downs and her gold Balenciaga slingbacks, arm sweeping in a display of mock-graciousness toward the inside of the apartment. "Please, come on in."

I step across the threshold, taking her in. "Really, Esme?"

It's all I can think to say. She's been missing since yesterday sometime, not with Hunter, or Dad, or one of her friends. She's been right here with my ex because apparently, they are sleeping together.

"We should sit." She pulls out two chairs at Jamie's small glass dining table. Watching her move through his apartment with such ease makes my stomach clench.

My eyes dance around the room, an open kitchen/living/dining setup leading to the bedroom in the back. Evidence of my sister is all around. I register her familiar rose-gold laptop on the dining table, her phone with its flashy carnelian case beside a juice glass on the kitchen counter, one of her paperbacks tented on the coffee table, her bag slung over the shoulder of the couch.

"How long has this been going on?"

Since Jamie broke up with me in July? Or much longer than that?

"Please sit." She peers up at me from her seat at the table. I drop my bag to the rug and perch stiffly on the edge of the second chair.

"He's out getting bagels," she says after a minute. "He'll be back soon."

"And you're together. You and Jamie."

She slouches back in her chair. "Yesterday I came here to end things. It's run its course, but he doesn't seem to agree. We've been talking."

I take in her bare legs, the bottom of Jamie's shirt barely dusting her thighs. She told Hunter she'd been feeling guilty about the relationship, but I wonder now if that was a lie to make herself look better in her half brother's eyes. Did she regret starting it, or is she simply ready to move on?

"What the fuck?" I spit out. "How long?"

She rolls her shoulders back, straightens up. "Not as long as you deserved."

My stomach knots. "And what does that mean?"

"You've been lying to me," she hisses. Her pretty eyes flash. "For years."

Her words land like a blow to my chest, knocking the wind out of me. Because Esme doesn't just know about Nolan, her biological father. She knows that *I* know—have known since we were kids. She knows I kept Nolan a secret from her.

"How did you—?" I start to ask, but she cuts me off, lifting the lid of her laptop case.

"Sunday, June 8," she begins to read from the screen. "Is it eavesdropping if your father has become unhinged, if he is threatening to expose a dangerous secret that will tear your family even further apart? Jane sits on the big bed in their dad's New Haven home, twists the phone cord between her fingers, thinking. She didn't ask to be the responsible adult, but she knows one thing for sure: it has fallen to her to change the course of the story.

"Wednesday, June 11. For days, I sleep, head wrapped in a thick white bandage, blond wisps sticking out, body wired to a battery of machines. They speak for me, beeping and blinking my will to remain in this world. *Stay alive stay alive stay alive.* I dream of my family, hovering over me, bickering, fretting, bargaining with God. My sister has no bargaining chips to offer. She's made her choice, and now the consequences flow as through a broken dam into a new universe of her creation, wave after unbridled wave, no return."

"I wrote that," I whisper. "The point of view is changed, but those are my words. From my journals."

A slow smile plays across my sister's face. "Are they? According to Victoria Shaughnessy and everyone at Brenner & Reed, what you heard is an early excerpt from my memoir. Seems like they're my words now."

My mind is reeling. Esme found my journals—*stole* my journals.

This is how she uncovered the secret I've been keeping for fifteen years: that her real father was a surgeon from Carson City, Nevada, named Nolan Bristow. That the horrible car crash that nearly ended her life wasn't a misguided teenage joyride, but my own Hail Mary pass to keep Dad from doing something rash, something that might result in my little sister being torn away from me. I was thinking of myself, yes, but I was also trying to *protect* her. And in doing so, I hurt her, badly. And I kept the truth about Nolan a secret, something clearly unforgivable in her eyes.

Which is why she stole Jamie away from me. Esme has always loved a good revenge plot.

And her memoir—an exposé about Carl, but also a rewrite of our twisted family history from her point of view. The family history I *wrote*.

"That's plagiarism. You can't—"

"Oh can't I? Because the way I see it, *you* stole from *me*. I had a chance to meet my real father, but you were so dead set on making sure I didn't get the one part of this fucked-up family that was mine and mine alone, you nearly killed me in the process."

I am speechless, stunned. Carl deserves the takedown Esme is planning in her book. He's never been held to account for years of misconduct with his students, and she has every right to be furious with him for jeopardizing her well-being when she was thirteen just to hurt Mom. His actions were selfish and cruel; on that we can wholeheartedly agree.

What I did was selfish, too, but does she really think I was cruel? Surely I'm not on par with Dad in her eyes.

"That's not how it happened," I splutter. "I was trying to protect you!"

"Bullshit," Esme hisses. "You were only thinking about yourself. You were stuck with an emotionally abusive dad, and you didn't want me to have anything different or better. You *loved* doing it, too, didn't you? Keeping a secret, knowing more than me about my own *parentage*. Feeling superior, like you always have. And in the process you kept my real father from me."

"Dad would have been fine with sending you away," I say softly, the shock of my sister's words reverberating all around me. "He was trying to hurt Mom, and you were going to be collateral damage."

Esme laughs and snaps her laptop shut. "Of course you would see it that way."

"What other way is there? If Nolan won joint custody, you would have had to go to Nevada. He was a total stranger. You could have wound up across the country, all alone."

I lock my eyes with hers, needing what I did all those years ago to have been the right decision, needing it to have not been in vain.

She shakes her head slowly back and forth, tucking one lock of blond hair behind her ear. "Did it ever, for one second, occur to you how miserable I was in Branby? It's not like we had a happy childhood, Jane. Why exactly did you think I started drinking so young, sneaking out all the time, breaking Mom's flimsy rules? I *dreamed* of escaping. You took that away from me!"

My jaw unhinges slowly. That *can't* be how Esme saw things. "But you could have been sent away *from me*," I gasp.

She narrows her eyes, and I feel suddenly small. We were inseparable then. She *needed* me. At least, I always thought she did. Suddenly, I'm not sure who's rewriting history—Esme or me.

"You nearly killed me," she says through clenched teeth.

"I know." My voice trembles, the weight of what I did crashing over me again. "And I know it was selfish—I would have been so lonely without you. But I swear to god, Esme, I did it for you. I did it for *us*."

"That's your story," she says. "But it's not mine. You hid the truth from me for fifteen years. If I hadn't found your journals last Thanksgiving, I never would have found out. You *never* would have told me."

My mind flashes to that horrible weekend, Esme storming out of Old Boney with no explanation, then refusing to come home for Christmas. That's what this is about—what her whole return home has been about all along.

"You stole my chance to meet my real dad before he died, to get away from Mom and Carl," she continues. "Tit for tat."

Tit for tat. I thought whatever affair she'd been having was to get back at Mark, but *I* was her target. And she stole my story, too, turned it into a lucrative book deal under her name. Esme has always been one to eschew confrontation for revenge, but I never thought she'd sharpen her knives against me.

I thought my sister loved me, underneath it all. I understand longing for escape at thirteen; what child doesn't fantasize about a new, better family, town, life? But to still feel that way at twenty-eight, to still, with the benefit of all this time, be incapable of seeing a fantasy for what it was?

Then to lash out at me like this? It hits me that in all her scheming and unraveling, she's destroyed my new relationship, too. Because I was willing to do anything for her, even if it cost me Dylan.

And for what?

"We're done here." My chair scrapes back from the table, and I reach down to scoop up my bag.

"No, we're not." Esme hurries to follow me, but I have nothing else to say. I'm nearly to the door when there's the sound of a key turning in the lock, and we both freeze. The door swings open, and Jamie steps into the apartment clutching a newspaper, two coffees on a cardboard tray, and a brown paper bag. His eyes dart between the two of us.

"Jane." His voice is weak. His keys clatter to the floor.

"Was just leaving," I say, pushing past him and out into the hall. I always thought I'd be the kind of woman to blame my partner—not the other woman—if he cheated on me. And Jamie is far from blameless, but this affair is so clearly by Esme's design, a carefully orchestrated revenge scheme.

Of course Jamie fell right into her plan. He's always been best in a crisis, and once the drama of my move home to Branby and my fraught decision-making about Mom's care had subsided, Jamie began to step back. Surely it didn't take much keen observation on my sister's part to gauge his character. She made herself vulnerable to him, a damsel in distress, and Jamie fell for her act—hook, line, and sinker. His savior complex made him an easy mark.

I thought what we had was real, that Jamie was strong and smart and compassionate. But he was weak, so quick to leave me for the more enticing Connor sister. I take one look behind me, at Jamie's surprised face, and wonder if I ever really knew him at all.

"Jane, wait." Esme's voice spills into the hall, but I keep walking. She's spent the past three weeks observing me. I haven't told her about reuniting with Dylan, but she's figured out that I'm over Jamie. She didn't come here to end things because she feels guilty; she came here because Jamie is a pawn in her game, and she no longer needs him.

When I call the elevator, the door springs right open, and I step inside with a sigh of relief.

On the ground floor, I hurry off the elevator and down the hall, past the courtyard, then through the lobby, saying a silent prayer I haven't been towed or gotten a ticket. By some miracle, the car is sitting there, untouched, and I dig in my bag for my keys, overwhelmed by the sudden need to be behind the wheel, driving far away from my sister and her cruelty.

I wrench open the driver's side door and collapse onto the seat. But before I can start the ignition, get my seat belt on, Esme is flying out of the building, still wearing only Jamie's shirt and her gold sling-backs, and hurtling herself across the front of the car and into the passenger's seat. She shuts the door and reaches for her belt.

"What are you doing?"

"Coming with you. We're not done talking."

I have half a mind to reach across and shove her out into the street, but I suck in an angry breath and jam the key into the ignition instead. With a quick glance in the side mirror, I pull the car into traffic, then cut left onto Eighty-Second, headed toward Third Avenue, then eventually the FDR. Flashes of that Saturday night nearly three weeks ago come back to me: picking Esme up at the Monarch Hotel in the driving rain, my sister evading my questions as I clenched the wheel tight and drove us to Connecticut. Jamie's flight had left the day before, or at least I thought it had.

But Jamie is a liar.

"Were you meeting him that night?" I ask. "That Saturday, during the storm."

"No." She's staring out the window as I drive farther uptown, not looking at me. "I was supposed to go over there after dinner with Mark, supposed to go with Jamie to San Francisco that night, but I'd changed my mind about all of it. I was trying to give you a chance, Janie."

My head whips toward her. "Give me a chance?"

"That's why I called you, why I came back to Branby. I could have gone anywhere after leaving Mark, could have just booked a room at a different hotel, but I wanted to give you a chance to come clean about the past. I was home for nearly three weeks, and you failed."

"Jesus, Esme. I didn't realize our relationship was a test."

"Fifteen years ago, you almost got me killed. These past weeks, I've been nothing but nice to you. I thought maybe you'd feel a little bit of remorse, admit what you'd done, but you never did."

I turn right at East Ninety-Sixth, headed toward the FDR North ramp. *Nothing but nice* is debatable, but we've had our moments. Now I realize none of it was real. The hurt that's been simmering in my stomach turns to an angry boil.

"Over the past ten months, you stole my journals, rewrote them as your own, and seduced my boyfriend. That's not normal behavior, Esme." My voice pitches to a near scream. "I kept a secret to protect you from Dad's angry whims, to keep you home with Mom and me. Can't you see that?"

"What I see is a punishment commiserate with the crime," she snarls. "You hid the truth from me, and I nearly died for it. I took my story *back*. You stole someone important from me, and I did the same. Now you know how it feels."

"That's not—" I start to say, but she barrels on as I merge onto the FDR, foot jamming down on the gas.

"*You* hurt *me*, Jane. Don't you get that? Jamie, the memoir, that was payback. Fifteen years later, and you can't even accept responsibility for everything you stole."

I weave left, then right, dodging the slow-moving traffic on the highway. My throat is thick, tears blurring my vision, but I don't swipe them away. I have only ever tried to protect Esme—then, now, always. Yes, I was driven by my own interests, too, but only because I loved her. For fifteen years, I have felt the horrible, crushing guilt of that crash, how I emerged unscathed while she was battered and broken. For fifteen years, I have tried to make it up to her in every possible way. But what happened was an *accident*. It was stupid to drive drunk like that, to put us both in danger, and I have apologized to her thousands of times for what happened that night. But I won't apologize for my intentions—stopping the ill-conceived family meeting, the disastrous events Carl would have set in motion, events that would have only hurt Esme.

"Wow," she says when I've been silent too long, white-knuckling the wheel and nudging the pedal farther and farther toward the floor. "Nothing? You're unbelievable, Jane. And slow the fuck down."

I can't find the words. Esme read my journals over Thanksgiving. Any time over the past ten months, she could have come to me, talked to me. But instead she went for the jugular, sabotaging my relationship, profiting off the writing I set aside to get my business degree, to make sure Mom was cared for. And *Dylan*. The tears misting my vision spill over, become full-blown sobs. Everything I have done for Esme in the weeks since she came home, putting her health and safety above everything else, has destroyed my future with him. She's taken that from me, too.

All my life, I have wanted nothing so much as the happiness my parents never found—a *good* marriage to a *good* partner. Esme has always been able to read me like a book, knew how deeply my desire runs. The vile truth of it lands like a blow straight to my chest: my sister *hates* me.

"We are not the same," I say through clenched teeth. Up ahead are signs for the Major Deegan Expressway. It's not a route I would normally take, but I merge back into the right lane. "I'm always thinking about you, Esme. Don't you get that? What you did was *malicious*. There's something wrong with you."

"Careful!" Esme yells, her arm flying out to snatch for the wheel as I take the exit for the bridge, too fast, tires squealing beneath us.

But maybe there is something wrong with me, too. Because all this time, I have put Esme first, and why? Because she is my sister. Because fifteen years ago, I made a costly mistake, and every day since, I have lived in her debt. But she doesn't deserve my kindness, my unflagging devotion. She is heartless, manipulative, cruel, and I am done being her doormat. I am done making the good choice.

I have lost Jamie, now Dylan, and worst of all, I have uncovered the truth about my sister. She is exactly as callous and self-absorbed as she appears; the girl I thought lay buried beneath never existed at all.

She never apologizes, and she never says thank-you. She is incapable of change.

There is no path forward for us, no healing from this.

The Willis Avenue Bridge stretches before me, below, the Harlem River. I jam my foot to the floor, weaving wildly around the other cars.

"What are you doing?" Esme shrieks. "You're going to lose control!"

But she's wrong. Because never in my life have I been so in control. I see us in Mom's car together, speeding away from Dad's terrible judgment, my senses numbed by vodka. I see myself three Saturdays ago, thunder clapping overhead, rain smearing the windshield, trembling all the way to the Monarch to rescue my sister. I see myself choosing her again, and again.

But today is crisp, lovely, not a cloud in the sky. My senses are sharp. For the first time in a long time, everything is perfectly, brilliantly clear. The guardrail is low. I jerk the wheel to the right, and as we sail over the concrete, toward the water, my sister's screams fill the car, but all I feel is a perfect, steady calm.

Then a bright flash of pain.

Then nothing.

FIFTEEN

GONE

I leave my car double-parked a block down from Jamie's twelve-story high-rise on Lex, a few feet shy of the police cruisers and emergency vehicles already blocking the street. I drove as fast as I could from Monte Viso, white knuckles gripping the wheel and foot inching down on the gas the whole way, but I'm relieved to see Marrone and his team were even faster.

I was wrong about Mark, but this is not another false alarm. If I'm right about this, the man inside apartment 8L is not the person I thought he was, not even close. The thought makes me shudder.

After discovering Jamie went to Monte Viso last night, right after the cameras conveniently went out, I went further back in the security database, and my suspicions were confirmed: Jamie was at Monte Viso, too, when he was supposed to be in San Francisco—when Esme went missing. He lied about the trip, just as he lied about being in Manhattan last night.

In the Monte Viso parking lot, head spinning, I immediately went back to Mom's journal. I'd thought she'd muddled the time-line, mixing past and present, confusing Esme and me, but what if she'd gotten it exactly right?

The new doctor is not a good man; he'll only hurt Jane in the end. They think I don't know, but I've seen them together, the way he walks her to the elevator after our visits, his hand on the small of her back. The lingering looks she gives him, pink creeping into her cheeks. Esme won't listen to me, she's too stubborn. I'll have to talk to the doctor, tell him this has to stop.

Was Mom lucid when she wrote that? Jamie walking Esme to the elevator after visits Esme never told me about, Jamie's hand on the small of my sister's back. The new doctor—not Dr. Yu, but Dr. Paulson, whose role has become muddled in Mom's mind. It would make Jamie the link between everything: Mom, Esme, and me.

And Jamie is a liar.

My mind flashed then to Dylan, the shoe and dress at his job-site, both soaked with Esme's blood. Then to Jamie at my house the night before, going through Esme's planner with me. I'd pulled up Dylan's website, showed him the location where Dylan was working. I carelessly gave Jamie the idea to go to the site before I did, where he planted the evidence to frame Dylan.

The more I think it through, the clearer it becomes: It's Jamie, not Dylan, who has been holding Esme all this time. Because he and Esme have been having an affair. And Mom found out. Mom, who could tie Jamie to Esme, when I believed my sister and my ex-boyfriend had never met. Mom, who confronted the "new doctor" about what she'd seen, who had to die so Jamie could bury the truth about what he'd done to my sister. How desperate must Jamie have been to lead her into traffic, ensuring she'd never share what she knew?

Now I race through the open building doors, heart pounding in my throat, then through the lobby, past the courtyard, and toward the elevator bank.

The ride to the eighth floor is interminable, but when the

doors finally open, I careen down the hall, across the threshold, and into Jamie's apartment.

The open-plan kitchen/living/dining area swarms with NYPD. A uniformed arm shoots out, hand gripping my shoulder. "Miss, you can't be here." She tries to steer me back toward the door.

"Wait," I protest, eyes skating around the room, frantic, until they land on Marrone. He has Jamie pinned over the small glass dining table, his hands in cuffs. "Where's my sister?"

"Jane," Jamie mumbles. His cheek is pressed to the glass. He looks ashen and small.

"She can stay," Marrone says to the officer gripping my shoulders. Then, to me, "Your sister's going to be okay. She's in the bedroom."

At the back of the apartment, paramedics swarm the entrance to Jamie's room. The truth, hard and unassailable, settles like a stone against my chest, pressing out all the air. With a shudder, I break free from the officer's slackening grasp and rush to the doorway.

Inside, Esme is sitting up in a hospital bed that has been shoved between Jamie's queen and the wall, speaking to a pair of medical workers. A thin white bandage is taped to the back of her scalp where the hair has been clipped away. She's painfully thin, dressed in a grubby pair of sweatpants and one of Jamie's button-downs, and deep hollows are carved beneath her eyes. Thick leather straps dangle from the bed rails, and I watch my sister rub at her wrists, where a few moments ago, the straps bit into her skin.

"Esme," I breathe, and her gaze breaks from the paramedics and lands on me.

For the past two days, ever since Dylan was taken into custody, I've entertained the thought that I might never see my sister alive again. On the heels of Mom's passing, I'm not sure I could have handled the loss. Tears rush down my cheeks, and a powerful surge of relief flows through me.

"Janie." She makes a move to stand, legs wobbly beneath her, and a stocky paramedic with close-cropped black hair rushes to help her to her feet.

"She's very weak," he cautions me. "It'll take a while for the drugs to wear off."

I step forward, not bothering to swipe at the tears staining my cheeks, and draw my sister into my arms. *Safe.*

"I'm so sorry," she mumbles into my shirt. "For absolutely everything."

There hasn't been so much food in the Old Boney kitchen since Esme's college graduation party. While she rests on the living room couch, a throw pulled over her small frame, I pack tea sandwiches and crab cakes into ziplocks and scrape hummus and spinach artichoke dip into the largest containers I can find.

"We'll have to throw another party tomorrow," she mumbles from the couch. "Just to get rid of it all."

"Hah." I jam a large bag of cheese cubes into the crisper drawer, then search helplessly for a space large enough to house the vats of leftover dip.

Mom's funeral was this morning at Calvary Presbyterian. After hours of entertaining and accepting condolences from most of Branby, the reception is finally over, and for the first time since Esme was rescued three days ago, then admitted to the hospital, then finally brought home last night, the two of us are truly alone.

I'm glad to finally have this time together, but not quite sure where to begin. There's so much to process. We've been going through the motions since she came home last night, but we haven't really talked about any of it. I abandon the rest of the leftovers on the kitchen island and cross over to sit on the couch. She scoots her feet into her knees to make room for me.

For a moment, we sit in silence before Esme finally breaks it.

"I can't believe she's really gone. I should have spent more time with her there at the end."

"But you did go to Monte Viso, at least a few times," I say tentatively, recalling Mom's journaling. "I think she was aware of more than she let on." I want to lay into her about Jamie, and I'll get there, but comforting Esme is so familiar, and we both know our roles.

"Those visits were mostly selfish," she admits. "And after everything I've gone through these past three weeks, I want to be honest."

"So tell me what happened. All of it." She's already given her statement to the police, of course, but I need to hear it from her directly.

"I checked into the Monarch on Thursday, after leaving Mark. Recently, the bar there had become my spot when I was in Midtown, which was a lot lately, with the book stuff. It was so perfectly mediocre, and there was zero chance of running into anyone I didn't want to see. But after two nights at the hotel, I was ready to get out of the city, and I wanted to come to Branby. To give you a chance to come clean about the past."

"I—" I start to say, but Esme holds up her hand. I let her talk.

"I'd told Mark I'd meet him for dinner, but he only wanted to talk about the prenup, and I had nothing to say. I called you instead. When you told me you weren't coming to pick me up, I was pissed as hell. I had another drink, then another, and then I called Jamie from the burner I always used with him."

"Burner?"

"Mark had a habit of snooping through my regular phone, so." She shrugs. "Anyway, I told Jamie San Francisco was off. I'd started the affair to hurt you, to get back at you for lying to me, but I didn't give a shit about meeting his family. Leaving Mark made it clear—I needed to go home for a while, to see if there was anything worth salvaging between you and me."

"Oh," I say, struggling to process all of this.

"Jamie was so mad when I called. We'd been scheduled to fly out on Friday, but I'd already backed out once. He'd moved our flights to Saturday night; he thought I'd change my mind. After I told him no again, he hung up and drove straight to the Monarch. I was so shocked when he called me from the street outside, I went out to meet him."

She picks at the edge of her blanket. "If you'd come to pick me up, I never would have gone to his place. I know what happened isn't your fault, but in the moment, it felt like the last straw. I was upset and distracted, and I left my regular phone at the bar."

My mind jumps to my first frustrating conversation with SI Marrone. "The police gave me the runaround about unlocking it."

Esme tucks a strand of hair behind her ear. "Nothing on there would have tied me to Jamie. I made sure of that, because of Mark. And the last time I used my laptop was at the hotel, so even if they had unlocked my phone, it wouldn't have led them anywhere."

I press my lips between my teeth, not quite ready to forgive Marrone, but it's time to let it go.

"What happened after you left the bar?" I ask.

"I got in Jamie's car. Biggest mistake I've ever made."

I nod; I know something about big mistakes, choices you can't take back.

"I still can't believe you were sleeping with him," I say softly. It's the truth I've been dancing around since the moment Esme was found. Once, I would've buried my hurt down deep, denying it was even there. But I'm done living that way. If Esme and I have a shot at coming back from this, I'm going to need to start telling her how I feel, and she's going to have to do the same. No more of her obfuscation and lies. And no more of the lies I tell by not saying anything at all.

Esme nods, and the guilt and hurt in her eyes is so strong it looks like she might cry. "I was so mad at you, after I found your journals. I wanted to hurt you, and I knew you loved him. It made perfect sense at the time—tit for tat. But after these past three weeks . . . Everything is different now. It was horrible of me, and I truly am sorry."

I'm sorry. It's the second time Esme has said those words in the past three days, and until this moment, I didn't realize how hungry I've been to hear them.

I breathe deep. "What matters most is that you're safe. But what you did hurts, and I want to understand."

She nods, grateful.

We both know it's going to take a lot more than one conversation to heal from everything that's happened. But I meant what I said: my sister is home safe, and that's the most important thing.

"What happened next?"

Esme twists around on the couch, tucks her feet beneath her. "I've never seen him so furious. I explained that my decision to leave Mark had nothing to do with him, that it was just for me, but he felt duped. He'd left you to be with me, which, again, I'm sorry. I wanted him to break your heart, but I never really planned to be with Jamie long term. I was done."

"Christ, Esme."

"I'm a bitch, what can I say. I've never been very good at talking. It's easier to lash out."

I shake my head, but we both know it's true. "And Jamie took it badly," I prompt.

"To say the least. We were in his kitchen, screaming at each other; the flight was delayed because of the storm, but it was still scheduled to take off. He said I was going to get on it. I told him to go fuck himself. That's when he shoved me, hard. My head snapped back, hit the wall."

Her fingers trail up to the close-cropped patch at the back of her head, blond hair about three weeks' growth. The bandage is gone, but a puffy pink scar mimics those remaining from the car crash fifteen years ago—the large one on her arm and the smaller, but much deeper one on the right side of her skull, hidden beneath her hairline.

"My head felt like it was going to explode. I told him I was going to ruin him—report him to the cops, spill every detail on social. Make sure he suffered." She presses her eyes closed. "I wasn't thinking clearly, for obvious reasons. I thought he'd back down, apologize. But he slammed me into the wall again, harder the second time. I blacked out."

If I'd driven into the city to get Esme, if she hadn't gone with Jamie that night, if Jamie hadn't lashed out at her, everything would be different. But would it be better? If Jamie hadn't lost control, he'd still be hiding the darkest part of himself, moving through the world as a compassionate doctor, intent on helping others. And he was that, but he was this other thing, too—a man used to calling the shots, who reacted with violence when he didn't get his way.

If none of it had happened, if he hadn't been caught, some-day he would have hurt some other woman, and maybe her story wouldn't have had a happy ending. And what about Esme and me? Would she have delayed ending things with Jamie, kept sleeping with him behind my back? Would her resentment about what I did fifteen years ago have kept festering forever? What would that have meant for the two of us?

"The second time he hit me, I passed out," Esme says. "When

I came to, maybe a few minutes later, I bolted for the door. But he yanked me back, and the pain in my head was so intense, I was sick to my stomach. All over his pretty white kitchen floor." She snorts. "I told him to get off of me, let me go, but it was obvious he was terrified. That I'd go to the cops, go to Instagram. Make good on my promise to ruin his career."

"He injected me with something that made me even sicker," she continues. "Fentanyl maybe, some kind of opioid. My head stopped hurting, but I was so out of it. He dragged me over to the bedroom and locked me inside. I remember being slumped against the door for a while, wanting to get up, but I could barely move."

"Jesus," I mutter.

"Eventually, he came back into the room and pulled me onto the bed. I was so fucking scared. His eyes, Jane. They were *cold*, I don't know how else to describe it. That's when I knew for sure he wasn't going to let me go. He had another vial with him. I thought it was more Fentanyl, and I tried to fight him off, but he had me pinned, all his weight, crushing me. He jammed the needle into my arm." Her hand moves to her shoulder, the ghost of the pain clearly still there. "I lost a bunch of time then. Days, I think. He made sure I stayed out while he decided what to do with me."

"What does that mean?"

"He put me in a medically induced coma, I don't know for how long. When he brought me out of it, I was gagged and strapped to a hospital bed. He'd hurt me, then drugged me, and now he was holding me hostage. It was incredibly fucked up—and we both knew it. But he was in so deep, I don't think he saw a way out." She shudders. "He told me if I tried to get away, he'd kill me, and I believed him. He was feeding me through an IV drip, and there were bottles of toxins lined up beside the fluids."

"Oh my god."

"For days, I was sure I wouldn't get out of there alive. You didn't know we'd even met, and besides, he was supposed to be in California."

I think back to that phone call with Jamie, the day after Esme went missing. I'd called seeking his help, and when I heard noise in the background, I assumed he was with his family, in San Francisco, where he was supposed to be. He didn't even have to lie; I made an assumption he never corrected. My stomach clenches. I hate that I never questioned Jamie—but he manipulated me.

"I can't believe I ever thought Dylan did this to you," I say. My mind travels to our conversation at his jobsite last Monday. "Were you two back in touch? Why did you get coffee that Saturday in June?"

Esme sighs. "The weekend we moved Mom into Monte Viso, Jamie gave me a ride to the train. As he was dropping me off, I spotted Dylan across the lot. I dodged Jamie's kiss, turned it into a hug, but Dylan gave me an odd look. I thought the two of you might have reconnected, that he might recognize Jamie as your boyfriend and tell you what he'd seen.

"So I met him for coffee a few days later, saying I wanted to discuss a landscaping project. I was prepared to convince him that he didn't see what he thought he saw between Jamie and me, but it turned out he hadn't spoken to you in ages. He wasn't suspicious at all, so I stayed and we talked—about you, mostly."

I shake my head slowly, processing. "Jamie acted so supportive these last couple weeks, but he was just using me to keep a close watch on the investigation. When I figured out that coffee date in your planner was probably with Dylan, I basically fed him to Jamie. And then I played right into his hand, going to the site the next day."

Esme reaches over and places a hand lightly on my knee. "What Jamie did wasn't your fault. And you couldn't have stopped him anyway. If you hadn't found my slingback, he would've called in an anonymous tip. And if he hadn't homed in on Dylan, he would have found another target. By that time, my head injury had healed, and Jamie was getting desperate. He was going to figure out a way to frame someone for my death."

My stomach churns, and I shut my eyes for a moment, letting the horrible truth about Jamie—*my Jamie*—wash over me.

"And your blood on the clothing?" I ask, prying my eyes open and resting my gaze on my sister. "It was fresh."

She nods. "He drew my blood that morning. He wouldn't tell me why."

For a moment, both of us sit in silence. Then Esme says, "Have you talked to Dylan?"

I shake my head. "Not really. I called as soon as he was released, but he wasn't ready to talk. Understandably. I got him thrown in jail."

"Only because Jamie's plan worked—for a few days, anyway."

I nod. "I'd love to take Dylan to dinner, to apologize. But I'm giving him space for now. Maybe someday he'll forgive me for doubting him."

There's a knife twist of shame in my gut every time I think about it, but Jamie knew how emotionally frayed I was, and he took advantage. By the time he planted the evidence, I could barely see straight. I couldn't see Jamie for the deeply damaged person he is, and I couldn't see through the sheen of suspicion he cast over Dylan, either.

Esme leans over to rest her head against my shoulder. "Everything that happened, it's all *my* fault. Dylan's arrest. Mom's death."

I run my fingers through her hair, and tears prick at the corners of my eyes. "What you did was really messed up, but you can't blame yourself for what Jamie did to you—or to Mom."

Mom. Once again, the knowledge that she's gone slams

through me. The tears that had threatened to spill a moment ago come streaming down my cheeks.

Esme nods, head bobbing off my shoulder. Then she slips her hand into mine. "Part of me knows you're right, but . . . I reacted in the worst possible way to what I learned from your journals. I'm truly sorry for sabotaging your relationship with Jamie—and not just because he turned out to be a psycho!"

I laugh, and then we're both laughing, and it's not okay, but it feels better than anything has felt in a long time. This tentative truce with my sister.

"And for stealing your journals," she adds when we've both recovered.

My jaw tenses again. Apparently, Esme's big deal book deal resulted from a proposal written in large part by me. She not only read my journals last Thanksgiving, she copied them. And then she tweaked them just enough, made my childhood her child-hood. I want to lay into her about plagiarism and ethics and how I gave up writing for the responsible career that would keep Mom in excellent care for decades. But there's nothing to be gained by exploding at Esme now. There will be time to talk about all of this when we're both a little less drained.

Instead, I say what I should have said a long time ago.

"I get why you're angry with me, for keeping Nolan from you all those years ago. I never should've gotten in the car that night." My eyes travel to my sister's arm, to the mark that's haunted me all these years, a physical manifestation of a choice I at once stand by and deeply regret. "But please believe I wasn't trying to keep you from having a better father than Carl or that I didn't think you deserved the truth. I was scared they were going to take you away from me."

She nods, real tears streaming down her face. "I was so angry when I read your journals. There was this one entry where you acknowledged how selfish it was, keeping Dad's threats a secret.

And I snapped. It *was* fucking selfish! That was all I could think about, how wrapped up you were in your own interests. For years, I fantasized about escaping Carl, escaping Branby. And you took that chance away from me."

"I—" I start to protest, but Esme holds up a hand.

"That's how I used to see it. It's why I lashed out—Jamie, the memoir. But these past three horrible weeks changed everything. You should have told me the truth, but I know you were trying to protect me. I get it now. I would have been terrified of being left alone in Old Boney without you, too."

I flash her a big smile.

"I'm so sorry, Janie."

"I'm sorry, too. I can't undo the choices I made, but if I could, I'd go back and find a way to tell you the truth."

I'd tell my sister about Nolan, somehow, someway. In hindsight, it's clear that holding fast to that secret nearly cost us everything.

But I can't go back, only forward, one decision spiraling into a million others, into a life I could never have planned, and I can't unmake. All I can do is live with my mistakes, accept the reality I've created, and keep going, buoyed by the hope of becoming the kind of person who makes better choices than my past self ever could.

"I didn't believe him," Esme says after a minute, breaking me out of my reverie. "When Jamie told me Mom was dead. Even after all those days trapped in his apartment, I didn't think he had it in him."

I shake my head slowly back and forth. Until a few days ago, I never would have believed Jamie had *any* of this in him. But the truth is, I didn't know Jamie at all.

Or maybe I just couldn't see what was right there in front of me. He always was best in a crisis, and once the drama of my move home to Branby and my fraught decision-making about Mom's care had subsided, he began to step back. Surely it didn't take much keen observation on Esme's part to gauge his character. She made herself vulnerable to him, a damsel in distress, and Jamie fell for it—hook, line, and sinker. His savior complex made him an easy mark.

Then when Esme didn't want him anymore, he couldn't handle the rejection. Being needed has always been the thing that makes him tick.

Esme twists around on the couch until she's facing me head-on. She takes both my hands in hers, and I draw in a shallow breath.

"Jamie was like a caged rat," she says. "After he slammed me against the wall the first time, he could have stopped right there, driven me to the hospital. But he was so afraid of what I could do—press charges, call him out online, end his career. So instead of doing the right thing, he doubled down, keeping me prisoner."

"One bad choice led to another."

My sister nods. "He would have done anything to not get caught. Eventually, he would have killed me." Her voice trembles, but her eyes are locked with mine. "But you made sure that didn't happen. Without everything you did over these past three weeks, no one would have ever tied Jamie to me. I'm home because of you, safe because of you. Thank you, Jane."

I squeeze her hands tight. First an apology, now gratitude, both genuinely delivered and genuinely felt. Evidence of the human capacity for change, that there is a path forward for Esme and me. We can heal from this.

She lets her head fall against the back of the couch. "We're pretty messed up," she says after a moment. "Both of us."

"We are," I agree. "But maybe we can try to be a little less messed up, together."

I let my head fall beside hers on the couch, my brown hair intermingling with her blond until you can't tell where she ends and I begin.

SIXTEEN

EPILOGUE

The view of the bay is gorgeous at midday. Blue on blue on blue, gulls swooping overhead. The cottage we've rented for the summer has a wide front porch overlooking the water; I sit in my favorite adirondack chair, laptop balanced on my knees, and stare out at a lone white boat, a small vessel with red trim, headed this way.

"Another tea?"

I drag my gaze away from the water and up to Dylan's smiling face. He lifts my mug from the arm of the chair and leans down to kiss the top of my head.

"I was thinking I'd go in soon," I say. "Make us some lunch."

"Keep working. There's chicken salad in the fridge and that sourdough we picked up in town yesterday. I'll put some sandwiches together."

I'm barely working, but I take Dylan up on his offer and allow my gaze to drift back to the boat, now ringing its bell as it pulls up to a dock several cabins down. Farther out, the wind bats a few wispy clouds around the sky, but there's no rain in the forecast. It's a truly perfect coastal Maine day, the first week of September.

It's been nearly a year since Jamie's arrest, since the charges against Dylan were dropped. Eventually, Jamie will be prosecuted in two separate trials—homicide in Mom's case and kidnapping and assault in Esme's—but trial dates have not yet been set.

Dylan put off that first dinner a handful of times, but when we finally talked, he accepted my apology without question. We were both puppets in Jamie's desperate ploy to escape the deep hole he'd dug. One dinner led to another, then another, and by the cold tail of winter, Dylan and I had found our way back into one another's lives for the first time since we were kids.

We hadn't been together long when he shared with me the truth behind our breakup so many years ago and his struggles with alcohol, which reared back up when he returned to Branby. His history with addiction, paired with the evidence Jamie planted, made him the perfect suspect for the police. But after his release, Dylan recommitted to his recovery, and he's been back on track for months now. We're both a work in progress, but we are working. We are happy.

It's hard to reckon with something so good coming out of Esme's ordeal, Jamie's betrayal, Mom's death. But every day, it gets a little easier to let myself enjoy what we've found.

I snap my laptop shut and straighten in my chair as Ray Covey's boat approaches. The Covey family has operated the mail boat around the islands for decades, and Ray has been a near-daily visitor to our dock this summer.

"Heavy one for you today," he calls as I head down and reach out to accept the small stack of letters from his satchel. Then he produces the brown cardboard box I've been waiting for all week, hefting it from a wobbly metal cart onto the dock. "Shipment of bricks?" he jokes.

"Something like that." I grin. "It's from my publisher. Advanced copies of the book I cowrote with my sister."

"Ah, fancy." Ray gives me an appreciative nod. "Lots of writers up around these parts, especially in the summers. I'll be looking for your name in the *New York Times*."

I thank him and heave the box and my laptop up to the cottage as the clouds overhead start to multiply, blocking out the afternoon sun. "Dylan!" I call out. "They're here!"

It took Esme and me six months of sending chapters back and forth to finish the memoir, a story of our childhood under the shadow of our father's literary prowess and anger and deceit, but also of the secrets we've kept, the ways we've hurt one another, of Esme's capture, and of my search for my sister. Victoria thinks it's bestseller material, and of course I hope she's right, but as I slice through the tape with a pair of scissors and lift the first galley from the box, what hits me is a sense of relief. Esme and I will never have the kind of happy, easy relationship I imagine some siblings enjoy. But through writing this book, we've been more honest with each other than I ever thought possible. We may never fully recover from the hurt we've inflicted on each other, purposefully or not, but with *Retaliation and Rescue*, we've accomplished something true.

"It looks so official." Dylan joins me at the table, wiping his hands on a kitchen towel, and lifts another copy from the box. "'Cowritten by Jane Connor and Esme Connor.' Your name comes first."

I smile. "One of several terms we worked out in the contract, after I realized how much of my writing was used in the proposal she'd sold."

"Smart," he says, placing the galley back into the box. "Putting that business acumen to work."

Little by little, Esme and I are learning who we are to one another in this life post-Jamie, two adults who share a difficult past and hard truths, but who are bonded by true affection, who are finally capable of establishing boundaries and saying what we mean.

Outside, thunder grumbles softly, and the first fat drops of rain splatter against the wide picture windows overlooking the porch.

"Speaking of, we should eat. I need to hop on a Zoom at two. If the Wi-Fi holds."

For now, I'm still at Empire Lenders, working remotely for the summer. But I'm keeping my eye out for new opportunities. Victoria's interested in reading the novel I've been slowly drafting on the weekends, if I ever finish. And I've been looking at careers in copywriting and book marketing. Nothing that will pay as well as Empire, but I'm set to close on the sale of Old Boney at the end of the month, and with Mom's care no longer part of the equation, I can afford to take a pay cut.

"Copy that." Dylan disappears back into the kitchen, and I clear the books out of the way so we can sit at the cottage's small dining table.

Halfway through lunch, the rain turns into a full-on downpour, and the lights flicker overhead. Dylan and I both tap at our phones; the Wi-Fi out here is notoriously fragile.

"There she goes," he says, flipping his screen face down. "Guess you got out of your Zoom."

"I wish." I shove the rest of my sandwich into my mouth and push back from the table. "We've already rescheduled with the client twice," I say around a mouthful of chicken salad. "I have to be there."

I zip my laptop into its case and throw my keys and phone into my bag, then hunt around the closet for my rain boots and an umbrella.

"You're going to drive in this?" Dylan eyes the dark gray sky skeptically through the windows. "Why don't you let me take you?"

"Not necessary." I give him a quick kiss and sling my bag over my shoulder.

"Jane." He places a hand gently on my elbow. "Are you sure?"

I look back outside. The rain is coming down in earnest, but there's daylight streaking through the gray, and it's hours from sundown. The rain will probably pass before I make it to the main road.

I nod. "I'll be at the library, or the coffee shop with the good scones. Back in a couple hours."

Then I throw up my umbrella and make a dash for the car. Inside, the usual anxiety begins to prickle along the back of my neck, but I slip the key into the ignition and switch the radio on low. My hands are slippery from the rain, and I rub them against the front of my leggings. It's not a long drive into town—a twisty but quiet road through the woods, then a straight shot once I hit the main drag. Easy.

I back out of the drive, then turn onto Weymouth Lane, lightning crackling overhead. The rain is coming down harder than I realized, and I crank the wipers all the way up. I'll take it slow; I have time.

From its spot poking out of my bag on the passenger's seat, my phone chimes, then again, then again. I readjust my grip on the wheel and keep inching along, eyes fixed on the road. In a moment, the Pretenders croon from the tinny phone speakers, the custom ringtone I have set for Esme.

Thunder rumbles, loud and angry, and for a second, lightning floods the car with intense white light. The storm is directly overhead now, threatening to swallow me up. I focus on the windshield wipers battling the rain, remind myself that I am not seventeen, am not drunk, am perfectly capable of making this drive.

Esme's call can wait.

I breathe in, reset, and by the time I hit the first light, the storm has abated to a steady drizzle. When the light turns green, I keep my eyes on the road ahead and drive.

ACKNOWLEDGMENTS

Tremendous thanks to everyone at Emily Bestler Books and Atria for taking such good care of *The Split*—especially my editor, Lara Jones; publicist, Camila Araujo; marketer, Maudee Genao; editor in chief, Emily Bestler; publisher, Libby McGuire; and editorial associate, Hydia Scott-Riley. To managing editor Paige Lytle, copyeditor Douglas Johnson, production editor Liz Byer, designer Danielle Mazzella di Bosco, art director James Iacobelli, interior designer Erika Genova, and proofreader Tania Bissell—many thanks to you all for your enthusiasm and incredible creativity and attention to detail in bringing this book to life.

Much gratitude as well to my agent, Erin Harris, who has seen me through multiple books now and whose dedication never wavers. And to Joelle Hobeika and Josh Bank at Alloy Entertainment for first whispering the words "sliding doors" and lending your incredible editorial gifts to this project.

Thank you to my dear friends for your unfailing enthusiasm and support for my writing. Special shout-out to Ivy and Dana for the Nutmegger insights! And to the writer friends who cheered me on from the book's very early stages—particularly Kara Thomas, Rachel Lynn Solomon, and Karen M. McManus.

And to my family—especially Mom, Dad, Aunt Sally, Sonia, and Lissette—thank you for always believing in me! To Osvaldo and Ramona, I love you.

Finally, to the booksellers, the librarians, and bloggers across platforms—thank you for getting my books into the hands of readers. I truly would be nowhere without you. And to you, reading this book: thank you most of all.